Wakefield Press

TROUBLE is my Business

Lisa Walker writes novels for adults and young adults. She has also written an ABC Radio National play and been published in the *Age, Griffith Review, Big Issue* and the *Review of Australian Fiction*. Her recent novels include a young adult coming-of-age story, *Paris Syndrome* (HarperCollins, 2018), and a climate change comedy, *Melt* (Lacuna, 2018). She has worked in environmental communication and as a wilderness guide, and recently spent six months in a Kmart tent in outback Australia. Lisa lives, surfs and writes on the north coast of New South Wales. *The Girl with the Gold Bikini*, her sixth novel, introduced teen PI Olivia Grace. *Trouble is my Business* is the second Olivia Grace novel.

For Simon and Tim

TROUBLE
IS MY
BUSINESS

An Olivia Grace mystery

LISA WALKER

**Wakefield
Press**

Wakefield Press
16 Rose Street
Mile End
South Australia 5031
www.wakefieldpress.com.au

First published 2021

Cover designed by Liz Nicholson
Cover and title page illustration by Jessie Brooke
Edited by Jo Case, Wakefield Press
Typeset by Michael Deves, Wakefield Press

ISBN 978 1 74305 844 2

 A catalogue record for this
book is available from the
National Library of Australia

 Wakefield Press thanks
Coriole Vineyards for
continued support

CHAPTER ONE

Walk on the wild side. If you believe in synchronicity, I'm your man.

Adjusting my glasses, I eye Rosco's Bumble profile. I've become an expert on dating profiles since Rosco and I parted ways a couple of months ago. If I didn't have skin in the game, I'd tell him it needs a makeover.

Rosco and I created our Bumble profiles when we were working together. It's a professional tool, he said. You can make contact with a suspect or sniff out an infidelity case. While we'd never used it for work, we'd swiped right on each other just for laughs. So now I can check out his profile as much as I want.

Scooping an ice cube out of my drink, I wipe it across my forehead. Here on Nan's little balcony, a northerly breeze blows in off the beach, but it's still scorching. The winter jacket I'm knitting for Nan's terrier, Kevin, lies on the table next to me. It's hard to imagine he's ever going to need it.

'I'm going to exterminate you.' A pistol points at the space between my eyes. A Vegemite-smeared face looms behind it. Jacq pulls the trigger and a jet of water hits my forehead.

'Ain't no way ya gunna exterminate this gal,' I drawl. In my rulebook, gangster roles require an American accent. I pull off one of my thongs and hurl it at my sister.

Jacq dodges, squirts me in the face again, and races away across the loungeroom.

I'm back on Bumble when *We wish you a Merry Christmas* interrupts my scrolling. I knew I'd regret letting Jacq fiddle with my ringtone. It might be late March, but on my phone it's Christmas all year round. Not that I have to listen to the tune often. Most of my friends would sooner run naked through Surfers than make a phone call. The only voice calls I get are from old people and telemarketers.

Deserting a *sincere, financially independent sports-lover*, I pick up. 'Hello?'

There's a pause.

Telemarketer. I'm about to hang up, when someone speaks.

'Olivia? It's Estelle Watson.'

'Mrs Watson?' Old habits die hard. Abbey's mother will never be Estelle to me.

'It's about Abbey ...' Her voice falters.

A queasy coldness fills me. Clutching the phone to my ear, I sink lower in my chair.

Mrs Watson talks and talks. Eventually her voice dies away.

My throat has seized up, but I squeeze the words out. 'I'm so sorry. I'll be there.'

I bang the phone down and close my eyes. *Abbey.*

It's a month since Abbey and I got together on one of her rare visits to the Goldie. We hadn't seen much of each other since she moved to Byron. Abbey was living her dream life and I, well ... wasn't. It made things uncomfortable between us.

Our last meet-up had gone particularly badly. I'd stormed out of the Cavill Avenue cafe, leaving my coffee half-drunk on the table. My departing words to her replay in my mind. 'Butt out of my life. You don't know what you're talking about.'

Abbey said I was putting my dreams on hold. 'How come you gave up on being a PI? Is studying law what you really want to do? Don't forget, life—'

'Is not a dress rehearsal,' I intoned. It's one of Abbey's favourite sayings. 'Save it for the motivational calendar.' I knew she was right though, and it hurt. Being a PI had been my dream since forever.

The roar of the sea penetrates my thoughts. Inside, Jacq sings in her usual random way. 'The little dog danced to see such fun and the mouse ran away with a spoon.'

Now Abbey is missing, and I might never get the chance to say I'm sorry.

❁

Two days later, I turn my blue Honda Jazz with the go-fast stripes south toward Byron Bay. I hadn't wanted the stripes, but second-hand car buyers can't be choosers.

If my car reflected my personality, I'd be a secretary who wishes she were a racing-car driver. Which I'm not. I'm a law student with unfulfilled aspirations to be the Nancy Drew of the Gold Coast.

'Try finding a car that says that for less than $5000,' I mutter to the guy in the red midlife-crisis sports car beside me. He looks straight through me as he zooms past. I pull down the mirror to check I'm not invisible. No, still there, but I've had better days.

The reason Abbey's comment stung is that only a couple of months ago, my dream of being a PI was right on track.

❁

I was working with Rosco at his agency, Gold Star Investigations, for the summer. Rosco and I had made the tricky transition from childhood friends to work colleagues.

After a rocky beginning, I was all set to become a partner in the business. The only difficulty was breaking this news to Mum and Dad.

My parents had gone trekking in Nepal for six weeks. Over this time, Jacq and I were with my Nan in her unit near Surfers Paradise. Nan had seized this opportunity to attempt to mould me in her image. Blingy fashionista is far from my usual style, so I was keen to get home.

As Mum and Dad's return drew nearer, I rehearsed ways to tell them I was going to be a permanent PI. They weren't impressed by my job at Gold Star Investigations, but they'd thought it was just for the summer. It wouldn't be a popular move. What parent dreams of having a daughter who trails villains around the mean streets?

Get the law degree, Mum always said. *After that, you can do what you want. Education is the key to a good life. A degree will open doors.*

Mum teaches outdoor recreation at TAFE, so education is in her blood. Dad lectures in zoology at the uni, so he follows her lead on this. Mum and Dad talk about education like it's the elixir of life. I know where they're coming from, but I don't believe education only happens at school and university.

Being a Gold Coast PI isn't like being Sherlock Holmes, Dad said. *There are too many low-lifes out there.* Dad is a big Sherlock fan. Between Dad and my nan, who is mad about Nancy Drew, I got plenty of childhood exposure to fictional detectives. It's no wonder I always wanted to be a PI. For me, it's the ultimate aspiration.

Despite Mum and Dad's pep-talks, I knew what I wanted. I didn't need to spend four years studying law to be a PI. It would be a complete waste of time.

I was sure I could talk them around. The trickiest part was the finance. I wanted to buy into Rosco's business. An equal partnership was the only way it would work. I'm not good at taking orders from Rosco, and I was sick of being assigned all the boring cases. I needed more control.

I had some cash saved, but I needed to dip into my money from Gran. Dad's mum, my gran, died a few years ago and left Jacq and me a small inheritance. Unfortunately, it's held in trust until I turn twenty-one. Mum and Dad have to sign off on any spending before then. It's for my education and career, her will says. This education thing runs in the family. Buying into Rosco's business fits the career angle and I planned to argue I'd be getting a fast-track degree in the university of life.

I had my arguments all figured out. But then, everything changed.

CHAPTER TWO

I tune the radio to Lighthouse FM as I get close to the Bay.

It's a few months since I've been to Byron, but the radio station sounds the same. A girl with a high-pitched voice is speaking. 'The problem is, only ten per cent of our essence manifests in this earthly plane so we're, like, handicapped.'

Luna. I smile. Luna Nakamura and I became friends when I got tangled up with her whale activism a while back. The last time I saw her, she was going off on a boat with Sea Shepherd, but it looks like she's back in town.

'I so know what you mean, Luna, but what can we do about it?' responds another woman.

Turning right along the beach road, I lose track of the interview. Mrs Watson said Abbey's friends were having a vigil at Wategos Beach. The purpose of this vigil wasn't clear, and it presented a fashion challenge I'm not sure I've surmounted.

Vigil sounds semi-formal, but Wategos Beach means bikini. A semi-formal black bikini could work. Considering I've come straight from a tutorial at uni though, my best black T-shirt and cargos will have to do. Also, bikinis are not generally my thing.

As soon as I pull up at Wategos, it's clear I have the dress code wrong. Standing in a circle of frangipanis on the beach is a cluster of the type of people who thrive in Byron Bay.

Tanned, fit and beautiful, they are all wearing outfits that make the most of their assets. Backless tops, topless backs. Rings in their ears and rings on their toes. And that's just the guys.

As I get out of the car, I see a poster fixed to a signpost. *Have You Seen Abbey? Disappeared while night surfing at The Pass.* Abbey never used to be into night surfing, but no doubt she's trying new things now she lives in Byron.

Abbey's face is beneath the words – her hair blowing across her cheeks. I swallow as I stare at her picture. She'll turn up soon. It's all a misunderstanding.

Swapping my driving glasses for sunnies, I trip across the sand like the bad fairy at Sleeping Beauty's christening. Sand grates inside my sandals as I make a beeline for the only person I know, Mrs Watson.

She looks as out of place as I do, with her grey hair and leather handbag. A bead of sweat runs down her cheek and lodges in the neckline of her sensible summer frock. Relief passes over her face as she sees me. She takes my hand and squeezes it, her brown eyes swimming. Mrs Watson is a single mum and Abbey is her only child, so that makes this extra tough.

A guy with red hair in a ponytail and a freckled nose moves to the front of the crowd. 'We are here to call on the community's support to find our dear friend Abbey.' His green eyes sweep the gathering and come to rest on me. He's good-looking in an intense, prophet-like way.

Lowering my eyes, I watch the waves wash away an elaborate sandcastle. *Abbey* is pressed into its side in shells.

'The universe gave us Abbey and now ... it has taken her away.'

Startled, I look up, meeting his eyes. This seems pessimistic. She's only been gone a few days.

He goes on for a while about the universe's plan for Abbey. This involves atoms resonating in time and a butterfly flapping its wings.

I tune out. Abbey is more realistic than that. *Not everything happens for a reason, Ol,* I hear her say. My eyes fall on the sandcastle again as it topples and Abbey's name is washed away. I don't like the symbolism.

At the end of the speech, the ponytailed guy and a few others paddle out on surfboards to throw flowers into the sea. They catch a wave back in, their bodies silhouetted in the setting sun.

The golden twilight is wasted on me. I want to leave. I don't know these people, Abbey's friends. Abbey and I have grown so far apart since school. I'm not sure whose fault that is. Abbey has seemed to have trouble getting up to the Gold Coast. I told her I'd come to Byron, but she was lukewarm on the idea. I sensed she didn't want me mixing with her Byron friends.

Mrs Watson is in a group near the shoreline. I walk down to say goodbye. It's hard to get a word in, so I stand awkwardly to one side.

The red-haired surfer, now dripping wet, looks me up and down. 'You a cop?' His voice is low and flat.

Several people swivel, their eyes flicking to each other.

Under the combined weight of twenty pairs of eyes, I take a step backwards. Sweat breaks out under my armpits. I don't know why he's so hostile.

Mrs Watson rescues me. 'Olivia's an old friend of Abbey's. I'm so glad you made it Olivia.' She clutches my arm and draws me aside. 'It will mean so much to Abbey that you came. She always says she's never had another friend like you.'

Guilt stabs at me. *Butt out of my life ...*

Abbey has been missing for nine days now. Her surfboard floated in on a remote beach two days after she'd disappeared. The police found a goodbye note in her house. It seems like she deliberately paddled out to sea, not planning to come back, but ... I don't believe it. She has to be around somewhere.

❀

The forty-minute drive back to the Gold Coast in the dark gives me plenty of time for reflection. Abbey and I have our differences, but she's important to me. I replay our last meeting over and over. Abbey gave no hint she had problems. Having problems is my role.

One of Abbey's favourite songs, 'Ocean Eyes' by Billie Eilish, croons from the radio. The car lights ahead of me blur as I cling to the wheel. Winding down the window, I put my head out, gulping for air as the wind dries my wet cheeks.

Once, I knew Abbey's hopes and dreams. Her life in Byron Bay over the last couple of months is almost a complete blank to me though. *Ocean eyes.*

Abbey was night surfing. I try to picture it ...

❀

The moonlit foam rushes past the rocky point. Tomorrow the surfers will jostle in the line-up, but for now Abbey has it to herself. It's not a heavy swell but sucking up on the sand. There's not much room for error.

Picking up her leg-rope so it doesn't snag, she feels her way down seaweed-coated rocks. The surge sucks at her calves. Timing her jump, she leaps, board beneath her. A few quick strokes and she is where she feels most at home, waiting for a wave.

Legs dangling in the water, she lets waves go by, feeding on the energy of the night. She needs this, the cleansing power of the ocean.

The sea is warm at the end of summer. It would be easy to slip in and swim away.

❁

As I turn off the highway and drive through the canyon of sparkling skyscrapers to Nan's place, I try to block the memory of Abbey's last words to me. *You're not living Olivia, you're existing.*

It stung. Working at Gold Star Investigations hadn't been perfect, but it had made me feel alive. Did I make the right decision when I left? I didn't have any other choice. Not after that Skype call.

CHAPTER THREE

When Mum and Dad's faces appeared on my phone screen, I assumed they wanted to confirm their airport pick-up time.

I'd been finalising a business plan to show them Gold Star Investigations was a good investment. Rosco had given me all the facts and figures. After a slow start, his PI business was booming. It wasn't only the Gold Coast that was crying out for PIs; the Byron Bay business was going through the roof. I planned to hit Mum and Dad with it all on the way back from the airport.

We waved at each other as they came into focus. They looked weather-beaten, and thinner than when I saw them off six weeks earlier. Mum's short hair was sticking up from her head. A string of turquoise beads hung with a Buddha circled her neck.

'Cool necklace,' I said.

She touched her beads. 'It reminds me to cut off from confusion, hostility, and attachment. Let go of trivial matters ...'

'Nice.' I was a little thrown. I'd never heard her talk like this before. Mum is a dynamo. She keeps the whole family on schedule. Without her, both our trivial and non-trivial matters would descend into chaos. I decided to move on. 'What time does your flight get in?'

They exchanged a glance. Mum fingered her Buddha.

After a long pause, Dad spoke. 'We've changed our flight plans.'

Something about the way he said it made me nervous. 'So, when are you getting back?'

'Your Mum and I are …' He cleared his throat. 'We're staying on for a while to volunteer in a monastery in Kathmandu, teaching English to the young monks.' His voice was upbeat.

'Wait. What? But …' It didn't make sense. Were Jacq and I trivial matters to be let go of?

'They need us here more than you do,' said Mum.

Right. I bet those monks agree with Mum that education is the key to a good life.

'I hope you understand.'

I didn't. Mum and Dad's lives revolved around me and Jacq. The trip to Nepal came out of left field, but I'd encouraged them to go. They loved hiking and the Himalayas were on their bucket list. I'd told them Jacq and I would be fine for a few weeks.

'It's been life-changing coming to Nepal,' said Mum. 'I had no idea how stuck in my ways I'd become. The people here live in the moment. It's so inspirational.'

Live in the moment? If anyone told me six weeks ago that Mum would say that, I'd have laughed in their face. Our weekly calendar was a colour-coded Excel spreadsheet that Mum created every weekend. She printed out four copies, so every member of the family knew exactly what was going to happen and when. We were not a *live in the moment* family.

'Jacq can stay with Nan if you want to move home,' said Mum. 'The tenants move out tomorrow. I know uni starts soon.'

Unfortunately, Jacq came into our bedroom just then. 'What? No.' Jacq's voice rose to a squeal. 'I am not staying with Nan by myself. I am not. She makes me wear dresses and clean my nails and ... what's happening? Why aren't you coming home?'

'There are children here who need us more than you do,' said Mum.

Jacq's brow furrowed. 'No they don't.'

This was fair enough. I was having trouble with the concept too.

'You and Olivia have school and university to look forward to. And Nan to look after you,' said Mum.

'I don't want Nan looking after me. I can look after myself,' Jacq said.

Considering Jacq's just turned seven, this wasn't quite true.

'Livvie can drive me to school,' she added.

'Olivia will be busy at uni,' Dad said.

'Don't you have to come back for work?' I said.

Mum and Dad glanced at each other again.

'I've resigned from my job at TAFE,' said Mum.

I blinked. It felt like an earthquake had rocked the room. Mum had worked at TAFE forever. She loved it. Didn't she?

'I've got long-service leave,' said Dad.

I cleared my throat. 'How long will you be there for?'

'Who knows? All we have is now,' said Mum. 'Buddha says the trouble is you think you have time.'

Mum didn't sound like herself. She is the most practical person I know. I'd never heard her mention Buddha before.

'We don't know,' said Dad.

'But—' This was not an auspicious time to hit them with my business plan. So, I bit my tongue about wanting to be a PI, about using Gran's money. It wasn't a conversation to have over Skype, especially with Jacq in the room.

At that stage, the connection crackled and broke. Their faces vanished.

Jacq and I stared at each other, wide-eyed.

'I hate those other children,' said Jacq.

'I won't leave you here alone with Nan. I'm sure Mum and Dad will come back soon.' It was inadequate, but all I could think of.

Later that night, Dad called me back. 'Your Mum's at evening prayers.' Cymbals clashed in the background.

'What's going on with you two?'

He sighed. 'Your mum hasn't been happy for a while. I know she puts on a good face, but she's questioning her life. I think she's having a midlife crisis.'

Crisis and *Mum* do not go together. 'She seemed okay last time I saw her.'

'She's been craving adventure. That was why we came to Nepal. I'm hoping she gets this out of her system, and we can come home soon. I can't leave her here by herself. She's ...' he hesitated, 'unpredictable.'

The turquoise necklace. The Buddha quote. All we have is now.

'I don't want you to feel like you have to look after Jacq. Your Nan ...'

I swallowed. 'No, it's okay. Jacq won't stay with Nan by herself. I'll help.' I couldn't tell Dad about my PI plans. He had enough on his plate. I would need to rethink.

Over the summer it had become clear to me that PIs work irregular hours. I'd had several run-ins with Rosco about not being available because I had to look after Jacq. Becoming a partner would only make things harder. It wouldn't work.

Studying law made sense. The hours were predictable.

The uni had even offered me a scholarship, so it made sense financially too. Maybe when Mum and Dad came back ...

The way things turned out, it was lucky I made this decision. Nan turned out to be even less helpful than I'd expected. She met a new man, Donald, a youthful fifty-eight-year-old ukulele player. Their whirlwind courtship left little time for grandmotherly duties. I was left carrying the can.

So, just like that, I gave up on being a PI. Sometimes I wondered if I'd been looking for an excuse. I'd loved being a PI over the summer, but it was challenging. In the books I read, the PIs were always so sure of themselves, so logical and brave. Living up to my fictional heroes was tough.

If I never tried, I'd never fail. I would always be the Nancy Drew of the Gold Coast in my mind.

CHAPTER FOUR

Abbey lets the waves go by, feeding on the energy of the night. She needs this, the cleansing power of the ocean. The sea is warm at the end of summer. It would be easy to slip in and swim away.

The town's lights seem far away, but in the lull between waves, a warm breeze carries a guitar twang from the Beach Hotel. She imagines the loud conversation and frantic quest for pleasure. She's glad she's not there.

Across the gleam of the bay, mountains press against the stars. Her eyes trace the familiar shape of each valley and peak.

A movement on the beach catches her eye ...

❀

'Pure puffery,' says my Criminal Law lecturer. Her slash of red lipstick matches her business suit and she wields her laser pointer like a lightsaber.

I slouch in my seat and try to make myself invisible. My mind is on Abbey, not Criminal Law.

Puffery. I write it down. It sounds like something you might buy in a bakery. My fellow students have already adopted a law-speak that's foreign to me. I must have missed the course in sounding like a law student. They begin sentences with, *a reasonable person would say.* Or, *if you trace the chain of causation.* Or, *the agreement we made is void.* I write down new phrases whenever I hear them. I figure sounding the part is half the battle.

Law is demanding. There is a ton of reading, which I am not keeping up with, and the lecturers are scary. Professor Anderson, my Criminal Law lecturer, is the scariest of all. Each lecture, she calls on students at random to give summaries of relevant cases.

My pulse races as I watch today's first victim get a tongue lashing and a cross against his name. I'm not sure what that means, but it can't be good. I know when I'm chosen, I'm going to fluff it, so I'm in a constant state of anxiety. So far, my invisibility shield has worked, but my luck will run out one day.

My life is so hectic, I don't have time for the reading. I'd always thought Mum's weekly spreadsheet was over the top, but it's starting to seem like a good idea.

As Professor Anderson introduces a new case study, I hide my phone under the desk and scroll to my oldest photo of Abbey. There she is – golden-brown hair, tanned skin, long legs. I'm next to her – average hair, pale skin, solid legs. We look about thirteen.

Abbey and I met in our first year of high school. We were practically Siamese twins until the end of Year Twelve. Things weren't the same after I pulled out of our long-planned trip through South-East Asia at the end of school. Abbey teamed up with Frannie instead, while I stayed home to work at Gold Star Investigations. I couldn't let the opportunity go by.

'Sophie Cartwright, summarise Nixon versus Drewe.'

I jolt upright as the girl next to me stands. Professor Anderson's search beam is in my vicinity.

'A reasonable person would say ...' Sophie gives what sounds to my ignorant ears like a flawless answer.

Professor Anderson nods. 'Fine.' This is practically a standing ovation.

Sophie sits, her cheeks flushed with triumph.

In the first week of law, Professor Anderson informed us that we are all in competition with each other. 'To get ahead in law, you need to improve your CV by getting internships. These are in short supply and go to the highest achievers.'

My classmates have decided I am no threat to their ranking, so they are friendly enough. Our lunchtime conversations revolve around two things. How many hours they studied last night – *a lot* – and which firms they plan to get internships at – *the best ones*.

These discussions make me nostalgic for PI talk with Rosco. Stake-outs, undercover disguises and creepy clients are much less cutthroat than the law.

❀

On my way home from uni, I rush into after-school care. Nan is at the beautician, so I'm on Jacq duty. For a retired person, Nan has a lot of commitments. I am on Jacq duty more often than not.

Jacq had a sleepover last night at Donald's penthouse with Nan, so she is excited to see me. She runs out so fast she almost knocks me over. She has become clingy since Mum and Dad deserted us. I can't blame her. Prioritising Buddhist monks ahead of me and Jacq is a little hurtful.

I press my nose against Jacq's soft cheek and squeeze her tight before she wriggles away to deliver her news.

'Nan and Donald let me stay up till nine o'clock on the Play Station. And eat chocolate after dinner.'

Clearly, it was party time at Donald's place while I was in

Byron. I put on my sternest face. 'Tonight, to make up for it, you'll be in bed by seven o'clock. And dinner is broccoli. Nothing else, just broccoli.'

'No,' wails Jacq. 'I'll die if I have to eat that stuff.'

I relent on the broccoli, but Jacq doesn't resist going to bed early. She's worn out.

After she's asleep, I make myself a Milo. Nan is at a ukulele convention, so I don't have to listen to her *tut tut* about how fattening Milo is. My level of caring about the calories in Milo is zero out of ten.

Slumping onto the couch, I flick through Spotify. To the haunting melody of 'Ocean Eyes', I sip my Milo and look through my photos of Abbey again. What happened to her?

I come to the selfie from our meeting at the cafe in Surfers. Abbey has a fresh fruit juice and a vegan slice in front of her – she's become a strict vegan since moving to Byron. I've got a coffee and two enormous scones. Abbey is wearing a halter-neck top and her sun-streaked hair is falling over her shoulders. My T-shirt has a splash of red on the front where I've spilt the jam from one of my scones. We are leaning toward each other, but our smiles are strained.

In her last couple of years at school, Abbey tossed up between two career choices – journalism and environmental science. She loved writing, but environmental issues were her passion. When she got back from Asia, her mind was made up. She enrolled in environmental science at the university near Byron. Abbey had always dreamt of living at her family's beach shack in Byron Bay. I understood why. She'd taken me down there when I was in Year Ten, and I'd fallen in love with the place at once.

Abbey seemed completely happy with her life. Almost sickeningly so. *I'm living the dream, Ol.*

I put down my phone and pick up my knitting but give it away after about fifty dropped stitches. Kevin will have to wait for his coat. I don't understand. Why would Abbey throw it all away?

CHAPTER FIVE

Across the gleam of the bay, mountains press against the stars. Abbey's eyes trace the shape of each valley and peak.

A movement on the beach catches her eye. Irritation twitches through her as a familiar face takes shape in the moonlight. Grasping the rim of her board, she pulls it around and paddles for a wave ...

❁

'Did you wet your bed Livvie?' Jacq jumps on top of me, her new-normal morning routine.

Outside, the sea is roaring. I must have fallen asleep on the couch. I guess Nan didn't notice when she came in. Or, more likely, she stayed at Donald's again. That means I'm on school duty.

I squeeze Jacq's warm body and breathe in her little-girl smell. 'No, felt like sleeping somewhere new.' I close my eyes again, holding onto oblivion. My head thumps and there's something sharp poking into my back. I dig around underneath me and unearth the tangled remains of my knitting.

'Time for *Bluey*.' Jacq pulls away from me and turns on the television. She's never allowed to watch morning television, but she knows when her prey is weak.

As I close my eyes again, I remember last night's Skype call.

Mum's late-night calls have become a routine of sorts. She

has a short timeslot free between teaching and prayers. Dad sometimes joins in. He tries to be upbeat, but his face droops when he thinks I'm not looking. I take it Mum's midlife crisis is still in progress.

For someone in the midst of a crisis, Mum is blissfully happy. Happier than I've ever seen her. I assumed frantically busy and super-organised was her happy place, but no. A Buddhist monastery suits her better. I've given up asking when she's coming back. She gets vague and ends the call soon after. I've decided to act like teaching English to Kathmandu boy-monks is the new normal. I'm hoping it will blow over.

❁

Last night, the connection was crackly as usual.

Mum waved as her face appeared on my phone. She was wearing a polar fleece jacket and beanie and her cheeks were pink. Tufts of short, dark hair poked out from the beanie.

'How are things going there, Olivia?' she asked.

I hesitated. These calls were frustrating. The short timeslot, the poor connection and Mum's vagueness made it hard to talk. But she did ask, so I blurted it all out, speaking quickly to get my words in while I could.

I told her about Abbey's disappearance. How guilty I was about what I said to her at the cafe. How I was sure she would turn up, but it still made me anxious.

After a pause, Mum spoke. 'I'm sorry, I didn't hear any of that – the connection, and the monks are chanting ...'

I gritted my teeth. Why wasn't she here? Busy as she was, Mum always found time for a chat. Not anymore. Cymbals clashed behind her. Over and over. The noise was deafening. 'What's happening there?'

'The monks are practising the Lama Dance. It's amazing here. I'm learning so much.' The cymbals pause and her next words are clear. 'Did you know there are two mistakes one can make along the road to truth – not going all the way, and not starting?'

The words cut through my annoyance. 'Did Buddha say that?'

'Yes. It's time for evening prayers now. Goodnight darling. Namaste.'

Namaste? 'But—'

Mum's face vanished.

I raised my hand. 'Goodnight.' It was hard to get used to Mum not being there when I needed her.

Feeling fragile, I plod through the 'off to school and uni' routine. I wish I could spend the day on the couch in my trackies. Making Jacq's lunch is my least favourite activity. Peanut-butter sandwiches would be easy, but Jacq informed me nuts are forbidden. Mum made tasty, nutritionally balanced lunches for Jacq and me, five days a week. She never complained. Not to mention the tasty, nutritious dinners every night that we all took for granted.

There are two mistakes one can make along the road to truth: not going all the way, and not starting ... It's lovely for Mum that she's getting so enlightened, but what about me? Where is my road to truth?

In the uni car park, I pull down the mirror to check my appearance. *Bad idea, better not to know.* In the morning rush, personal grooming has become an optional extra. I slam the car door and head for class.

Mrs Watson said she would tell me as soon as she heard

anything about Abbey so, in the absence of an update … Abbey is still missing. Where has she gone?

⁂

'You look tired, Olivia. Were you up late reading Brown versus Hodges?'

I lift my head off the desk as Sophie slides into the seat next to me. Sophie is the style queen of first-year law. She's wearing a tight-fitting yellow dress with matching shoes and her blonde hair is sleek and shiny.

If I didn't feel like the walking zombie from hell before she arrived, I do afterwards. My outfit of crumpled cargos and a worn-out T-shirt is not lawyer-in-training material. I haven't kept on top of my washing.

The first week of uni, Sophie had asked me if I was into normcore. I'd had to consult Google. It turned out the normcore fashion trend focuses on looking nondescript. Khaki cargo pants are in, colourful dresses are out. Designer purses are out, backpacks are in. It described me to a T.

'Why yes, I am into normcore, thank you for asking,' I'd replied.

It was a revelation. I wasn't fashion-challenged, as I'd thought. No, I was at the forefront of a cutting-edge trend. Today though, I may have slipped below the standards of normcore. It only works if you give the impression you could dress well if you chose to. This is not my look at the moment.

'Uh, yes, Brown versus Hodges. That was an interesting case,' I mutter. 'A lot of puffery going on.'

'I know, right?' says Sophie. 'I can't believe how misleading and deceptive the witness was. The jury bias was not insignificant too. I was up until midnight studying it all.'

I nod. 'A reasonable person would say they should have acquitted.' I am pulling this from nowhere. I have no idea what Brown versus Hodges is about.

Sophie's eyes widen. 'Do you really think so?'

'Absolutely.'

'Oh, I missed that conclusion, thanks.' Sophie scribbles in her notebook.

I don't feel guilty. My chances of overtaking Sophie in the class rankings are nil. Luckily, today my invisibility cloak works again, and Professor Anderson doesn't call on me. I sense her eyes rest on me at one stage though. The hair on my neck stands on end. My odds of being picked are shortening. I'd better get on top of that reading.

It's a relief to get home, after picking up Jacq from after-school care. Nan is out somewhere as usual. Pulling on the extra-big T-shirt that's my glamorous lounging-at-home outfit, I lie on the bed. Outside on the balcony, Jacq bounces a basketball against the wall, making my head throb.

I checked my phone all day, but there's still no message from Mrs Watson. Stretching out my feet, I close my eyes, and remember how I met Abbey. It was the first week of high school ...

'Is this seat taken?'

I slid my notebook and pens along the lab bench to make room. 'Go for it.'

A girl slipped onto the bench next to me. Abbey hadn't gone to my primary school, but I knew who she was. I'd seen her at the inter-school swimming carnival last year. She wore red Speedos and sliced up and down the pool like a shark. When she won the finals, she did a fifty-metre victory lap underwater without coming up. My friends and I decided she was a show-off.

I wondered why she'd chosen to squeeze in here. There were plenty of other spots to sit.

She put out her hand. 'Hi, I'm Abbey.' Her fingers were warm.

'The name's Grace, Olivia Grace.' I blushed as soon as I said it. I sounded like an idiot. Dad and I had just watched the latest James Bond movie and I was going through a 007 phase.

But Abbey smiled like she got it. 'Watson, Abbey Watson.' As the teacher came in, Abbey pulled a leaflet out of her backpack and gave it to me.

I eyed the heading – *March Against Climate Change*. So that was why she'd sat beside me. She was recruiting. I should have known someone like Abbey wouldn't befriend someone like me unless she wanted something.

'You should come along.'

'I might.' I stuffed the leaflet in my pocket and opened my notebook. I wouldn't. I was as worried about climate change as the next person, but marching wasn't my thing.

I'd forgotten about the march by the time the day came around. But as I walked down the street toward school, the sound of chanting drifted toward me.

What do we want? Climate Action! When do we want it? Now! About ten placard-carrying kids straggled around the corner. Up the head of the marchers, someone in a panda suit held a sign – *There Is No Planet B.*

A bunch of older kids at the bus stop whooped with laughter. 'Check out the mad panda,' said a girl with bottle-blonde hair and hoop earrings.

The panda's furry head had a sideways tilt, and the creature kept tripping over its feet. As it shuffled past, its head fell right off. The girl in the suit paused to pick it up, and as she straightened, her eyes met mine. It was Abbey.

Abbey wasn't a show-off. She was standing up for what she believed in, and she didn't care if she looked stupid doing it. I stepped off the pavement, righted her furry head and joined the march.

That's Abbey: always on the go, never a minute's pause for self-doubt. She is the exact opposite of me, but I jumped into her slipstream and stayed there for years.

CHAPTER SIX

Opening my eyes, I stare at the bedroom ceiling. Jacq is still bouncing a basketball along the balcony. Its noise reverberates through Nan's flat. Abbey and I were so close – what happened?

I find Abbey's song on Spotify and press it. 'Ocean Eyes'. I still can't process it. It's like a raft has been pulled from under me. I'm even mixing my metaphors. Abbey would be shocked.

The song stops and the apartment is silent. Jacq must have moved on from basketball. If I were still a PI, I would try to find out what happened to her and where she is. But I'm not a PI, and my life is hectic enough as it is. I should leave it to the professionals. It's not like I'm the only one who knows how to investigate.

But then Mum's words flash into my head: *there are two mistakes one can make along the road to truth, not going all the way and not starting.* This seems very pointed. Very targeted at me. According to Buddha, if I want to find the truth, not starting would be a mistake. This is not just another case, not to me. It's Abbey.

A memory of Abbey from not long after we met pops into my mind. We were lying on top of a sand dune at Main Beach, dripping wet from the surf ...

Abbey rolled toward me, the sand sticking to her body. 'What are you going to do when you finish school, Ol?'

'Be a PI, like Nancy Drew. How about you?'

Abbey propped herself up on her sandy elbows. 'All I know is, I'm moving to Byron. I'll figure the rest out once I get there.'

I'd never been to Byron Bay, but Abbey made it sound like an enchanted land. *The rainforest comes down to the sea, and the water is full of dolphins ...*

'Beat you to the bottom of the dune,' she said.

'Eat my dust.' I flung myself over the edge.

Abbey overtook me, tumbling down the sand, her hair trailing behind her. We crashed into each other at the bottom and broke into fits of giggles.

Abbey held out her little finger. It was coated in sand. *Best friends forever. Pinkie promise.*

I linked my little finger to hers, the sand grains grating between us. *Pinkie promise.*

Pinkie promise. I might not be a PI, but this is personal. I need to know what happened to Abbey. To find her. My heart thumps and my mind starts to buzz. I know this feeling. It's the feeling I get at the start of a case. My body has made up its mind before my head.

Sure, I'm busy, but I can give this one weekend. If I don't, I won't be able to think of anything else. I'll have a poke around, see what comes up. It won't be an investigation, just a casual ... exploration. There's nothing wrong with that, is there?

But where to begin? The key to Abbey is Byron Bay. It means so much to her.

My mind circles the idea, before plunging in. *Yes*, I'll need to return to the Bay. The tricky part will be lining Nan up to look after Jacq for the weekend.

'Hawaiian spaghetti for dinner,' says Nan as I come into the kitchen. Tonight, she is wearing a floor-length kaftan with a hibiscus design. Our life is all about Hawaii since Nan discovered ukulele. Israel Kamakawiwo'ole is singing 'Somewhere Over the Rainbow' on the sound system. I know it's Israel Kamakawiwo'ole, because as of this week, he is Nan's favourite musician. Nan might be sixty, but her enthusiasm for new experiences never wanes.

I had no idea Hawaiian spaghetti was even a thing, but it appears I've lived a sheltered life. As it turns out, Hawaiian spaghetti is not bad. Even when Nan's no-carb diet means shredded zucchini takes the place of spaghetti.

'Can't you taste the Aloha spirit?' Nan forks up a twirl of pineapple, pork, and zucchini-spaghetti.

'Maybe you should have cooked it on Aloha temperature,' says Jacq. 'It's a bit burnt.'

'Very punny,' I say. It's a laugh a minute around here.

After Jacq goes to bed, I try to figure out a way to ask Nan to look after her for the weekend, so I can go to Byron. Nan's weekends are usually booked solid with social events, so it's a big ask.

'I've seen you on that dating app. Have you met a nice boy yet?' Nan asks as we do the dishes.

'No.' My chances of meeting a nice boy on Bumble are non-existent, since I never swipe right.

Nan sighs. 'That's a shame. You know that's how I met

Donald, don't you? I changed my profile to say I played the ukulele, to get his attention.'

'Was it a problem when he realised you didn't?'

'No.' Nan points at me with the washing-up brush. 'I took some lessons before our first date. There's no need to let a lack of musical talent stand in the way of true love. Why don't you let me set you up with someone? My friend Maureen's grandson ...'

'No. No way. Forget it.' Nan's tried to palm off the sociopath grandchildren of her friends on me before. I have no wish to spend another evening listening to a greasy-haired boy explain *World of Warcraft*.

'I know you think you've got forever, but you're not getting any younger. Before you know it, you'll be too old to have babies.'

I screw up my face. 'I'm eighteen, Nan. Babies are ... not a thing for me right now.'

Nan sniffs and scrubs at the saucepan. 'You're wasting the best years of your life.'

Suddenly I have a brainwave. 'Actually, a nice boy asked me out to dinner in Byron Bay this weekend. It's a shame I can't go ...'

It works like magic. Nan agrees to look after Jacq for the weekend. 'Have you heard from your mother lately?' she asks as she passes me the clean saucepan. 'She told me she was keeping in touch with you the last time we spoke.'

'Yes. She calls every now and then.'

Nan shakes her head. 'I knew it wouldn't end well. Nepal. They should have stuck with New Zealand. Where did I go wrong with her?'

Since Nan and Mum are about as unalike as two people can be, it's hard to know how to reply.

'Buddhism.' Nan snorts. 'Don't you get mixed up with anything like that in Byron Bay.' She retires to her room with her ukulele.

I slump on the couch under the breeze of the fan and spoon Milo out of the tin. So, I'm going to look into what happened to Abbey. She has to be out there somewhere. Where should I start? I'm out of practice with this investigating game.

As I suck on my spoon, I trawl through my conversations with Abbey. She'd said she was trying to stop a development in the rainforest near Byron Bay. She mentioned a group she was working with. *Bush Buddies?* No, Forest Friends. I'd pictured a group of shaggy-haired people hugging trees. Maybe that's a good place to begin.

The chimes of 'Merry Christmas' interrupt my pondering. *Mrs Watson or a telemarketer?* I pick up my phone. 'Hello?'

'It's Rosco.'

CHAPTER SEVEN

Rosco. My stomach churns as I hold the phone to my ear. Why is *he* calling? Rosco and I haven't spoken since I told him I was leaving Gold Star Investigations two months ago.

True confessions time. Rosco and I weren't just colleagues, we were ... at the start of something. Things hadn't got further than a few kisses, but they had been exceptional ones. We were like Princess Leia and Han Solo – our chemistry was sizzling. Or that's what I'd thought.

I hadn't expected him to react the way he did, when I told him I was leaving the agency.

He went all quiet. He was taken aback – which was fair enough; it would have come as a surprise. He felt let down. I figured he'd get over it, so I decided to give him some space.

After a couple of days, I sent a follow-up message. I kept it casual. *Hey, what's up?* When he didn't reply to that one, I tried again. After about twenty attempts to compose a message that would say *why didn't you reply to my last message?* without actually saying that, I settled on *hi.* He didn't reply to that one either.

I could have tried calling him, but phone conversations are so icky. A voice call is an effort at the best of times, let alone when someone is ghosting you. I do voice calls for work reasons only. There are too many ways for a phone call to go wrong.

Rosco's non-response to my texts was message enough. It was obvious our personal relationship was over as well as our professional one. That hurt.

So now, hearing his voice is strange. Why is he calling?

'Mrs Watson asked me to look into Abbey's disappearance.' His voice is crisp and professional. As if we'd never been anything to each other. As if he hadn't been ghosting me for months.

'Oh.' This shouldn't surprise me – it makes sense she would ask him. He's the PI, not me, but still ... it's me who was Abbey's friend (*is* Abbey's friend), not Rosco.

'I have some questions,' he says.

I swallow. 'Okay. Shoot.'

He dives into his interview. 'Were you and Abbey close lately?'

'Not as much as we used to be. She didn't come up to the Goldie much.'

'Did she give you any sign of suicidal thoughts?'

'No, not at all.'

'Was she using drugs?'

'Drugs? Abbey? Why?' I straighten.

There is silence on the end of the phone.

This is why I hate phone calls: it's so hard to work out what's going on. Does he know something he's not telling me? I fill the silence. 'No. She never even used to drink. She said it made her feel stupid. Do *you* think it was suicide?'

He pauses. 'I couldn't say.'

'I'd like to hear what you think.'

'Okay.' His voice is slow. 'My reading is she paddled out to sea then ... either passed out and slipped off her board or had a fall and hit her head. She was seen at the Beach Hotel that evening. Maybe she'd been drinking ... or taking something else. She must have been a long way out or ...'

His voice drifts off, but I know what he means. *Her body would have washed up.* I blink. But Abbey isn't dead, just missing.

'Maybe she didn't mean to come back,' he says.

'No, I don't believe that, I ...' My voice trails off. *What do I know?*

There is silence again.

'Is there anything else you can tell me that might help my investigation?' he says.

'You might be better off speaking to her friends in Byron Bay.'

'Thanks, hot tip.'

'You're welcome.' We never used to speak to each other like this.

There's another silence.

'I saw you updated your profile on Bumble,' he says.

My gut squirms. He's been on Bumble. That means he's dating other girls. Or thinking about it at least. And he saw my stupid profile. 'I saw yours.' I shouldn't have said that. He'll think I'm cyber-stalking him now. I suppose I am. But only in a non-obsessive, well-adjusted way.

Again, there is silence.

'Okay, well if you think of anything relevant, give me a call,' he says.

The fact I'm heading to Byron myself might be relevant, but I'm not going to tell him that. In the brief pause before he hangs up, I almost say *I miss you*, but I breathe until the urge passes.

Rosco's call stirs up feelings I've worked hard to damp down. Tapping on Bumble, I examine his picture again. He looks like a surfer-boy, but beneath that exterior lurks a Mariana Trench of hidden depths. My Geography teacher used to say that if you put Mount Everest in the Mariana Trench, it wouldn't break the surface. That's a lot of hidden depths.

I eye the words beneath his picture. *Walk on the wild side, if you believe in synchronicity, I'm your man ...*

According to my research, creating a good dating profile is both an art and a science. You should *share who you are* but *keep some mystery. Look your best self* but *keep your silly side.* And be either *authentic and attractive,* or *high achieving but fun-loving.*

Rosco isn't doing any of these things. But despite his uninspiring profile, my guess is he's getting plenty of swipe-rights.

I tap on my own profile. *Olivia – law student, eighteen years old, likes skydiving, competitive chess and gourmet cooking.* When I say *likes,* what I mean is *might like.* I've never done any of these things. It's probably as close to the truth as most of the profiles I've read though. I edit it – *Doesn't believe in synchronicity or walking on the wild side.*

As I put my phone down, Rosco's voice echoes in my mind. *Maybe she didn't mean to come back.*

CHAPTER EIGHT

A familiar face takes shape in the moonlight. Grasping the rim of her board, Abbey pulls it around and paddles ...

Wave after wave rolls past the point. A guitar falls silent, the moon inches westwards, the lights of the hotel dim. As the lighthouse beam swings around again, a board floats, drifting with the current.

I wake, sweat-soaked and dry-mouthed, my sheets in a tangle.

My invisibility cloak holds up at uni the next day – I am not called on in lectures. This is fortunate, as I can think of nothing but Abbey and my coming weekend in Byron. *Maybe she didn't mean to come back.*

That night, I ring Mrs Watson. Her voice is soft as we go through our greetings.

'I'm going to Byron Bay this weekend,' I say. 'I wondered if there was anything you need me to pick up?'

'Actually, there is something. Abbey borrowed my best gardening shears when she was here a month ago. I need them for the roses. Would you mind picking them up from the house?'

'I'd be happy to.'

'Drop in on your way and I'll give you the key. Why don't you stay there? There's no point in paying for accommodation if you don't have to.'

I hesitate. *Do I want to stay in Abbey's house?* The idea of being there without her is weird. But it will help me get inside her head. 'Thank you, that would be great.'

'I still can't understand it ... it makes no sense at all.' There's a muffled sob on the end of the line.

'I know.' I'd like to say something comforting, but words fail me.

After Mrs Watson hangs up, I make a Milo. What am I trying to do with this weekend in the Bay? I'm not a PI anymore. I should leave it to Rosco. My throat clenches as I remember his phone call. He treated me like just another source. He won't be happy about me meddling in his case. I'd better make sure he doesn't find out.

My phone rings with a Skype call from Mum. I start to tell her about Abbey again.

'Sorry darling, I didn't hear most of that, the connection ... did you say you're going to see a play?'

I suddenly feel very tired. I can't have this conversation right now. 'I'm going to Byron Bay, on a bit of a mission ...'

'That's great.' Mum is suddenly crystal clear. 'Buddha said one moment can change a day, one day can change a life and one life can change the world.'

Is she talking about me, or herself? I'm getting used to Mum's Buddhist proclamations, but I'm never sure what to make of them. I ask her what it means.

'Maybe ...' says Mum. 'You want to change?' Cymbals clash in the background. 'Time for prayers.'

I wave goodbye, and she hangs up.

Change. I walk out on the balcony and smell the salt air. I remember how out of place I was at the ceremony at Wategos.

That red-haired guy with the ponytail had thought 1 was a cop. 1 look at my pale legs, my khaki shorts. I'd stuck out like a sore thumb.

If I'm going to be investigating, 1 need to fit in. 1 don't want the people who saw me at Abbey's service to recognise me.

My pulse gives a leap of excitement. When 1 was a PI, 1 had a grab-bag of disguises for every occasion. Transforming into someone new was one of the things I'd enjoyed best. While 1 am most at home in my sub-standard normcore look, inside, there's a girl who loves dress-ups. Disguising myself releases something inside me. It's like being an actor, I'm free to assume a new role.

Maybe you want to change? 1 finish my Milo, an idea stirring. I'm pretty sure it's not what Mum or Buddha had in mind, but ... *it's makeover time.*

Plonking my glass down, 1 make a call. An answering machine picks up. 'I'd like to make an appointment for tomorrow afternoon. The name's ...' 1 pause. I've had enough of being boring old normcore Olivia. Inspiration strikes. 'Nansea. That's N-A-N-S-E-A.'

Yes, 1 will reinvent myself as Nansea. Nansea is the kind of girl who gets her man, never takes no for an answer, and always looks stylish. Nansea, in fact, is the long-lost hippie cousin of Nancy Drew. *Peace out.*

On Friday afternoon, 1 skip the last two lectures. Back home, 1 open the doors of the cluttered wardrobe I'm sharing with Jacq. Nan's spare clothes are in there too, so it's lucky I'm a minimalist dresser, or the wardrobe would explode. So, what would Nansea wear?

Not cool babe, 1 hear her say as she inspects my clothes.

Nansea is coming to life already, and she wouldn't waste a minute with my black and khaki clothing collection. I grab my usual uniform of T-shirt and cargos. It's time to get tanned.

Abbey and I once had a flirtation with fake tan. We pretended no-one noticed our orange-tinged faces, or our brown knuckles and palms. This time though, I'm doing it like a pro. *Tanning in your own private cubicle,* the website had said.

My heart flutters as I open the door of *Tan Magic.* I'm a low-maintenance girl and this is out of my comfort zone, but Nansea is not the type of girl who rocks lily-white legs.

The blonde and bronzed young woman behind the counter gives me a quizzical look. Her dazzling white lab coat implies that tanning is scientific, important, and not far removed from curing cancer. This is reassuring.

'I've got an appointment. The name's Nansea.'

Her sculpted eyebrows lift a fraction. 'What colour would you like today Nansea?' She pulls out a series of before and after photographs. 'Regular bronze, celebrity tan or tangerine dream?'

'Tangerine dream.' If I'm going to tan, I want to tan properly.

'Excellent.' She pulls back a curtain and gestures like an air hostess toward a cubicle. 'Have you been in one of these before?'

I shake my head. The cubicle is shiny white and looks technical, like a time-travel chamber. I'd better not end up as a suntanned medieval serving wench.

She starts her briefing, indicating with her hands like a flight attendant. 'You put your clothes here. There is paper underwear if you want, or you can get an all-over tan. It's best to wear the shower cap. When you're ready, step into the cubicle and press the button. The tanning mist comes in four cycles. You should vary your pose like so.' She demonstrates four different poses, her arms rising and falling.

My armpits sweat as I watch her. What if I can't remember the poses? Will I end up tangerine swirl instead of tangerine dream?

'Close your eyes when the mist reaches your face. When you're finished you can wipe off the excess. Use wet wipes on your hands and feet. Enjoy.' With a practised smile she turns and leaves, pulling the curtain behind her.

I peer into the cubicle and consider, then reject, the paper underwear. Stripping off all my clothes, I put on the shower cap and step in. Ready for take-off.

I press the button and a loud humming begins. There's a hiss and cold, wet spray hits my feet and makes its way upwards. It's up to my stomach before I remember to assume the first position. As it hits my face, I close my eyes and hold my breath. The spray stops for a moment and I turn around, remembering to clench my fists. Suntanned palms are a bad look.

Three more times, the spray works its way up my body, before the humming stops. I step out, pull off the shower cap, and wipe myself with a towel. Gazing into the mirror next to the cubicle, I blink. *Is that me?* I'm not sure how I feel about it. I turn and peer over my bronzed shoulder.

Well, hello, says an inner voice I'm coming to know as Nansea.

Unlike me, Nansea is a bronzed beach babe and proud of it. I pull on my clothes.

'Wow,' says the attendant as I come out. 'You look different.'

'Thank you.' Different obviously means better. A terrible thought strikes me. 'Is there any way of removing the tan?' I don't want to shock the law class on Monday with my tangerine skin.

41

'No problem.' She leans down and pulls out a plastic packet. 'If you need to take it off, wipe yourself with these towelettes. Soak in a bath and use a loofah to remove any remaining patches.'

I pay up. It's time to hit the clothes shops before Nansea's next appointment at the hairdresser.

CHAPTER NINE

I crawl out of bed on Saturday morning, catch sight of myself in the mirror and almost squeal. *Who is that girl?*

It's quite a transformation. My teeth flash white in my tangerine face and my blonde-streaked hair looks amazing. Grabbing two hair elastics and a fistful of bobby pins from Nan's dresser, I add the final touch. I tilt my head. Are the Princess Leia side-buns a mistake? No, they are totally Nansea's style.

You rock babe, says Nansea.

I like this Nansea voice. It is cheery, optimistic and confident. It is just what I need. Unlike me, Nansea has no doubts about solving the mystery of Abbey's disappearance.

I pull on my new bare-midriff halter neck top, floaty skirt and purple thongs and check myself out. The dolphin tattoo on my shoulder is a groovy touch – temporary, of course. Some piercings would be cool, but I have law school on Monday. I pull on some Indian bracelets instead. They chink against my arms as I walk from the room.

Jacq looks up from her Rice Bubbles as I come in. 'You look colourful, Livvie.'

I bury my face in her fluffy hair for a moment, breathing in the smell of shampoo. 'Are you looking forward to spending the weekend with Nan?'

'Yeah ...' She sounds doubtful.

'Do you like Donald?'

'Mm hm, he always buys me ice-cream and lollies.'

I would say something to Donald about junk food, but I can't afford to get him offside. 'Great.'

Nan's eyes widen as she comes into the kitchen. She was out last night, so she's missed my makeover. She takes in my hair, my tan and my outfit. Her eyebrows twitch. 'Fake tan is so slimming, isn't it?' Nan is a black-belt in backhanded compliments.

I don't let her get me down. 'Body-shaming is so last year, Nan.'

'Be back by five o'clock tomorrow. Donald and I are going to a ukulele play-along. Don't be late.'

Waving, I give a Nansea-like twirl and head for the door.

❧

Mrs Watson lives in Broadbeach, a ten-minute drive away. I pull into the driveway of her red-brick house and knock on the door. She opens it, wearing a thick blue dressing gown, her hair still flattened from sleep.

'Yes?' She peers at me, her brow wrinkled.

'It's me ... Olivia.'

'Olivia?' She fumbles in the pocket of her dressing gown and pulls out her glasses. Sliding them over her ears, she stares at me. 'Why so it is. I didn't recognise you. What have you done to yourself?'

I shrug, embarrassed. 'Felt like a change ...'

She smiles, her tired face brightening. 'It suits you. Come inside, I'll get the key.'

I wait in the loungeroom while Mrs Watson disappears up the corridor. Their house hasn't changed. The glass-fronted cabinet in the corner still displays Abbey's sporting trophies.

Swimming, soccer, athletics ... You name it, she did it. Abbey and I were complete opposites in that way. The only sport I ever got into was surfing, and I never excelled at it.

Mrs Watson returns and presses the key into my palm, wrapping her hands around mine. 'There's something else ... The police phoned and asked me what to do with Abbey's surfboard. They've finished with it now.'

I picture the board floating in on a wave, riderless.

'Can you look after it? Until Abbey comes back.'

'Sure.'

'You should use it. Abbey loves that board. Look, there's a picture of her on it.' Mrs Watson points to a framed photo that has pride of place on the coffee table.

Abbey is wearing red board shorts and a black bikini top. Poised on the nose of the board, her toes curl over its rim and her body arches backwards as she rides the lip of the wave. I know a tricky move when I see one.

A piece of notepaper lies on the table beside the photo. I recognise the scrawl of writing and the signature. *Abbey*. Pulling my gaze away, I meet Mrs Watson's eyes.

'It's what she left, in her house. Would you like to read it?'

I nod, both dreading and longing to hold Abbey's words in my hands.

Mrs Watson hands me the note.

It is brief. *It's not the way it used to be. I don't want to go on anymore, Abbey.* Chewing my lip, I place the note back on the table. I'm such a bad friend. Why didn't I know she was depressed? 'Do you think ...?'

'No. I don't.' Her voice is suddenly, uncharacteristically, fierce. Then she smiles, as if to apologise.

'I don't think so either,' I say, smiling back. 'Was she happy, in Byron?'

Mrs Watson's brow wrinkles. 'I suppose so. She always wanted to live there. She was so busy lately though. I didn't see as much of her as I wanted to.'

'No, me neither.'

I glance back at Abbey's picture, my eyes fixing on the leg-rope leash that circles her calf. 'Wasn't she wearing a leg rope? When she disappeared? She always used to.'

Mrs Watson's soft voice quavers. 'No, I don't think she was dear. Or the board would still have been with her, wouldn't it? Unless the leg-rope broke?'

But if it broke, the end would still be on the board ... I don't want to upset her, so I drop the subject. Not everyone uses a leg-rope, and maybe Abbey changed.

We walk down the hallway, Mrs Watson shuffling her slippers beside me. I hesitate at the door. 'Mrs Watson, Rosco rang me ...'

Mrs Watson nods. 'Yes dear. I asked him to look into Abbey's disappearance. He's a private investigator now. He's a lovely boy, isn't he?'

A lovely boy who stopped returning my messages.

'It's inexplicable, the way she disappeared ...' Mrs Watson's voice trails off.

'I know, it is strange.' I almost tell her I'm looking into it, but she might tell Rosco. Besides, I shouldn't get her hopes up. I only have a couple of days, it's not likely I'll find out anything useful. This weekend is mainly about settling my guilt.

I give Mrs Watson a hug and get into my car. I glance in my rear-view mirror as I turn the corner. She is gazing after me.

The traffic is heavy, but by nine o'clock I'm through the Gold Coast bedlam and over the border into Tweed Heads.

I zone out on the freeway until I see the sign pointing to the old highway. I remember how I drove it with Abbey the first time we went to Byron ...

The old Holden discharged a puff of smoke as we climbed the range.

'You can do it Maisie.' Mrs Watson patted the dashboard.

Abbey stuck her hand out the window, swooping it in the wind. 'Three days in Byron Bay, yahoo!'

We chugged past dark-forested mountains. 'Wollumbin, Mount Neville, The Devil's Marbles, The Sphinx ...' Mrs Watson named the peaks.

The mountains appeared mysterious and inviting, almost enchanted. They looked like the kind of place you could disappear.

The roar of the traffic pulls me back to the present. Byron seemed like paradise when we got there, but I soon found out it wasn't. I accelerate into the fast lane, leaving the memory behind.

CHAPTER TEN

First right out of Byron Bay, follow the road past the water tank ...

I pull into the driveway of the Watsons' holiday shack. It's been ages since I've been here, but it's still familiar. A tangled bush dripping with red flowers pokes through a picket fence. As I get out of the car, the hum of a tractor from the paddock next door carries toward me on the breeze.

A colourful hammock hangs on the verandah. I'm in no hurry to go inside, so I slip into it and swing, enjoying the sun on my face as I gaze toward the sliver of sea. Sliding from the hammock at last, I fit the key into the door. It feels invasive to go in, but I'd better get on with it. Opening the door, I step inside.

The corridor is cool, and I wander from room to room, my steps loud on the wooden floor. So many memories of Abbey flood back, I almost expect her to run out of one of the rooms.

How good was that surf, Ol?

I imagine her damp footprints on the floorboards ahead of me.

Abbey's bedroom is at the end of the corridor. It is unnaturally tidy for the Abbey I remember. A computer has pride of place on the desk, but there are no papers, no notebooks. Abbey always used to keep a notebook. Perhaps the police have taken them.

I gaze around, but I don't know what I'm looking for – something to fill in the gaps.

A pile of magazines has been shoved under her bed. I drag them out. *Eco Life, Simply Living, Small Planet* – they all have articles by Abbey. Environmental science might have won out as Abbey's career choice, but she still loves to write.

The planet needs people who can communicate, Ol.

I leave the magazines on the bed, I'll read them later. On my way back to the front door, I stop to inspect a large corkboard filled with thumb-tacked photographs. Abbey often printed out her photos. My breath catches as I see the faded square down the bottom.

Two tangle-haired girls peer into the frame. Abbey took it one evening at a picnic at Wategos Beach. She'd held the phone out as we leaned our heads together, arms around each other. Our conversation had taken a philosophical turn that night.

Do you think this life is all we have, Ol?

I hope not, Ab. It's going to take me more than one go to get it right.

Guess I'm still not getting it right. I unpin the photograph and stick it in my shoulder bag. As I straighten, something catches my eye – a calendar on the kitchen wall. Walking over, I scan the last month. There are notes here and there in Abbey's messy writing, reminders to pay bills and article deadlines. The most recent entry is a scribble of letters. My pulse thumps as I notice the date. It's the day she disappeared.

Her writing is hard to read. I used to joke Abbey would make a good doctor – she had the illegible scribble down pat. I run my fingers over the pen marks, trying to make them out. It looks like an *A*, followed by a dash, then *FAP*. I tilt my head to the side and stare at the letters. *A – FAP.* It doesn't ring any bells, but it could be important.

I google the letters. Maybe it's the name of a restaurant, or a bar. There is a *Fins* and a *Francesca's*, but nothing that matches with *FAP* or *A – FAP*. My mind returns to Abbey's notebook. It must be around somewhere. It might have more detail on this mysterious note. Where would she have left it? As I gaze at the calendar, a memory returns ...

Abbey and I were having a study-in at her house; exams were starting soon. I'd lifted my head from my notes to see her lying, eyes closed, on the couch.

'Hey, what are you doing? Exams start Monday. You'd better get into it.'

She opened her eyes and tapped her forehead. 'I'm implanting the information.' She pulled her notebook out from under the cushions and brandished it. 'I'm absorbing it from under the pillow. You need to let your brain make connections.'

I scoffed. But she got straight distinctions, so maybe there was something to it.

Walking over to the couch, I lift up a pillow, and ... *Bingo.* A blue notebook is tucked underneath. Picking it up, I flick through notes about her days and outlines of stories. Nothing catches my eye until the final page. In a flowery doodle, Abbey has written *Fallen Angel's Plaything.* Creeping vines decorate the words, snaking their way through the letters.

Fallen Angel's Plaything. FAP. I look at the calendar again. *A – FAP.* The *A* is separate from the other letters. Is it a name? At our last meeting, Abbey had hinted that there was someone new in her life. I tried to get more out of her, but she said it was early days. She didn't want to jinx it. The letters could be something banal of course. A shopping list – *apples, fruit, Ajax, potatoes*. Am I being too Nancy Drew?

No, it's as suss as a five-day-old salmon steak, hisses Nansea.

Nansea is my kind of gal. I slip the notebook into my bag with the photo. It's time to head down to town.

Letting myself out, I shut the door. The hammock sways in the breeze as I drive off.

❋

I find the poky office of Forest Friends in the back streets of Byron. It's nestled between the aromatherapy shop and the Indian imports. Parking my car, I sit for a minute, listening to the radio. Luna is on again.

'Right now, it's the new moon, which is, like, an excellent time to start projects. It's a new cycle and the beginning of an expansion that lasts until the full moon,' she says.

'Wow, so what can we expect over the next couple of weeks as we move toward full moon, Luna?'

'Well, in the first quarter we take advantage of the seeds sown in the new moon. Things will come to a head. This is a time for building, creating and planning.'

'What about the full moon? What can we expect then?'

'Kapow. We all go crazy at the full moon. Emotions run high. It is a phase of romance, relationships and feelings. We are, like, in full bloom.'

I smile. I'd like to catch up with Luna, but seeing as I'm undercover, I'd better not. Byron's a small town, word gets around. Turning off the radio, I get out of the car.

Through the window of Forest Friends, I see a familiar face.

It's the red-haired dude with the ponytail from the ceremony at Wategos. Anand? No ... Ashok. Indian-inspired names are popular in Byron Bay. I think it reflects an interest in Eastern religions. He's sitting on a blue rubber ball at a cluttered wooden table, his eyes fixed on a computer screen. His green singlet and loose cotton pants look like they need a wash.

I take a deep breath. It's my first investigative interview for a while. Can I still do it?

Once a PI, always a PI, says Nansea.

Ashok's head comes up as I open the door. 'Yeah?' His fingers are still on the keyboard and a string bracelet dangles from one sinewy wrist.

'Hi. I'm Nansea. A friend of Abbey's.'

His brow furrows. 'Haven't seen you round before.'

That's good – my disguise is working. 'I've been away for a while. I'd like to talk to you about Abbey.'

His eyes flicker over me. 'I'd rather not, but ... if you must.' He types a few words and hits print. 'Shoot.'

Moving closer, I raise my voice over the noise of the printer. 'Can I buy you a coffee or something?'

'I don't drink coffee and I've got a deadline. What is it, exactly, you want to talk about?' He shuffles the papers on his desk.

'I want to learn about her life here.' I take a punt. 'Does the term *fallen angel* mean anything to you?'

His green eyes narrow and meet mine. 'Why?'

'Want a coffee now?'

He stares at me for a moment, clicks his mouse and shuts the laptop. 'I drink peppermint tea, if you're shouting.'

He locks the door of the office behind him and walks ahead

of me down the street and into the nearest coffee shop. I almost jog to keep up.

Inside, I order a latte and a chocolate muffin. Ashok sticks with peppermint tea.

'What was Abbey working on with Forest Friends?' I ask, as we sit at a table near the window.

Ashok rolls his eyes. 'There's lots of stuff going on – mainly developers wanting to build resorts. They call it eco-tourism to make it sound sweet, but it's a marketing gimmick. Byron Bay can't take any more, but the big money from Sydney and Melbourne want—'

'What was Abbey doing?' I cut into his rant.

'Writing letters and articles, organising protests, putting out news releases. Same as the rest of us.' Ashok crumples a paper napkin in his hand.

I pause while the waitress puts our orders on the table. My stomach rumbles. It's been a long time since breakfast. 'Back at the office, it seemed like *fallen angel* meant something to you.'

Ashok taps his teaspoon on his saucer. 'I was intrigued, that's all. What's it about?'

'It's something I found in a notebook at Abbey's house. It doesn't ring any bells?'

'Nope.' Ashok's eyes meet mine. 'What do *you* think it means?'

I shrug. 'Maybe nothing.'

'What's your interest in this anyway?'

I've just taken a bite of my muffin, so it takes me a while to reply. 'Abbey is a friend ...' I swallow. 'Do you think she killed herself?'

'If you know Abbey, you'll know she can be moody.'

Moody. That's not a word I'd have used about Abbey. I take a slow sip of my coffee 'Did she have a boyfriend in Byron Bay?'

'There were lots of guys around her.'

'Including you?'

He flicks his head up and shreds his napkin.

I take that as a yes.

Ashok stands, scraping his chair backwards. 'I've got to get back. If I don't get this submission in by Monday, the Council won't look at it.'

'Do you know anyone else I can talk to about Abbey?'

He shakes his head. 'Why don't you try her journo contacts? She used to write articles for all the papers and magazines around here.' He turns to go, before swinging back to face me. 'She was up and down, the last few weeks. Everyone thinks it's all peace and love here in Byron Bay ...'

'How do you mean?'

Ashok looks cagey. 'I'm speaking generally. There's a lot of sharks around town.'

'You don't know anyone else Abbey was working with?'

Ashok shrugs. 'Try Adam McBean. He calls himself a freelance botanical consultant.' His voice is scornful. 'He and Abbey used to hang around together. You'll find him at the market tomorrow. He performs there. Gotta go.'

'Peace out.' I give him the peace sign.

He leaves without returning my greeting, which is strange. I watch him weave through the traffic, his red ponytail swinging. He's certainly keen to get back to the office.

CHAPTER ELEVEN

As I finish my coffee, I survey the street. Past the hippie chic and expensive chic clothes shops, a sandwich board reads *Learn to Surf.*

I stare at the sign. Didn't Abbey say she was doing some casual work at the surf school?

Give it a whirl, says Nansea. *You could learn something.*

It's not a bad idea. I leave the cafe, cross the road and go in. A suntanned teenager tears his gaze away from a TV screen on which a surfer rides a skyscraper-sized wave. He gives me a vacant smile. 'Hi.'

'I want a surf lesson,' I say.

'The lesson's from twelve till two. You can take our bus from here or meet Rosie up at The Pass car park.'

'I'll meet up there.'

He writes my name on a clipboard and glances up. 'Hey Rosie, how's the surf?' he calls.

A solid woman with short, sun-bleached hair is at the door, a surfboard under her arm. She has the shoulders of an Olympic swimmer. 'It's unreal, super clean.'

'Nansea is one of your students for the twelve o'clock,' he says.

'Hi Nansea, I'll see you there.' She gives me a smile, her face crinkling into salt-encrusted lines. 'You're going to love it.'

I step out into the sunshine with an hour to spare. Time for a visit to the police station.

❀

Byron Bay Police Station is an unthreatening Queenslander-style bungalow. The door jingles as I go in. 'How can I help you?' asks the young dark-haired policewoman behind the counter.

'My name's Nan – I mean Olivia Grace. I'm here to pick up the surfboard for Mrs Watson.'

The policewoman disappears into the back room. While I'm waiting, an Asian surfer in board shorts comes in, his spiky orange hair still wet from the surf.

'Lost wallet,' he says, his voice forlorn.

'The police will help you.' I point at the counter. After a couple of minutes, a side-door opens, and the policewoman carries out a surfboard. It's about eight-foot long. Pink on the bottom, hibiscus flowers on the top. *Pretty.* She props it against a wall.

No leg-rope? says Nansea.

'Was there a leg-rope?' I ask.

The policewoman glances at the board. 'If there had been, it would be still attached. Sign here.' She passes me a clipboard.

'Are you sure about the leg-rope? She always used to wear one.'

The policewoman frowns. 'There are a lot of surfers around here who don't wear them. As I said, it would still be attached if there was one. If there's nothing else?' Her gaze turns to the surfer.

'Lost wallet,' he says.

I let it drop. I sign for the board and she passes it to me. My fingers tingle as I run them down its smooth edges. *Was this the last thing Abbey saw?*

'You okay?' The surfer is gazing at me.

Air rushes into my lungs and I lift the board. 'I'm fine.'

❀

At The Pass, I get out and gaze at the sea. Masses of bodies crowd the water. Someone has painted *Locals Only* across the rocks. I don't like their chances. My stomach lurches as I see a poster attached to a signpost. It's the one I saw at the Wategos vigil – *Have You Seen Abbey?* Abbey's smile in the picture is infectious. I almost smile back. And Ashok said she was moody.

'Better get in quick while the wind's offshore.' A suntanned surf god puts his surfboard on the rusty Holden next to mine. He ties his board to the roof and pulls off his rash vest, revealing a muscled torso.

'Yeah, looks unreal. Nice and sparkly.'

The blond god gives me a quizzical look, as he towels himself off.

'The water's clear too.' I look at the waves with my best old woman of the sea expression. 'I bet it's warm.'

The surf school minibus pulls in, full of backpackers with sunburnt faces.

'Over here Nansea,' calls Rosie out the window, blowing what's left of my cool. 'We'll get you kitted out.'

'Better go to my lesson,' I say.

The blond god rolls his eyes. 'Make sure you stay out of the way of the real surfers.' He jumps into his car and backs out.

I glare after him. *Good looks aren't everything, mister.*

❀

Fifteen minutes later, I'm lying on a foam learner board on the sand. Lined up beside me are the backpackers: three girls and three boys. I haven't brought Abbey's board to the beach. I'm not ready to ride it.

What if I put a ding in it? Abbey would kill me. There's also the odd feeling I got when I touched it … as if it has something to tell me.

'Paddle, paddle, paddle, look behind you and jump to your feet … like so.' Rosie leaps to her feet and lands in a semi-crouch.

In our matching pink lycra tops, we look like a troupe of drunken gymnasts. Even though I'm the only one who's done this before, I'm not the star of the class. Many of the backpackers leap to their feet with more agility than me. A group of smirking kids with surfboards stops to watch us.

'Hope you're getting a laugh out of it,' I pant.

Rosie decides we're ready to hit the water. I put my board in and paddle out, reminding myself to impersonate a beginner surfer. As it turns out, I'm one of those method actors who take things too far. I am Joaquin Phoenix learning guitar from scratch to play Johnny Cash. Or Heath Ledger ranting and raving in a hotel room for a month to get inside his role as The Joker.

I've never been a stand-out surfer, but usually I can at least get to my feet and ride the whitewash into shore. Today, courtesy of my strenuous dedication to the Stanislavski method, I cannot.

Time and time again, I paddle for perfect little waves, struggle to my feet and fall straight off. It doesn't even feel like I'm acting. My skills have totally deserted me. Soon my arms are limp, and I'm bruised in places I don't even remember hitting. It's as if I've never surfed before in my life. Method acting is powerful stuff.

Rosie takes pity on me. She pulls my surfboard out through the slop and turns it round. 'Okay, Nansea. I'm going to push you off on the next wave. Give it all you've got. Go girl.'

Suddenly I'm on my feet and gliding down a sparkling wave. 'Yay, yippee, yahoo!' I holler in a fake Scandi accent. When you're in Rome ...

'That's the way Nansea!' calls Rosie. 'Okay, that's the lesson for today. Let's head for the bus.'

This is a relief. I once saw a documentary about turtles coming ashore to lay their eggs. I've never seen any creature look as exhausted as those old dears, pulling themselves up the sand. That's what I'm like as I drag my surfboard up the beach. The sand seems to have got wider. I'm grateful when Lars, a handsome Swede, grabs my board off me as I get to the car park and hoists it into the bus. I've got to say, those method actors earn their money. It's exhausting.

'It was a lot of fun, yes?' says Lars. 'Now we are going to drink beer if you would like to come?'

I shake my head. 'I'm pooped.'

'Well done everyone,' says Rosie. 'If you ever need another lesson or want to hire a surfboard, you know where to come.'

As the backpackers file onto the bus, I realise I haven't asked Rosie about Abbey. But how to raise the subject?

She saves me. 'You've got your own surfboard have you, Nansea?' She gestures toward my car. 'You didn't want to use it for the lesson?'

'No. It belongs to a friend. Abbey. You might know her?'

Rosie's blue eyes turn serious. 'Yes, I know Abbey. I was so sorry to hear ...' Her voice trails off.

'Do you know her well?'

'No, just to chat to, you know how it is. She's a hot surfer. Used to rub a few people up the wrong way though.'

'Why's that?'

Rosie wraps a towel around her waist. 'Some of the dinosaurs don't like it when a girl's taking waves off 'em. Cactus, that guy who drove away as we got here, he and Abbey were always at it.' Rosie waves at a passing surfer. 'Yo Paulie. I saw you get a mad one.'

Cactus. That would be the rude surf god. I shift from foot to foot on the hot asphalt. 'You mean fighting?'

'Yeah. Whenever she turned up, he'd fume. You wouldn't believe the way surf rage gets to people sometimes. I guess it's the crowds, but hey, that's Byron Bay – everyone wants to be here.' Rosie glances up at the bus. 'I'd better truck on. Keep up the surfing.'

I wave to the backpackers as they leave. Lars presses his nose up against the window and gives me a sad puppy-dog look. I'm sure he'll get over it in about five seconds.

It's only two o'clock, but I'm shattered. I'm out of practice with the rigours of investigation.

❋

Back at Abbey's house, I flop into the hammock. Swaying to and fro, I recap what I've learnt. Abbey used to argue with Cactus. She was probably having a thing with Ashok. And she worked with a so-called freelance botanical consultant called Adam McBean. I picture a middle-aged man in a floppy khaki hat. Hopefully I can track him down at the market tomorrow.

As the sun sets, I crawl out of the hammock and into the shower. My buns have been trashed in the surf, so I re-make them. We method actors like to stay in character. Refreshed,

I make myself a cheese sandwich, and sit on the verandah couch, enjoying the frogs' twilight chorus. A ute drones past and disappears into the shadows. The lighthouse beam shines in the distance as darkness falls.

Suddenly, it is very dark. Is it always this dark in the country? Behind me, the house creaks. It sounds like someone is tiptoeing up and down the corridors. I know no-one's there, but it's spooky. I lean back on the couch and try to enjoy the solitude. The house creaks again. No, it's no good. The silence is too creepy, I need to talk to someone.

I pick up my phone and look through my contacts, but who's going to be home doing nothing on a Saturday night? Only boring old me. I told Nan I have a date with a surfer. I'm going to need to make something up to satisfy her curiosity. Or ... I really could have a date? I scroll through Bumble, but there's no-one who takes my fancy. *Except for Rosco.*

I know I shouldn't, but I can't resist. I check his profile again. A snort bursts from my nose. He's stolen my fake-hobbies. Instead of, *if you believe in synchronicity, I'm your man,* his profile now says, *enjoys skydiving, competitive chess and gourmet cooking.* He's taunting me.

I'm going to have to get some new hobbies now. Pulling up my profile, I write. *Enjoys trainspotting and collecting china cats, seeks someone with similar interests.*

No-one's going to swipe right on that, says Nansea.

This is true. I guess I'm not all that keen on the idea of a Bumble date.

Why don't you follow up with Rosco? Find out where he's up to with his investigation.

It's an idea, but maybe not a good one. On the positive

side, he'll be someone to talk to, plus I'll be progressing my investigation. On the negative side ... my gut squirms as I remember my unreturned texts. No, I can't call him. He'll think I'm chasing after him.

But he called you the other day, says Nansea.

Excellent point Nansea. He's established a precedent. We are fact-sharing on Abbey's case. Although ... he wouldn't see it that way, seeing as I'm not officially on Abbey's case.

Call him, squeals Nansea.

Okay. I'll call him. Even though I hate talking on the phone. I need to get over it. I can't go through life with a phone phobia. Not all of my communication needs can be taken care of with a text message. I'm going to call him. *Here I go.* My heart patters as I scroll to his number. He won't answer anyway. Who answers their phones? *No-one.*

Rosco answers on the third ring. 'Olivia?'

I like the way he says my name. It makes me warm. I was silly to be nervous. It's Rosco. We played Star Wars together when we were kids. We had our own special language. *May the horse be with you.* It was our little joke. I put him on speaker.

'What can I do for you?'

I swallow, my nerves returning. He sounds so businesslike. Not at all like he used to when we played Star Wars. I clear my throat and adopt a similar brisk tone. We are two colleagues sharing information. That is all. Only he doesn't know I'm an unofficial colleague and it would be better if he doesn't find out. 'I wanted to see how your investigation is progressing.'

'It's not really any of your business, but it's slow. There are a few rotten fish in this sea.'

'What aspects, exactly, are you investigating?' I sound like

I'm channelling someone from another era. Sherlock Holmes perhaps. *You see, but you do not observe ...* It must be a side-effect of nervousness. This is why I need more phone conversation practice.

'As I said, it's not any of your business, but ... there are people round the Bay I need to keep my eye on. Can't say too much more.'

He's holding out on you, squeals Nansea. *You should meet face to face.*

'I'm in Byron Bay at the moment as it happens.' I scratch at one of my buns. 'We should meet up and compare notes.' *Compare notes.* I shouldn't have said that. 'Not that I have any. Notes.'

'I'm afraid I'm tied up at the moment. And Olivia ...' He pauses. 'As I said, it's none of your business.'

I gulp. He doesn't want to see me. I shouldn't have rung him. I already knew he didn't want anything to do with me.

'I know what you're like,' he says. 'You get involved in things that don't concern you. Mrs Watson hired me. You are no longer an investigator. That was your choice. I know Abbey was ... is, your friend, but you need to stay out of it. Things could get nasty.'

I try to think of a comeback, but only manage a Sherlock Holmes-ish 'humph'.

'Goodbye Olivia.'

'Goodbye Rosco.'

He doesn't hang up though and neither do I.

'I'm quite interested in trainspotting as it happens,' he says.

My stomach squirms. He's taunting me about my profile again. I shouldn't have written such stupid stuff. 'That's almost as bad as collecting china cats.'

He laughs. 'Goodbye Olivia.'

I salvage my pride by summoning Nansea. 'Peace out.'

I drop my phone beside me on the couch and lean back. 'Not any of my business, huh? Well, Rosco ...' I assume a pompous English accent. 'It is my business to know what other people do not.' It's a quote from Sherlock Holmes and *The Adventure of the Blue Carbuncle*. One of Dad's favourites.

A snort of laughter emerges from my phone – it turns out neither of us have hung up.

Stabbing the *end call* button, I take a drink of Milo to cool my burning cheeks. No wonder I hate phone conversations. They are the devil's work.

CHAPTER TWELVE

I wake late to the sound of a whip bird and groan as my phone call to Rosco rushes back. My cheeks burn again. Why did I ring him? And worse, why did I impersonate Sherlock Holmes? It's out of character. Nancy Drew, maybe, but not Sherlock ...

Don't worry about it, babe, says Nansea. *He thought it was funny.*

Maybe. Or maybe not. He was so cool with me. *It's not any of your business, Olivia ...* Rosco wants me to stay away from Abbey's case. Well, I will most likely be doing just that after today.

When I sit up, a sun-speckled glimpse of sea beckons beyond the trees. The day is too beautiful to obsess about what Rosco thinks. I'll die if I don't swim right now. My task for this morning is to track down the khaki-hat-wearing botanist at the market, but ... swimming comes first.

Dragging on my faded Speedos, I drive down the hill to Broken Head. Some surfers are carving up the waves off the rocky point. I'm tempted to grab Abbey's board and head out there, but I'm not ready to use it yet. It feels like acknowledging she's gone.

Instead, I dive under the waves and do a gentle breaststroke, feeling my muscles loosening up. The water is all it had promised, cool and fizzing like champagne.

Afterwards, as the sun dries the salt on my body, I saunter up the beach. Wrapping a towel around my waist, I follow a narrow walking track onto the headland. Some banksias are in bloom behind me. A strong smell of honey wafts from their yellow flowers. Out past the rocks, three dolphins cruise northward. It's like paradise here, but Abbey's voice is in my head. A shiver runs up my spine.

People would kill for this, Ol.

Byron Bay Market is in full swing when I arrive. Old or young, the look is colourful and bohemian. No normcore here. I wander through the maze of stalls and impulse-buy a rainbow headscarf, which I arrange over my buns, and a silver anklet to adorn my tangerine-dream ankle.

Right on, babe, says Nansea.

After toying with some aromatherapy oils, I devour a huge piece of chocolate fudge. Sadly, my feet are too dirty for a reflexology massage. The market is bigger and busier than expected. I have no idea how to find Adam McBean. I don't even know what sort of performer he is. Does he have a botanical puppet show or make balloon flowers? Perhaps he leads a wildflower walk?

Sweat trickles from my armpits as I scan the stalls, my eyes coming to rest upon a red-lettered sign. *Tarot Readings.* I hover for a minute, checking out the woman inside the tent. She's focused on her client, who has her back to me. I've always been wary of anything mystical. It's hard to turn off my inner cynic. I get all the guidance I need by scoffing at the astrology readings in the newspaper. In Byron Bay though, consulting psychics is like popping into the chemist for Panadol.

The tarot reader looks down-to-earth. No headscarf, hoop earrings or dangling necklaces. Just a loose blue blouse, glasses and short, brown hair. As I'm about to move on, her customer moves away, and she glances up.

'Do you want a reading?'

Why not? Maybe she can give me a lead on where to find Adam McBean. And at least it will be shady in there. I take a seat.

The woman smiles, her brown eyes crinkling at the corners. 'I'm Beatrice. Are there particular questions you'd like answered today?'

She has an accent, possibly French. For some reason this gives her extra credibility. *Where to begin?*

'Relationships, career, life directions?' she prompts.

'Yes. All that please.'

'Anything specific?'

I shake my head.

'I always like to ask my clients, what sign were you born under?'

Maternity Ward? The penny drops. 'You mean star sign?'

She nods, her face passive.

'Taurus, but I'm not into astrology.'

She frowns slightly. 'Okay, let's see what we've got for you.'

She shuffles the cards and deals ten onto the silk tablecloth.

My eyes focus on a picture of a skeleton wearing armour, mounted on a white horse. A body lies on the ground under the horse's feet. That doesn't look promising. 'What's that about?' I point at the card, trying to sound relaxed and comfortable. *Alert not alarmed*, as the old anti-terrorist magnet on our fridge at home instructs.

'Is this your first tarot reading?' Beatrice's voice is reassuring.

'How can you tell?'

'The death card can be positive. It means you have reached the end of one phase of your life and are entering a new one. You are letting go of outworn ways of living.' She points at another card. Adam and Eve beside the apple tree. 'The Lovers. You may be about to start a romance. Or you have to choose between two lovers?'

I wish.

'The Lovers may mean you are about to make fundamental choices that will change the course of your life. You need to weigh up decisions carefully.'

I have no idea what she's talking about. 'Anything else?'

'You have a lot of swords.'

I examine the cards. There are swords everywhere – on the wall, in hands, stuck in the ground. 'What does that mean?'

'It could mean you have many decisions to make.'

Something about her voice makes me ask, 'Is there another meaning?'

She nods. 'The suit of swords is the most powerful and dangerous in the deck. Many swords in a reading can be a warning. You need to watch where you're going and be careful who you deal with.'

I swallow, wiping my sweaty hands on my skirt as my mind turns to Abbey. *Danger. A warning.*

Beatrice sweeps the cards together into a bundle and smiles. 'It seems you are on the brink of an interesting phase in your life. Do you wish to break out of your current lifestyle?'

The law lectures. Wrangling Jacq. The lack of excitement... 'Yes.'

'I would say, based on your tarot reading, now is an auspicious time to make those changes.'

I have no idea how to do that, but the reading has come to an end. I glance behind me and see a grey-haired woman in a yellow bikini waiting.

'I hope your reading has been useful,' says Beatrice.

'Yes ... thanks. There's one other thing. I'm looking for a market performer called Adam McBean. He's a botanical consultant. Do you know where I can find him?'

'Sorry dear, I'm filling in for Gaia, who usually has this stall. I'm not a regular.'

I back out the tent door into blazing sunlight. So ... big changes, a lover and danger. Not much different to the horoscope. Except for the danger, that's new.

I wander up and down the market lanes again, looking for performers. I'd better find him soon, I have to get back to the Goldie.

A crowd has gathered around an open area and loud music blares from a speaker. I stand on the outskirts and peer in. A young guy wearing a grey T-shirt and grey pants stands in the middle of the circle of spectators. A trilby hat perches on his head. Compared to the crowd around him, his look verges on normcore. His speaker is blasting out 'Dog Days are Over', by Florence and the Machine. I should keep looking for Adam, but I like this old song, so I pause to listen.

'Ladies and gentlemen, I am about to perform the death-defying Fish of Fate,' he calls. 'For this amazing act, I need a volunteer from the audience.' He has an English accent. There's nothing unusual about that. Byron Bay attracts people from all over the world.

He scans the crowd and I step back to show I'm passing by.

'The beautiful girl with the glasses and the buns!' he calls.

I look around for the victim. Wait a minute ... *buns* ... *glasses*. He means me.

The performer steps through the crowd and grasps my hand, pulling me forward.

Panic lurches in my gut. 'No, I can't ... I need to ...' I never volunteer for this sort of thing. Ever. Not since Billy Hunt pulled me out the front in his school play comedy routine. He made me hold a glass of water to the ceiling with a stick and I was stuck there for the whole act. Very funny. For everyone except me.

Placing his hands on my shoulders, the busker propels me to stand in front of a small trampoline.

Everyone is staring at me, and short of kicking him and running away, which is a little extreme, there isn't a lot I can do. I glare at him.

He smiles back at me, his teeth flashing.

It's a pretty great smile, so even though I resent him shang-haiing me into his act, I find myself smiling back. I hope this doesn't take too long.

'Now to perform the Fish of Fate,' he shouts.

He flings off his hat, revealing close-cropped platinum hair that shines in the sun. His olive skin and dark brown eyes suggest he's not a natural blond. He pulls off his T-shirt, exposing a smooth, brown chest.

I momentarily lose interest in trying to find Adam McBean.

He strips off his grey pants and ... underneath is a pair of multicoloured leggings.

I forget all about Adam McBean. I'll catch up with his wildflower walk later.

'Keep still.' He places a stuffed blue silk fish on my head. 'I'll be back,' he says in a deep voice.

'The Terminator?' I ask. Dad and I went through an Arnold Schwarzenegger phase a few years ago.

He grins. 'You had a wasted childhood too.' He walks about ten metres away, turns and runs full pelt toward me.

I want to close my eyes but cannot take them off him.

He jumps onto the trampoline, soars up into the air and somersaults above me.

I can't look up, or I'll lose the fish, but I can sense him floating overhead. There's a rush of air as he grasps the fish and lands on his feet beside me. I gasp, and the crowd cheers.

He takes my hand and holds it high. 'Thanks to my lovely assistant. That's the end of the act, please show your appreciation with gold coins or notes.'

We both bow.

The crowd disperses and I'm about to wander off, dazed by my encounter, when I remember why I'm here. 'You don't know a performer called Adam McBean, do you?'

He puts his hands up. 'Guilty.'

CHAPTER THIRTEEN

Well, who knew? I've failed the first rule of investigating – never make assumptions.

Adam McBean is not a middle-aged botanist with a khaki hat. He's a dangerously attractive acrobat. He looks, in fact, a lot like an angel, maybe even a fallen one.

I'm still in a tizz from having him jump over me, not to mention ... *well* ... so I just come out with it. 'I'm Abbey Watson's friend. I want to talk to you about her.'

He scans my face, and nods. 'I've got to pack up here. I'll meet you at the coffee stall in five.'

I head toward a nearby fig tree and, perching on a stool beneath it, order a coffee. Nearby, a dreadlocked old man dressed in flowing white plays the tom-toms. Beautiful hippie girls wander past with babies in slings. Belly-button rings are big here in Byron. Maybe I should get one.

When Adam turns up, he's back in his grey suit, his platinum hair hidden under the trilby. I prefer this more conservative look, it's better for my pulse levels.

Adam orders a flat white, and I get another to keep him company.

There's an uncomfortable silence while I rack my brain for

small talk. I give up. 'Do you know any reason why Abbey might have killed herself?' Not that I think she killed herself, of course. The second coffee is doing nothing for my nerves.

Adam looks startled. 'No.' His brown eyes meet mine.

I gulp my coffee again. 'Were you two together?'

'In a relationship?' He shakes his head. 'No, we're pals. I helped her with some botanical surveys. She railroaded me into it.'

But, didn't Ashok imply ...? 'Ashok told me you and Abbey were, you know.' I shift on my stool and bang the table, sending Adam's coffee slopping over. The brown stream runs across the table and trickles onto his pants. 'Oh no, I'm so sorry.' I search for something to wipe it up.

'It's okay. Chill.' Adam leans over to the next table and grabs a napkin, dabbing at his pants. 'You can't believe everything Ashok says.' He drains what's left of his coffee.

I watch the way his smooth, suntanned hand curls around the cup.

'Ashok was jealous of every guy Abbey spoke to.'

'Does the term *fallen angel* mean anything to you?'

Adam's brow wrinkles.

'It's something I found written in her notebook ...'

Adam drums his fingers on the table. 'Fallen angel? There's plenty of them around here.'

'Like who?'

'How long have you got?' His eyes slide away from me.

I'm reluctant to bring our conversation to an end. 'So, Ashok said you're a botanical consultant?'

'I'm studying botany at uni. I help out where I can.'

'Botany and acrobatics are an interesting career combination.'

Adam shrugs. 'They both pay next to nothing. There's an

oversupply of performers and environmental consultants in Byron Bay. Beats breathing the London fumes though.'

I get to my feet, fiddling with the wisps that are escaping from my side buns. 'Well … I guess that's all. Bye.'

Adam puts out his hand. His fingers are warm and hold mine for a fraction longer than the regulation one second.

My stomach flip-flops. I turn to go.

'Hang on a sec, what's your name?'

I swivel back. 'Oh, didn't I say? Nansea. That's N-A-N-S-E-A.'

He gives me a lopsided smile. 'Why don't you give me your number, Nansea? We can have another coffee?'

I play cool. 'I'm from the Goldie, I don't get down this way much. But, I guess …' I give him my number and he types it into his phone.

'Well, maybe I'll see you next time?' One brown eye drops into a wink and he turns and walks away.

I pull my eyes away from him with difficulty. As I head toward the carpark, my phone goes *ting.*

It was fun jumping over you, reads the text.

I look up, but he's out of sight. I smile as I click my phone off.

I've got half an hour until I need to head home. My weekend hasn't been as productive as I'd hoped. I don't have much of a lead. A loose thread is niggling me. Ashok. *Fallen angel* had rung some bells with him, though he pretended it hadn't. I'll call back there now and try to talk to him again.

When I pull into the office of Forest Friends, the door is shut and the blinds pulled. A piece of notepaper is taped to the window.

Forest Friends needs your help
Call Ashok on 0418 557 224

I punch in the number, reaching his voicemail. 'It's Nansea here. Abbey's friend. I've remembered there was more to Abbey's note. It said *fallen angel's plaything*, not just *fallen angel*. Can you give me a call if it means anything to you?'

I head toward the highway, my mind turning to the week ahead. I have a ton of reading to do for uni, and Jacq has an action-packed week coming up too. I've given this my best shot, but I haven't got anywhere. I should leave the investigation to Rosco now. He's the one who's getting paid for it, after all.

No, I won't be rushing back to Byron Bay. *It was fun jumping over you.* Not even for Adam. He might be the first guy I've felt anything for since Rosco, but I know trouble when I see it.

It is time to focus on the essentials. I need to pass law, look after Jacq, and, most importantly, persuade Mum to come home and take charge of our lives again.

CHAPTER FOURTEEN

I'm half an hour late home and Nan looks cross. She is wearing a bright red wrap dress and a fake hibiscus behind her ear. Donald hovers behind her in a Hawaiian shirt and a plastic flower lei. Despite their outfits, the Aloha vibe is in short supply.

'I told you we were going out, Olivia,' Nan mutters through clenched teeth.

She and Donald sweep out of the house, taking their ukuleles with them.

Aloha to you, too.

Jacq runs out of the loungeroom and I give her a hug. She inspects Abbey's surfboard, which I've carried up from the car. 'You bought a new surfboard?'

'I'm looking after it, for Abbey, until she comes back.'

I make dinner – hamburgers – and put Jacq to bed. When I pick up my phone, there's a voice message from Ashok.

'Nansea? I got your message. I'm going to check it out. Call me back.'

His annoying tone reminds me why I didn't tell him the whole story when I first spoke to him. I call back, but the number rings out. I yawn. I'll talk to him tomorrow.

At uni, Sophie gives me a blow-by-blow account of the *amazing, totally cool* party she went to at Surfers, with her medical-student boyfriend. 'What about you Olivia? What did you get up to?'

I don't know where to start. *This super-cute guy jumped over me. I had a weird phone conversation with my ex. I tried to figure out what happened to my former best friend who's gone missing.* None of these topics will fit into the sixty seconds before our lecture starts. I decide to go with my usual weekend activity. 'I took my sister to football. She almost scored a goal.'

Sophie's brow furrows as the lecturer comes in. My life doesn't provide a high standard of gossip. 'You must have gone to the beach,' she whispers. 'You've got a tan.'

I've scrubbed off the fake tan, but my skin still has an orange glow. The blonde streaks in my hair also add a touch of pizazz. Pity there's no-one around to impress. My thoughts return to Adam. I squash them. *No Olivia. He's way too good-looking. Trouble, trouble, trouble.*

But lots of fun, counters Nansea.

I ignore her. She'll go away soon. I don't need an undercover identity anymore. I won't be heading back to Byron. *The essentials – law, Jacq, Mum.* That's what I'm focusing on. As soon as I get this call to Ashok out of the way.

I call Ashok in all my class breaks, but now I get the *phone turned off or out of range* message. Should I get Rosco to follow up with him?

He left a message for you, not Rosco, squeals Nansea.

She's persistent. It seems the only way to get rid of her is to get this Ashok thing off my plate. Then I can return to what I should be doing. After Torts, I find a quiet spot on the grass, google Forest Friends and call their office number.

A girl answers. 'Hello, Forest Friends, Luna Nakamura speaking.'

Luna. That girl has her finger in a lot of pies. I don't want her to recognise my voice, so I put on an American accent. 'Is Ashok there?'

'Who is this?' she says. 'You sound familiar …'

'My name is Nansea,' I drawl. 'I'd like to speak to Ashok.'

'Are you a friend of his?'

'Yes. Is he there?'

'I'm afraid Ashok's had an accident.'

I lower my voice. 'What sort of an accident?'

'In the surf. He nearly drowned. He's, like, in a coma in hospital.' Luna's voice quavers.

My mouth goes dry. I hadn't liked him, but still … 'Will he be all right?'

'They don't know. The doctors say there's a fifty-fifty chance he'll come round.' She sniffs.

'I'm sorry. I hope he gets better.' I press the *end* button and stare out at the courtyard. What's going on in the surf? First Abbey, and now Ashok …

Something rotten is going on down there, mutters Nansea.

I sit through my class on criminal law but it's hard to concentrate. I keep picturing bodies face-down in the surf. Maybe it's a coincidence, but maybe not.

I get through the after-school rush and dinner in a blur. *Abbey and Ashok.* Am I making too much of this? Nan is out with Donald as usual, so it's just the two of us.

'Your face is wrinkly, Livvie.' Jacq spoons up my macaroni cheese special.

'Sorry.' I relax my facial muscles. 'I'm thinking.'

Jacq puts her chin on her clenched fist and pulls her face into a deep frown. 'I'm thinking too.'

After I get Jacq to bed, I sit down with a Milo. I replay Ashok's phone message. He'd left it just after four o'clock. Shortly after that, he'd almost drowned while surfing.

Pulling Abbey's notebook out of my backpack, I trace her last words with my finger. *Fallen Angel's Plaything.* Is it a clue? Ashok said he was checking it out. And then he almost died. I gnaw my nails, trying not to jump to conclusions.

Jump, jump, says Nansea.

Are the words a coded message pointing to her ... murderer? *That's a leap.* Why would anyone kill Abbey? I remember her note. *It's not the way it used to be. I don't want to go on anymore.* It sounds like a suicide note, but there are other ways to read it. My pulse thumps and I exhale slowly. Abbey will be okay.

I can't keep this all to myself. I need to talk to Rosco. He'll know what to do with it. I find his number. My finger goes toward it, and away. I don't want to call him. Every time I talk to him it's weird. But it's the responsible thing to do. It might help him with the case. Taking a deep breath, I press his number.

The phone rings once before he answers. 'Hi Olivia.' He pauses. 'Or should I say Sherlock?'

My cheeks burn as I remember my bizarre Sherlock Holmes impersonation. I press on, trying to keep my voice business-like. 'I need to talk to you about Abbey's case. A friend of hers, Ashok, a former boyfriend I think, had a surfing accident yesterday. He's in a coma.'

'I did hear that.'

'Isn't it a bit of a coincidence? Given how Abbey ... how Abbey disappeared.'

There's a brief silence on the end of the phone. 'You think someone is knocking off surfers?'

He's humouring me.

'I suppose that's one way of reducing the crowd in the line-up,' he adds.

He's joking, or I think he is, but his words remind me of the surfer, Cactus. What had my surf coach, Rosie, said? *You wouldn't believe the way surf rage gets to people here.* I stare at Abbey's surfboard propped up against my wall. If only it could talk. Tell me where she is.

I pull my thoughts back to Ashok. 'I found the words *Fallen Angel's Plaything* written in a notebook at Abbey's house. I told Ashok. I think he knew what it meant. He was going to check it out.'

'What makes you think *Fallen Angel's Plaything* is significant?'

'She had the initials *FAP* on her calendar the day she disappeared. It's a funny thing to write.'

'It was probably a piece she was working on.'

That's a reasonable explanation, but I don't buy it.

'I'll check out Ashok's accident,' he says. 'See if there are any suspicious circumstances. I've got a mate in the Byron Bay station.'

An image of the black-haired policewoman comes to mind. *I'll bet he's got a mate in the police station.* Something else occurs to me. 'Do you know if the police took any notebooks from Abbey's house?'

'No, I checked their report. They visited the house and found the note, but there wasn't much else. Looks like she might have tidied up.'

I wander across the room and run my fingers down the

smooth rim of Abbey's surfboard. 'What about the computer, did they check that?'

'Yeah, nothing relevant on it.'

'Isn't it peculiar there were no notebooks apart from the one I found? She was always writing.'

'Sometimes people when they ... don't like to leave a mess behind.'

There's a silence. I stroke Abbey's board. 'Abbey wouldn't do that.' She's finally living the Byron Bay life she always dreamed of. And besides, I just *know* she's still out there.

'You're keeping her surfboard, are you?' It's like he can see what I'm doing.

'For now. How did you know?'

'Mrs Watson told me.' There's another silence. 'Olivia.'

'Yes.'

'This is my case, not yours. You made it clear you don't want to be a PI anymore. Are you going to stay out of it?'

I hesitate. There's no reason for me to be involved now I've told Rosco what I know. He'll probably do a better job than me anyway. *The essentials – uni, Jacq, Mum.* 'Yes.'

'Terrific.' He hangs up.

Good phone call, I congratulate myself. I didn't do anything embarrassing. I'm getting the hang of this voice call business.

As I'm getting into bed, my phone rings with a Skype call. I snatch it up and Mum and Dad appear, wearing matching woolly hats.

I get in first, before Mum bombards me with words of Buddhist wisdom. 'Can I talk to you about a case?' I say, as soon as they come into focus. 'Rosco's case, I mean.'

'Of course,' they both reply.

'Okay, so ...' I take a deep breath. I'd like to talk to them about Abbey, but I don't know if I can. Not when the line is so bad, and they might have to go off and pray at any minute. No, I can't talk about Abbey like that.

So, I tell them about Ashok's accident. 'It's linked to a girl who's gone missing.' I don't use her name. 'I don't believe she killed herself but ... Rosco thinks someone ...' I force the words out, '... murdered her.' *Murdered.* I imagine the word bouncing off a satellite and into the monastery in Kathmandu.

There's the usual silence while my words make their way across the globe, then Mum blinks. 'That's terrible, Olivia. That poor girl...' There's some crackling and her mouth keeps moving, then the sound clears. 'Human existence is filled with suffering.'

I wish she'd leave out the Buddhist sayings and talk to me like she used to. Mum was always my go-to person for practical advice. No problem was too small. It's strange not to be her first priority anymore. Cymbals clash in the background. It must be almost time for evening prayers.

'It sounds like you can't let it go,' Dad says.

'The girl's ...' I swallow. *Abbey.* I still can't tell them that it's her, not while they're so far away. What's the point of worrying them? Not when there's every chance we'll find her. '... she's my age and so ...' I trail off. 'So do you think ... I should keep investigating?' The line crackles again, and I'm not sure they catch the last part. The cymbals clash. I don't have long.

'When watching after yourself, you watch after others,' says Mum. 'When watching after others, you watch after ... *crackle, crackle.*'

I clench my jaw. Talking on Skype is so stupid. 'Is that a yes?'

'Time for prayers,' she says.

'But—'

As their image fades, crackly words come through, from Dad. 'You must remember it is a capital mistake to theorise before one has data.' It's a quote from Sherlock Holmes, *A Scandal in Bohemia.*

'What the ...?'

Their woolly hats hover on the screen, then vanish like the Cheshire Cat from *Alice in Wonderland*. This makes sense because they are just as infuriating.

Great. Just great. Both my parents are completely useless and clearly, this bizarre Sherlock thing I've got going on is Dad's fault. It's rubbed off on me. I used to think my parents were a bit boring, but now ... I'd take boring over weird any day.

CHAPTER FIFTEEN

The lighthouse beam slides across the bay. It lights up hills, skims over the pointed finger of an ancient volcano. Around again it beams ... a shape in the water ... a body floating ... octopus hair trails in the surge.

❊

'Olivia Grace, summarise the Meow-Ludo Disco Gamma Meow-Meow case.'

My number is up. Despite my best efforts to remain invisible, the scary lecturer's finger is pointing at me. I had a terrible night's sleep and am not at my best. Even taking that into consideration though, it doesn't sound like she's speaking English. 'Pardon?' I say.

'The Meow-Ludo Disco Gamma Meow-Meow case. Summarise it.'

It still doesn't make sense. I open and shut my mouth like a dying goldfish.

Sophie puts up her hand and Professor Anderson nods. 'Meow-Ludo Disco Gamma Meow-Meow inserted the chip from an Opal public transport card into his hand. He was fined for fare evasion, but later acquitted as the judge acknowledged that any reasonable person would say he had paid for the fare. Mr

Meow-Meow claimed it was a not-insignificant win for cyborg justice.'

'Thank you, Sophie.' The lecturer's gaze turns on me. 'You are aware ten percent of marks for this class are given for participation, aren't you?'

I wasn't, but nod anyway.

She narrows her eyes. 'Do the reading.'

'I will.' I won't, but there is no other acceptable answer.

When I get out of class, I find a long message from Rosco on my phone. I get a strange feeling in my chest as I listen to his voice. *I've looked into the near-drowning. The police say there are no suspicious circumstances. He was surfing at dusk, no-one else around, big surf. He'd had a few drinks, which wouldn't have helped. Looks like he got hit on the head with his board. A dog-walker pulled him out of the water, but he hasn't come around.*

It sounds plausible, but I'm still not convinced. In fact, the longer I think about it, the surer I am it wasn't an accident. Someone – most likely a surfer – had it in for Abbey, and Ashok as well. Why?

For some reason, Dad's weird statement replays in my mind. *It is a capital mistake to theorise before one has data.* Am I theorising before I have data? Maybe. First, I should work out what *Fallen Angel's Plaything* means. As I drift through the rest of my lectures, the words run through my mind. Is there something a little sinister about them?

The essentials, I remind myself. *Uni, Jacq, Mum.* I should leave this to Rosco like I said I would.

But if I disappeared, wouldn't Abbey search for me?

The essentials.

But it's Abbey. *Best friends forever. Pinkie promise …*

All day, the alternative viewpoints argue in my mind. Should I get involved, or shouldn't I?

Driving home from uni, I come to a decision. I can't rely on the police. As far as they're concerned the case is closed. And Rosco has a lot on his plate, so he might not be giving this case the attention it deserves. I'm the one who knows Abbey well. I know how her mind works. And ... I seem to be the only one who thinks she's still alive. I owe it to her to sort this out.

Besides, I've missed investigating. It's like Buddha says, *when watching after others, you watch after yourself* ... I don't only owe it to Abbey, I owe it to myself. I can take care of the essentials and look for Abbey too. It will be an opportunity to see if I've got what it takes to be a PI.

You go, girl, says Nansea.

But how will I get back to Byron? I need to look after Jacq. Then I remember that it's Easter next weekend. Nan and Donald are going to a ukulele festival on the Sunshine Coast, and they offered to take Jacq. I'll have four days free. That's my chance.

I'll need to turn myself back into Nansea. I think of my Tarot reading. *Transform yourself and let go of outworn ways of living.* I won't do a half-hearted makeover this time. For a four-day weekend, a more comprehensive transformation is in order.

❋

Over the next couple of days, I call all the magazines Abbey wrote for and ask if she was working on anything for them. I get lucky with *Eco-vibe*. They tell me she was researching a piece on a Byron Bay cult.

'They're trying to push through an environmentally controversial building application,' says the girl on the phone.

This gets my antennas vibrating. Any cult would have motive to silence someone who might expose their shonky operation.

As it happens, cults and I go back a way. I seem to be the sort of person cult recruiters are attracted to. During my school days, no less than five so-called friends tried to recruit me into one particularly insidious cult.

They weren't successful. If I'm going to undergo mind control and alienate myself from family and friends, there have to be benefits. Ones that don't involve selling cleaning products.

On Thursday afternoon, I commence my transformation into the new, improved Nansea. It's a lengthy process, but it's worth it. Nan and Jacq have left for the Sunshine Coast by the time I get home, which is good. My new look is bound to provoke comments.

Before bed, I inadvertently find myself checking Rosco's Bumble profile. He now lists his personal motto as, *to a great mind, nothing is little.* I snort. It's a Sherlock quote. He's having a dig at me.

I tap on my Bumble profile and add my own personal motto, another Sherlock quote, which seems apt. *The game is afoot.*

❋

On Easter Friday, I head off on the familiar route to Byron Bay. I've got a big weekend ahead. *Four days of investigation.* My stomach squirms. I hope I can pull it all off.

You're a hot PI, you'll kill it, says Nansea.

She, at least, has no doubts about this mission. I wind down the window to feel the breeze. As a strand of hair flaps across my face, I'm startled again by its bright colour. Pink hair was a complete masterstroke. I also revisited Tan Magic. My tangerine-dream stomach bulges over the top of my stretchy bell-bottomed pants. With my fake belly-button piercing, fake butterfly tattoo, and bare-midriff top, I'm feeling groovy.

Lookin' cool babe, says Nansea.

I'll need to lose the pink hair before uni, but the hairdresser told me it's a snap. I just need to crush a Vitamin C tablet into my shampoo. Who knew?

As I drive, I review my suspects. Currently top of the list is Cactus, the surfer. He had motive and ability. I remember the note on Abbey's calendar. *A – FAP*. The sole point in Cactus's favour is his name doesn't begin with *A*. Or does it? Unless his parents are desert plant enthusiasts, they didn't christen him Cactus. I'll have to find out his real name.

I guess Ashok is out of the frame now, seeing as he was most likely attacked by the same person who attacked Abbey. That leaves Adam – *it was fun jumping over you* – and a new suspect I've nicknamed Charismatic Cult Captain, Citra.

As I take the turn-off to Byron Bay, I ponder what I've learnt about the Amalian cult so far. They worship Amal, a dead prophet representing the extraterrestrials who created us. Now, they wish to revisit Earth and guide us further. To bring about this miracle, we need to banish our guilt and fears and improve ourselves philosophically and emotionally.

The cult's website looked a lot like a dating agency. It invited me to choose someone I was energetically attracted to, to be my spiritual guide. Their well-groomed spiritual guides would get a lot of swipe-rights on Bumble. They all looked like pop stars.

There was a darker side though. A quick google found testaments from parents whose children had joined and cut them off from all contact. A journalist in America had received anonymous death threats. There was the mandatory celebrity member. Cleo, a rising rock star, had pledged herself to Amal and was planning a brood of half-alien super children.

I've booked into a free half-day Transformative Workshop with Citra, starting at ten o'clock today. I'm trying to stay positive, but the prospect makes my stomach churn. Transformative workshops are way out of my comfort zone. I hope it doesn't involve getting naked and sharing my innermost fantasies and fears. I'm not into that stuff. I think your inner psyche should be left inside where it belongs.

CHAPTER SIXTEEN

The cult headquarters turns out to be an old timber farmhouse in the hills outside Byron Bay. Flags at the entrance give it a cheerful vibe. The cult's logo, a spaceship within a circle, ripples in the breeze. Goats lean over the fence and bleat at me as I get out of the car.

A lank-haired girl in a sleeveless purple dress greets me at the door and assures me Citra will be here soon. She shows me to a large room scattered with beanbags and I lower myself into one of the few that isn't taken.

To my left, sit two plump men in Hawaiian shirts, who look like they lost their Gold Coast Theme Park tour bus. Across from me is a well-dressed woman in full make-up, with coiffed blonde hair. Her furrowed brow hints at hidden anger.

A stocky girl in shorts and sandals sits to my right and there's a mixed bag of hippies, both male and female. All up, about fifteen people have turned up to learn about Amal, our extra-terrestrial saviour.

One of the middle-aged men smiles at me. 'Here for some transformation?' He makes *transformation* sound like a washing powder.

I nod. *Yep, I'll take two, seeing as they're on special.* So far it's all humdrum, not at all like the sinister plot for world domination I'd suspected.

'Welcome to the house of Amal.' A commanding voice resonates through the small talk.

The chatter ceases. All eyes focus on the woman who has appeared in the centre of the room. I recognise her from the website, but she is more impressive in the flesh. Her black hair is drawn back from her face, and an ankle-length orange sarong clings to her body. A tattoo of the cult's symbol decorates one toned bicep. She's stunning, but a little frightening, like a prowling leopard.

I remember what I've read about her. Citra is the protégé of the cult's international leader. She left San Francisco a year ago to lead the Australian branch. Since they set up headquarters in Byron Bay, their following has boomed. She must be good at marketing.

The silence draws out as she circles the room, her piercing gaze meeting everyone's eyes. I try to look innocent.

Only when she has eyeballed everyone does she speak again. 'Welcome to the transformative workshop. I am Citra. You will all experience the presence of Amal today. First, you must all tell me what made you come here.' She points at one of the Hawaiian-shirt men. 'You start.'

As we go around the room, it becomes clear a mysterious force has guided everyone to enrol in the workshop. Everyone except me. One dreamy-looking hippie tells us he'd been about to go surfing. But the wind had mysteriously turned northeast, even though southerlies were predicted. He'd stopped for a milkshake and been guided to pick up a brochure in the cafe.

A chorus of *wow* and *awesome* greets this tale.

I don't have a cover story, but by the time my turn comes around, I've got the idea. 'I was heading out for a coffee, when I found I didn't have any money. It was weird, because I'd got some out the day before. The cafe I go to only takes cash, so I went to the ATM. Someone had stuck a poster about Amal on the wall, and I read it while I was in the queue and ... here I am.'

Yeah, wow, awesome.

The workshop deteriorates when Citra instructs us to improve the energy in the room by soundwave cleansing. She explains the process and hands us each a small pair of brass cymbals. We are to mill around making meaningful eye contact, healing each other with the energy of our chimes.

After ten meaningful eye contacts and cymbal healings, it's all wearing thin. I move on to the tangle-haired hippie who was guided here by a change in wind direction.

He smiles at me lovingly as he raises his arms above my head, blasting me with the force of his underarm odour. *Ting, ting.* The cymbals in his hands vibrate as he moves them from my head to my feet, clashing them together. He stands up and looks into my eyes. 'I sense a deep love and compassion within you.'

'Um, thanks.' My eyes dart from side to side. I'm surrounded by strangers gazing tenderly at each other. There is nowhere to run. Cymbals ring out as they give the gift of pure sound healing. *Don't let him hug me.*

Too late. My partner pulls me into a loving hug. A farmyard aroma envelops me. *Has he been sleeping with pigs? Why did I let myself in for this? Why? Why? Why?*

'You can thank your partner and return to the circle now.' Citra's voice resonates through the chimes.

Hooray.

My partner joins his hands under his chin and bows. I return his salute and sprint away. From the safety of my beanbag, I inspect my fellow transformees. None look any better for their sound cleansing.

All eyes focus on Citra as she circles the room. 'I can sense your energy levels and awareness are heightened. Tell me how you feel.'

One by one, the group tells her.

'Filled with joy and abundance.'

'Like I have no limitations.'

'Part of a group of loving friends.'

'I feel a deep sense of love and compassion.' This is my hippie friend with the personal hygiene problem.

It is my turn. My mind goes blank. *Like I'm trapped in a room of zombies* won't go down well. 'Quite tired … but filled with a deep sense of love and compassion.'

Citra nods with satisfaction at the litany of meaningful feelings. 'You have started your journey to enlightenment.'

Her eyes rest on mine and a tingle runs up my spine.

'Now, I am going to give you something to help in your journey.' Citra picks up a velvet bag and circles the room, placing a crystal into each set of hands. 'This is a gift for you. These crystals have been programmed to transmit Amal's thoughts. Hold your crystal to your heart and describe the feelings it transmits to you.'

I hold my crystal and try to look thoughtful. It is purple and pleasant in its own way, if lacking in transmissions. My fellow classmates are all gazing at their crystals intently. Some are murmuring to them. Maybe I got a dud one.

'Put your crystal somewhere safe,' says Citra.

I don't have any pockets, so I tuck it in my bra.

'Would anyone like to share with us what Amal has to say?' asks Citra.

One of the pot-bellied men puts up his hand. 'I don't think my crystal likes me.'

A giggle bursts out of me. I change it into a coughing fit.

Citra lowers her eyebrows at me.

'Sorry. Nasty cough.'

'You feel some antagonism?' asks Citra.

'No. It seems ... apathetic,' says the man.

'Give it lots of love,' says Citra. 'Soon you will be old friends. Anyone else?'

'I sense a deep love and compassion,' says the Pig Man.

Citra's mouth twitches. 'Excellent. Has Amal spoken to anyone else?'

The hand of the stocky girl in the shorts shoots into the air.

'Yes, Tarini?' says Citra.

'Amal says he is close.' Her bottom lifts off her beanbag with excitement. 'He will be among us soon.'

'Good,' says Citra. 'It is time for me to tell you about him.'

She moves to the wall and draws the blinds, casting us into shadow. A screen lights up at the front of the room. Tinkling music accompanies an image of Earth from space.

'Forty years ago,' says Citra, 'our leader, the prophet Amal, was visited by beings from outer space. They told him they had created the human race and he was their representative on Earth.' The screen now shows a picture of a clean-shaven man dressed in tight, shiny white clothes. He looks like Benny from ABBA. Nan is into ABBA, so, even though I'm not a fan, I know all their greatest hits.

A sweet smell fills the room. Citra must have lit some incense. I yawn. It's been a long morning.

'Amal has now passed over, but he still guides his people ...'

I wake to find I've been dribbling. I look around, wiping my mouth. All eyes are still focused on the screen, where Citra seems to be winding up. The picture shows an artist's impression of luxurious, space-age buildings. They nestle among tall palm trees and tangled vines. A man and woman, naked except for cleverly draped vines, relax beside a flowing stream.

'Our vision is that we will build a retreat and embassy where Amalians can relax and enjoy each other's company.'

I notice some knowing glances. *Did I miss the part about free love?*

'It will be a place where our creators can come to teach us how to achieve liberation from our human failings. To build this retreat, we need the support of all Amalians.'

Is she about to give us the financial bottom line?

Citra presses the power button, leaving the room in semi-darkness. 'I'd like you all to stand, join hands with your neighbour, and close your eyes. I will lead you in a meditation exercise where we call on Amal to guide us. Listen with open minds to what he says and make your decision on whether you wish to join our movement. I will provide personal help to some of you if you need it.' Citra starts to chant. 'Show us the way, Amal, show us the way.'

Everyone joins in, intoning the words over and over.

I am self-conscious at first, but the chanting grows on me. The repetition is mesmerising and with my eyes closed, my mind drifts. Out of the blackness, an image of a man in a tight white suit appears. I focus on him. Is it Amal? Am I having a religious experience? Is he about to reveal the meaning of life?

Waterloo. Oh, oh, oh, oh. The ABBA song insinuates itself through the chanting. My head sways to the music inside. 'Do you see him?' murmurs a voice in my ear. Citra's breath is hot against my skin and a spicy smell, like cloves, drifts toward my nose.

I nod.

'I sense a need for guidance in your life,' Citra murmurs. Placing her finger into the middle of my forehead, she presses. 'Hold onto that image of Amal. He is your guardian angel. He will help you.'

I concentrate on the image. *Ring, ring,* he sings to me. If there is a message, it's obscure.

The chanting continues. So do ABBA's greatest hits. It's not unpleasant, just weird.

'Wriggle your feet and hands and return to the present,' says Citra, interrupting 'Fernando'. 'Amal is among us and he is pleased so many wish to join him.'

She opens the blind and I blink as the light streams in. It seems strange that it's still a sunny day outside. Did I have a religious experience? Maybe not, but *something* happened. Around me, everyone looks dazed. Vacant smiles plaster their faces.

Citra moves around the circle. She touches foreheads and murmurs as she hands out forms.

She thrusts a piece of paper into my hand. It asks me to join the movement and pledge my donation. Twenty percent of my salary is suggested. This wouldn't be a problem, seeing as it's twenty percent of nothing. Everyone else in the room is scribbling madly.

I pocket the form and head for the door. I'd planned to ask her about Abbey, but if I stay too much longer, she might force me to sign on the dotted line. A lifetime of listening to Amal sing ABBA's greatest hits doesn't bear thinking about.

Citra catches my eye as I trot past.

'Thanks,' I mutter, not slowing my step. 'That was great. Really ... transformative. Bye.'

She steps in front of me and puts her hand on my arm, looking into my eyes. 'Are you sure you want to let this opportunity go? You came here for a reason. We can give you what you need.'

'I ... I need to think about it.'

'It may not be easy to return.' Her cool fingers curve around my arm. 'We need strong people who understand the truth when they hear it. You may be walking away from salvation.'

Salvation? She sounds like a missionary. 'I've always been indecisive.' My voice rises to a nervous squeak. 'Amal sounds cool and I like the look of the retreat, but I'm not into nudity, so ...'

'You're not a journalist, are you?' she says.

My heart skips a beat. 'No.' *What if I was?*

Citra gives me a hard look, like she's storing my facial details for later use. 'The truth is not for everyone.' She lets go of my arm and backs away as if I have an obnoxious smell.

I scurry past the bleating goats to my car, feeling like I've failed a test.

CHAPTER SEVENTEEN

'Chamomile tea, thanks,' I say to the waitress. *What's happening to me?* '... and a chocolate muffin.' *That's better.* I reach for the honey to add flavour to my tea and my crystal digs into my chest. I pull it out of my bra and narrow my eyes.

'Did you make me order this disgusting tea?' I mutter. It's still taciturn.

I'd ducked into the cafe to collect my wits after the workshop. Something weird happened in there. I need to get my thoughts straight. My hand goes to my bag for my PI notebook, but I remember I left it behind at Gold Star Investigations. Spreading the Amalian membership form face-down on the table instead, I find a pen. It's time for some analysis.

What I Know, I write on top of the page.

I take a sip of my tea, chase it down with a bite of chocolate muffin, watch the bongo player across the road and zone out. Five minutes later, the paper is still blank. I chew on my pen and admire my purple toenails. *Have those Amalians done something to my brain?* Or is it the chamomile tea?

'A triple-shot flat white please,' I ask the passing waitress.

I sense my crystal recoiling in shock. I expect the Amalians are all caffeine-free.

'And a sesame, tofu, honey, yoghurt bar.' Compromise is the name of the game.

When the coffee comes, I drain it in two gulps and poise my hand over the paper, waiting for inspiration ...

What I Know ...

– Abbey disappeared in suspicious surfing incident

– Ashok almost killed in suspicious surfing accident

– Citra building (nudist?) retreat in rainforest

– Abbey writing article on cult + trying to stop their rainforest development?

– Cactus hates Abbey – is it really because of surfing? Investigate

– Adam?

I nibble on my sesame bar. It tastes like something you might give a horse. I gaze at Adam's name. There's nothing to link him to Abbey's disappearance, but ... *It was fun jumping over you.* My pen moves away from his name, then back again. *Investigate,* I write. A girl's got to have some fun.

Now what? Alibis. I need to figure out what all the suspects were doing the night Abbey disappeared. I write my suspects' names – *Citra, Cactus, Adam,* and make a column down the side titled *Alibis.* I'll fill that in as I go along.

Proud of my efforts, I rest on my laurels, gnawing at my sesame bar. On the table next to me is an abandoned copy of the local weekly newspaper. I lean over and grab it. My sesame bar sticks in my throat as I see the headline. *Forest Friends President in Freak Surfing Accident.*

The photo shows Ashok perched on a wooden platform in a tree, holding a placard reading *End Logging Now.* The article mentions his passion for rock climbing and exploring. Luna gives a glowing tribute – *Ashok is an inspiration to us all. He is the most dedicated person I know. We are all devastated and send our best vibrations to him in hospital.* There is to be a *meditation for healing* on Ashok's behalf tomorrow. I note the details. It could be worth a visit. Finishing my sesame bar, I run down my list of suspects, and get to my feet.

Next cab off the rank is *Mr Surf God*, Cactus.

❀

I drive along the beach, pull up, and scan the waves. It's impossible to tell who is out there. Everyone looks the same from this distance. Opening the glove box, I pull out Jacq's toy binoculars from the spy set I'd bought her for Christmas.

My spy set had been my favourite toy when I was her age. I was forever sleuthing around looking for clues. Or writing coded messages in ink that only became visible when I squeezed lemon on them. Jacq loves her spy set too, but she'd been happy to lend me her binoculars for my trip to Byron.

The binoculars are cheap plastic, but they do the job. I focus on the bodies in the surf. None of them look like Cactus, but perhaps he'll show up soon. I need to engineer a meeting that won't raise his suspicions. I get back into the car and drive to The Pass. I pull a shopping bag out of the car, take Abbey's surfboard off the roof, and head for the toilets. It's time for my Bond Girl outfit.

I do know that Bond is a highly problematic hero, but what can I say? I love the over-the-top action sequences and campy vibe of the films. And besides, Bond might be a sexist psychopath, but those Bond Girls really rock.

I'd bought the lime-green bikini because the colour popped with my pink hair and fake tan. Now though, I have stage fright. Can I walk out of here in these two tiny strips of green? I am not usually a bikini-wearing girl. Well, except for that time I worked as a Gold Coast meter maid. But that was to make a point.

Go for it, babe, you're hot, says Nansea.

Let go of all limitations, intones the crystal from inside my bra.

It sounds a bit like Mum. I transfer the crystal to my bikini top, as it is now offering Mum-like advice. I hope these inner voices aren't going to become a problem. I had a lot of imaginary friends when I was a kid, but I thought I was over that phase.

I saunter out of the toilet, trying to act like a green bikini type of girl. A cool breeze blows on parts of my body that haven't been aired for a while. Humming *itsy bitsy, teeny weeny, limey greeny string bikini,* I pick up the surfboard. My humming stops abruptly as I feel Abbey's board, cool and smooth beneath my arm. As I head for the beach, I think of her. How many times would Abbey have done exactly this?

The sea is as touch-me-quick blue and crowded with surfers as usual. I pause near a surfer who's checking out the waves.

He eyes me over the top of his aviator sunglasses. 'Going to risk it?'

Risk what? 'I guess so. Why?'

He gestures at the surf school, who are conspicuous by their matching pink tops. 'Too many speed bumps.'

'Yeah, stupid surf school,' I mutter. 'I'm looking for a friend of mine, Cactus. Do you know him?'

'Friend of Cactus's are you?' He gives me a not-so-subtle look up and down. 'He'll be along soon. Unless he's resting up for the night.' He chuckles.

I nod, though I have no idea what he's talking about. *Is he a werewolf?*

'He's a madman, but I expect you know that.'

'Yes, ha, ha. Well, I'd better get in.' I walk to the water, feeling his eyes on my back. Pushing Abbey's board into the whitewash, I lie on it and start paddling out. It's strange to be on her board, to be lying exactly where she would have lain. I'm gazing dreamily at the pink hibiscus flowers on top of it when an enormous wave comes out of nowhere.

It smashes into me, pushing me off the board and into the water. I roll around like I'm on spin cycle, before it spits me out, right back onto the beach. As I come up for air, my head crashes into the board. Pushing it off me, gasping, I break the surface and flop back onto the sand.

'You dropped this,' says a man's voice.

Raising my head from the sand, I see Cactus. In his hand is my purple crystal, which must have fallen from my bikini top onto the beach. He's clearly got sharp eyes.

'Thanks.' I snatch it off him.

'Any time.' He pushes his board into the water and, with two strokes, cuts through the waves to the calmer sea beyond.

All obstacles are blessings of the guru, says the crystal as I tuck it back into my top. It still sounds like Mum.

I put the board in the water again. This time, I focus on the paddling, and make it out the back without too much fuss.

It's relaxing out here in the clear water beyond the waves. A stingray flaps its wings above the sand, like an underwater bat. A school of silvery fish darts past, so close I could pluck one from the water. My eyes come back to Abbey's hibiscus flowers again. I remember her telling me how she'd painted them herself ...

'Look out.'

Oh, no. A massive wave is coming toward me with a surfer on it. He's aiming right at me. It's Cactus. I paddle hard to get out of his way.

'Not that way,' he yells, doing a rapid cutback toward the whitewash. His board slices past my face.

There's no time for relief. The wave collects me with a loud crash, sweeping my board away as the water pushes me under. I struggle to come up, dog paddling frantically. *Which way is up?* I open my eyes wide. All around are foaming bubbles. I paddle harder. At last the wave passes, and I break the surface with a gasp, coughing and spluttering.

My board is still floating on the end of my leg rope. I pull it toward me and clamber on. I lie there, panting, before I remember my crystal. I feel inside my top, but it's gone. *Good riddance.*

A surfer points at me and shakes his head in the universal language for *no idea.* It's harsh, but true. I'm not on my game. I can't stop thinking about Abbey. Maybe I'd better get out of the water before I hurt myself. I scan the sea for looming waves and paddle for shore. A gentle wave lifts me, so I get to my feet and ride it all the way to the beach. At least I got *one* nice wave. Picking up my board, I trudge up the sand toward my car.

'So you *can* surf,' calls a voice behind me. 'Sort of.'

I glance around. It's Cactus. He wants to yell at me again. I walk faster.

'Hang on. I don't bite.'

I keep walking.

'I'm sorry I yelled at you.'

I stop and turn to face him. 'I'm sorry I got in your way. Now leave me alone, all right?'

'Can I buy you a drink?'

My jaw drops. *I'd rather be covered in honey and tied to an ants' nest.*

But Nansea kicks in. *You need to find out if he's got an alibi, babe.*

'Okay. When? Now?'

His brow wrinkles. 'I've got to get a few more waves. How about I meet you at the Beach Hotel in two hours?'

My mouth twitches. 'Fine.' At least I know where I stand, priority-wise.

'What's your name? I hear you already know mine.'

The surfer must have told him I was looking for him. 'Nansea. That's N-A-N-S-E-A.'

'Okay. Cool. See you at the Beach Hotel in two hours ... Nansea.' He turns and sprints back toward the surf.

I watch him go, mentally underlining his name in my suspect list.

CHAPTER EIGHTEEN

I go back to town to tidy up before my drink with Cactus. I'd booked a room at a backpackers this time. It was too lonely and spooky out at Abbey's house. I don't want to make any more ill-judged late-night phone calls. And it's harder to keep my anxiety to a manageable level when I'm in Abbey's empty home. Harder to believe I'll find her. I take a deep breath.

I inspect myself in the mirror above the sink. My tan's holding up well and my hair is still bright pink. It's time to bust out one of my new outfits, a stretchy blue dress teamed with lots of colourful necklaces.

Awesome, says Nansea.

I wander up the street to the Beach Hotel thinking about Abbey and Cactus. I've seen what he's like in the surf. Could Abbey be a victim of surf rage?

The inside bar of the hotel smells of sweat, smoke and beer. Four o'clock is happy hour. Backpackers crowd the tables, enjoying the transition from daytime surf to night-time party. A reggae band has the crowd up and dancing. Above the dance music, voices yell in every language of the affluent world. Byron Bay is still the coolest place on the backpacker circuit.

'Can I buy you a drink?'

A guy in a button-up shirt and pressed khaki pants comes into focus. He's trying for casual, but Brisbane casual is not the same as Byron Bay casual.

'She's with me,' says a voice behind me.

Mr Button-up Shirt shuffles away, a nervous look on his face.

I spin around. Cactus looms behind me. His hair is still wet from the surf and faded zinc covers his nose. Sand cakes his bare feet and salt water drips from his board shorts onto the wooden floor. A T-shirt hangs over one shoulder, leaving his muscled chest on display. I see why my admirer has bolted.

'Sorry to drag you from the surf.' I eye his dripping board shorts.

'Yeah, it's pumping. Still, a date's a date.'

I'm not in this for pleasure, so I smile sweetly. 'I'll have an orange juice.'

Cactus pats his back pocket. 'Damn, I've left my wallet in the car. Can you buy me a beer?' His voice is unapologetic.

Wasn't it him who asked me for a drink? The indignity of being an investigator. I roll my eyes and order the drinks, as well as a packet of chips. Cactus takes off with his beer, leaving me to trail him. He plonks himself into a vacant chair and takes a drink.

'Grab yourself a chair Nansea.' He gestures at the next table, where there's a chair free.

What a gentleman. Grinding my teeth, I drag it over to him.

'Cheers.' Cactus drains his glass. 'Any chance of another?' He must see the way my eyes narrow, because he adds, 'Take your time.'

'Thanks, that's awfully good of you,' I mutter, sipping on my juice. 'Were your parents into desert plants?'

Cactus's face wrinkles. 'What kind of a question's that?'

'What's your real name?'

'Antony.'

Hmm, another A ... 'So, why Cactus?'

'I had a wicked wipe-out a while ago, smashed my nose and cracked two ribs. My mate said *you're cactus* when he saw me. It stuck.'

Must be a surfer thing.

'I know why you're after me.' He takes a handful of chips from the packet and stuffs them in his mouth with a loud crunch.

'Pardon?'

'I recognised the board. It's Abbey's, isn't it?' He demolishes the chips.

'Huh?' Nansea's witty repartee deserts me when I need it most.

'What's your interest in Abbey?' He leans forward, pushing his sunglasses up on his salty hair. His blue eyes are sharp with intent.

A jolt of fear makes my mouth dry. I'd taken him for a dumb surfer, but he's no fool. 'She was a friend, that's all.'

His hand shoots out and grasps my forearm.

I try to shake him off.

'Now listen, Nansea. Don't make waves. There's a lot going on you don't know about. You don't want to get involved. Lay off, or you might get hurt. I'm telling you for your own benefit.' He lets go of my arm, pulls down his sunglasses and leans back in his chair.

I rub my arm where he'd grabbed it. It's not sore, I just want to make him feel bad. He's not going to scare me off that easily. Dispensing with subtlety, I get straight to the point. 'Where were you the night Abbey disappeared?'

'You're barking up the wrong tree, sweetheart. You'd be better off sticking to sunbathing.'

My hands quiver with the effort of not throwing my drink over him. I repeat the question.

'Which night was that?'

I tell him. *As if you don't know.*

Cactus pretends to think for a while. 'Now let me see. At a dance party in the rainforest.'

I suck on my lemon slice. 'On a Thursday?'

'Every day's party day in Byron Bay.'

He sounds sure of himself. How can he be so definite about what he did a month ago? I can't remember what I was doing that night. Probably the same as every weeknight, watching Netflix and going to bed early. 'Anyone who can corroborate your story?'

Cactus laughs. 'Quite the detective, aren't you? A few hundred spaced-out ravers. Want me to round some up for you?' He glances at his empty beer glass. 'Here, lend me your card would you, and I'll get myself another one.' He reaches for my purse.

I slap my hand on it and pull it toward me. 'What do you know about Abbey's disappearance?'

'Give me a break. I hardly knew her. Buy me another beer and I'll see if I can remember anything else.'

I pull out my ATM card and finger it. 'That's not what I've heard.'

Cactus stiffens and leans forward so his face is close to mine. 'Who have you been talking to?'

I flinch. He's worried.

Stick it to him, says Nansea.

'Someone saw you arguing with Abbey in the surf. You couldn't stand to see a girl surf better than you, could you?'

The tension drains out of his body. He laughs. 'I haven't seen a girl yet who surfs better than me. I'll give you some free lessons if you'll wear that green bikini.' He flashes his eyebrows at me.

Even investigators have their limits. And it's not like I'm even getting paid for this. I get up from the table, leaving my drink half full. 'Buy your own beers.' I put my purse back in my bag and stride out.

I get back to my room and sit on the bed fuming. *The nerve of him. Threatening me. And what kind of a guy asks a girl for a drink and forgets his wallet?* Cactus, aka Antony, is staying firmly on my suspect list.

It's close to dark now. What should I do next? My subconscious has an answer. Adam is next on my suspect list and his number is already up on my phone. *Adam McBean, the swoon-worthy acrobat and botanical consultant.*

Go on, have some fun, Nansea urges.

This isn't about fun. He's a suspect. My heart thumps and I press his number before I can change my mind. The phone rings for a long time. I'm about to hang up when he answers.

'Adam here.'

I almost drop the phone in fright. I guess I'm not a black-belt in voice calls yet.

Talk to him, Nansea screams.

'Hi, it's Nansea here. Abbey's friend?'

There's a pause. *He's forgotten who I am.*

'Hi Nansea, how are you?' He sounds pleased.

'I'm in town for the weekend. I wondered if you …'

'I'd love to.'

He would? 'Well, do you want to meet up somewhere?'

'How about I meet you at Charlie's at seven? It's an Italian restaurant.'

Not just drinks, but dinner. 'Okay, cool. I'll see you there.' I press *End*. Yeah, I'm killing this phone conversation thing. What was I worried about? One hour to get ready. I need some penetrating questions to ask him.

I put the penetrating questions on hold. Instead, I fling the contents of my bag onto the bed and try on every possible clothing combination. It's lucky I only have five tops, five bottoms and the blue dress I'm wearing, but still, it takes a while. With fifteen minutes to go, I slip back into the dress and race out the door. I'll think up some penetrating questions on the way.

I walk up the street to Charlie's, stop, and peer in the window. My stomach does a triple back-flip as I see him. Adam is sitting at a table near the back of the restaurant, wearing a black T-shirt and looking at his phone.

That's one sexy suspect, says Nansea.

I'm only in this for information, I reply.

Adam smiles as I come toward his table. 'Well hello there. You look different. I like the pink hair.'

'Yeah, you know. A change is as good as um, whatever ...' I trail off. My brain has turned to mush in his presence. Never mind penetrating questions, I'll be flat out acting normal.

'It suits you.'

I blush and sit down.

'Have you eaten here before?' we both say together.

'You go,' I say.

'No, you go.'

'I haven't.'

'Well, I have. I recommend the meatballs.'

'Meatballs it is.' I rack my brain for something else to say. The silence draws on. I need to get myself together – I'm out of my depth. I jump to my feet. 'I've got to go to the loo.' In the toilet, I lean against the wall, breathing deeply.

He digs you, says Nansea. *He wouldn't be here otherwise.*

This is not a hot date. He's a suspect. Sometimes investigators must use their sex appeal to get the answers they need. *Alibi, alibi, alibi,* I repeat to myself as I return to the table. *I am a Russian spy interrogating James Bond.*

Adam is texting but he slips his phone into his pocket as I approach. 'Are you okay?'

I nod, in what I hope is a sultry manner.

'So, tell me about yourself, Nansea.' Adam pours me a glass of red wine.

I'm not used to drinking wine, but I take a sip to buy some time. *Tell me about yourself ...* If you leave out the part about being a PI and a law student, it doesn't leave much.

Ad lib, babe, murmurs Nansea.

'I'm a dolphin trainer,' I blurt. 'At Ocean World.' *Where did that come from? Aargh.*

Adam leans forward. 'That must be interesting work.'

'Yes. I've seen things you wouldn't believe.' I take another sip of wine, while I imagine what those things might be. 'Training dolphins is not as glamorous as you might think. They can be annoying. That smile thing? It's just a front. You don't want to get on their bad side.'

'Wow. I've never heard anyone diss dolphins before. I always thought they were like the Mother Teresas of the sea.'

'Exactly. Don't get me started on Mother Teresa.'

Adam laughs.

After that, things warm up and our conversation becomes a bit like a ping pong game. He bats me a line, I bat one back. *Ping* – childhood in London. *Pong* – childhood on a hippie commune in the hills behind Byron. I made that up too, obviously.

'That still doesn't explain you.' Adam leans toward me.

'How do you mean?' I chase my Tiramisu around the plate with my spoon.

'You're like, incredibly changeable. I feel like you might do something unexpected any minute.'

'I have that feeling about myself too.' I bite my tongue. That sounded borderline psychotic. Am I not handling the Olivia-to-Nansea transition as smoothly as I imagined? I press on, telling him about my transformative workshop with Citra. '... and this guy said his crystal didn't like him ...' I giggle.

'Why were you at this workshop?' says Adam. 'I didn't have you down as the spiritual quest type.'

I'm about to make something up, when I decide I'll never get a better lead. 'I'm trying to find out more about Abbey. She was writing an article on the cult. Did she talk to you about it?'

Adam shakes his head. 'We never talked about her writing. I identified some plants for her every now and then. Helped out where I could.'

'What were you working on most recently ...' I stop with a gulp. Adam's hand is on my knee. My stomach turns over.

His hand is on your knee, squeals Nansea.

Thank you Nansea, I did notice that.

'An eco-tourism resort proposal,' he murmurs, in a husky voice.

He could be speaking Mandarin as far as I'm concerned. The words go in one ear and out the other. My heart is dancing a rapid fandango and I have a sudden urge to leap over the table and press my lips against his. Did Nancy Drew ever have a hot thing with one of her suspects? I don't think so. *James Bond, on the other hand …*

Adam locks his brown eyes on mine, while his finger strokes my knee. 'You don't know how sexy you are, do you Nansea?'

That's true, Adam, I don't.

CHAPTER NINETEEN

Adam's body presses down on mine. My stomach turns to treacle. He reaches behind him and his hand comes back, revealing ... a trailing mass of seaweed. He wraps it around my head and arms. It is clammy and tough. I struggle against its rubbery embrace –

'Help!' I scream, startling myself so much I wake up.

My sheet has twisted itself around me like a shroud and my body is slippery with sweat. I fling myself about, panting, until the sheet releases me. My dream fades as the walls come into focus.

Sharp fingers of sun stream through the window onto my face. *Take cover,* screams my fragile brain. Squeezing my eyes shut, I roll over to the shady side of the bed. I open my eyes a fraction and survey the room. My first impression was correct: it's empty.

Did I spend the night with Adam? I blink, sorting fact from fantasy. *No, I didn't.* I close my eyes again, as I remember the way my evening ended.

Adam had walked me back to my backpackers. He had his arm around my waist. It sounds demure when I put it like that, rather Jane Austen. In fact, it was anything but. My dress was thin, and I use the term waist in the loosest possible sense.

He came upstairs with me, and we kissed against the door. It would have taken just one step and we'd have been inside, on the beige carpet. Or on my bed. But something weird happened.

He's a suspect, Nansea screamed at me.

Wasn't Nansea all about having fun? Apparently not. Anyway, it put me right off. I pulled away, stuttered *bye, it's been fun,* and slipped into my room before he kissed me again.

Now, edging my body to the side of the bed, I roll out and stagger toward the kettle. Balancing the kettle in the sink and tearing at a sachet with my teeth, I produce a cup of coffee. Feeling like I've hunted and killed my own breakfast, I totter back to bed.

Cup in hand, I sink down, ready to indulge in some daydreaming. Adam really is super-cute. My toes curl and I let out a sigh.

He's a suspect, Nansea reminds me.

Yeah, you said that last night.

Soon, the coffee kicks in, spurring me to action. Perhaps we can have the all-important second date tonight?

Nansea raises an eyebrow.

It's business. A second date will allow me to progress my investigations further.

I scoop my phone off the bedside table and press his number, but it goes straight to voicemail. *Voicemail.* Is there anything more awkward than leaving a voicemail message?

I hang up and decide to text instead. *Hi.* I pause. *Would you like to come over and see my knitting?* I delete this and settle for *Call me back. Bye.* I press send, then realise it's a little terse. What's worse, I have used full-stops in a text. Everyone knows that full-stops in texts are passive-aggressive. Why did I use full-stops? *Why?*

I resist the urge to send another text without full-stops. We are not on double-texting terms.

After that surge of activity, I'm ready for a nap. I close my eyes, but they spring open again. *Damn.* The meditation session for Ashok is on this morning. It's the last thing I feel like. I close my eyes again.

What kind of an investigator are you? Nansea chides.

I'm getting a bit sick of her. Moaning, I drag myself out of bed and into the shower.

The meditation session is being held in one of the alternative therapy centres that scatter the streets of the Bay. It had better be close, or I'll have to lie down on the way. I'm so tired.

Luckily, it's not too long before I find The Waveroom. Dolphin songs and a brochure-covered wall greet me in reception, but there's no-one around. I glance at my phone. It's ten past eleven. I'm late. I guess they've already started.

The gentle squeaking of dolphins is calming. Maybe I really should be a dolphin trainer. They might not be the saints of the sea, but they sound like they should be. I inhale, enjoying the cinnamon aroma that wafts from the oil burner on the counter. My eyes fix on the puffy couch. *Maybe I'll sit for a moment and listen to dolphin calls ...*

You're here to do a job, screams Nansea.

She's become so strident lately. I suppose she's right though. I pull my eyes away from the puffy couch and see a carpeted corridor leading off from the reception area. Slipping off my thongs, I add them to the row of shoes stretched out beside the door and pad down the corridor.

A door at the far end is open. I peer around it, into a darkened room. In the flickering candlelight, I see about twenty people holding hands in a circle. Their eyes are shut. I watch for a while, but it's not very interesting. I'm about to sneak off again, when my stomach jolts.

One pair of eyes is open. It's a girl with brown hair to her shoulders, a hoop through her nose and a toned physique. *Luna.* Of course she would be here. I duck back around the corner. Did she see me?

From my hiding spot, I hear her speak. 'We are here to bring healing energy to our friend Ashok.' She begins to chant, in a high, clear voice.

I retreat back up the corridor and inspect the brochures on the wall. Luna's face is on the cover of one. I pull it out of the rack. When I met Luna a few months ago, she was a yoga instructor, but it appears she's branched out. The brochure tells me she specialises in chakra realignments – whatever they are.

I should talk to her about Ashok, but I'll hold off. She's busy and I don't want to blow my cover yet. I yawn; an afternoon nap is coming on.

It is mid-afternoon when I get back to work. Munching on a packet of chips, I pull out my *What I Know* list.

What I Know ...

– Abbey disappeared in suspicious surfing incident

– Ashok almost killed in suspicious surfing accident. **Talk to Luna,** I add. **Get chakra balancing?**

– Cult building (nudist?) retreat in rainforest

– Abbey writing article on cult + trying to stop rainforest development?

– Cactus (AKA Antony) hates Abbey – is it really because of surfing?

– Adam?

Next to *Adam?* I doodle *So hot!!!*

Not very professional, drawls Nansea.

I cross it out.

My alibi column is still bare, so beside Cactus I write – *investigate dance party in rainforest.*

My eyes rest on Cactus's name and I remember something the surfer on the beach said. *Unless he's resting up for the night.* Where would a surfer be at night? *Surfing duh.*

Rosco loves night surfing too. I hear his voice in my head. *You've got to wait until the moon's high. It's eerie, but it's awesome. Like outer space. Night surfing is best on the full moon, but any time from half-moon onwards is okay.*

So, what's the moon doing at the moment? Yesterday's local paper is on the floor. Picking it up, I flick to the tide and weather section. The moon is half-full tonight. I crunch on my chips.

So, what was the moon doing the night Abbey disappeared? I pull out my phone and google moon phases, putting in the date Abbey disappeared. The moon was full. *Hmm ...*

My phone rings. All thoughts of the moon whoosh out of my head as I hear Adam's voice.

'Yeah, five o'clock. That'll be great. See you there.' My pulse goes double-time as I put the phone down. Adam and I are meeting at the Beach Hotel this evening. *The second date.* I know what this means. My legs turn to limp spaghetti as I remember what Abbey said about second dates ...

It was the week before our final Year Twelve exams, and we were studying at Abbey's house. In our lunch break, the conversation had turned to sex, as it often did. Abbey had dated lots of boys and slept with two, so that made her an expert, compared to me.

My sexual history had been notable for its lack of sex. I was aware this made me a slow starter, but I had my reasons. I'd found romantic relationships tricky since I was assaulted on the beach when I was fifteen. I found it difficult to trust guys.

I'd gone out with three boys in high school, but there was no chemistry. Their kisses did nothing for me. I was starting to think I'd never find someone I liked enough to *do it* with.

'My recommendation is, if you find someone you like, you should do it on the second date.' Abbey bit into a banana.

I sucked on a spoonful of Milo. 'That's not too soon?'

'For most people, I would say, maybe five dates,' Abbey said. 'To be sure you really like them. In your case though ... you should get it over with.' She smiled. 'Then you can relax.'

She made this sex thing sound like jumping into cold water. I knew what she meant though. The longer I left it, the more anxious the idea of it made me.

'You don't need to be serious about them, just seriously attracted. Maybe choose someone who's more experienced than you.'

'Well, that narrows the field.'

Abbey laughed.

'Not,' I added.

Abbey flung her banana peel in the compost bin. 'Don't forget to use condoms.'

❀

Adam is only the second guy who has ever made my heart beat faster. Rosco was the first. Rosco and I had bucketloads of chemistry. Our kisses were dynamite, but our relationship didn't last long enough for things to go further.

So now, with Adam ... is it a good time to take things to the next level? I remember his warm hand on my knee, his soft lips against mine. Yes, the chemistry is there. With Rosco missing in action, Adam is the perfect candidate for first lover.

Apart from the fact that he's on your suspect list, shouts Nansea.

I ignore her. I have no evidence to connect Adam to Abbey's disappearance. Besides, becoming intimate with a suspect is a tried-and-true investigative technique. Possibly not for Nancy Drew, but it is for James Bond, and what's good for 007 is good for me, right?

James Bond is not an appropriate role model, shouts Nansea again.

She may be raucous, but she is probably right. I will reimagine myself as Jane Bond, a feisty, sexy, do-whatever-it-takes spy who always gets her man.

Am I about to become sexually active? My gut lurches. If so ... I need to address the condom question. Should I buy them, or will he have them? I wish Abbey were here. She was good at this sort of thing.

My chest tightens. *Abbey.* How did I let our friendship fade away like that? We used to be so close. I have to find her, to put things right between us. What would Abbey say if she were here right now?

You are in charge of your own destiny and sexual health, babe.

Abbey sounds a lot like Nansea, who seems to have given up her resistance to my proposed rendezvous. They're right. Picking up my purse, I head for Woolies.

Back home in Southport, most supermarket shoppers are efficient. They know where they're going and what to buy. In contrast, the shoppers in Byron Bay Woolies seem to:

(a) have never been in a supermarket before,

(b) have forgotten why they're there,

(c) need to find the chips and chocolate, dude, or,

(d) come from countries that drive on the right-hand side of the aisles.

It's total chaos.

I pick up a basket and jostle my way to the toiletries aisle. Once I'm there, I change my mind. If I just buy condoms, it will look like I have an urgent sex date. Which is not something I need to broadcast.

Backtracking to the fruit and vegie aisle, I place a bunch of bananas in my trolley. On second thoughts, I take the bananas out and replace them with a less suggestive pineapple. I add a few tomatoes to complete my *serious shopper* résumé.

Okay. Taking a deep breath, I stride toward the condom section. I have what I hope is a *might as well stock up on condoms while I'm here* look on my face. It's a difficult look to pull off.

Coming to a standstill, I scan the prophylactic display. It's overwhelming. That's the trouble with our society – too much choice. You can't just get condoms, you have to make decisions. Large or normal? Small isn't an option. Ribbed or unribbed? Novelty or standard?

Legends condoms in a collectible tin, or vibrating condoms with extra zing? muses Nansea.

If I choose standard, will it mark me as staid and conservative? But what will novelty condoms say? Nothing wholesome, I'm sure. Psyching myself up for sex is hard enough. Do I have to choose my position on the spectrum between vanilla and *Fifty Shades* first? Where is the condom that says *I'm a fun-loving, though inexperienced girl who might be open to experimentation if things go well?* My hand hovers between standard and novelty.

'Need any help?'

Fabulous. You can never find help when you need it, but when you don't ... 'Just looking,' I mutter through clenched teeth.

'I'd get the variety pack, try them all out.'

I turn around, my cheeks burning. They practically burst into flames when I see who's there. *Rosco.*

An empty shopping basket dangles from his hand and his face is neutral. Suspiciously so. 'Or would you like some recommendations?'

My mouth turns as dry as the Simpson Desert. I haven't seen Rosco in person since I told him I was leaving the agency. And now ... this is about as inauspicious as unscheduled ex-boyfriend encounters come.

Seeing him here in the toiletries aisle, I get a peculiar fluttery feeling in my chest. I blink quickly. I'm worried I might cry. 'I'm buying them for a friend.' I snatch the first packet of condoms my hand comes to and toss it in my basket.

'Not a good choice,' he calls after me as I march away.

I am well beyond embarrassment by the time I get to the checkout.

The teenage boy scans my rainbow-coloured party pack. His cheeks colour. 'Do you want a bag?'

'No, I'm fine.' I stuff the condoms in my backpack, along with the pineapple and the tomatoes. *Whatever. Mission accomplished.* I don't turn around to see if Rosco is watching as I walk away.

Whatever feelings he might have still had for me, I'm pretty sure this condom incident has squashed them. *Good.* I need to move on.

Back at my room, I shower, shave my legs, primp up my pink hair and shine my belly-button ring. I try to focus on Adam. The whole time though, I keep seeing Rosco's face.

He'd had a strange expression. Distant. As if he wasn't sure where he'd met me before. I comb my hair, brush my teeth and put on some deodorant. No, didn't he look ... wounded? Like Han Solo after that hurtful Ewok village argument with Leia. Where does he get off, looking like a wounded Han Solo? He was the one who ghosted me.

So Rosco saw you buying condoms? Big deal, says Nansea.

She's right. I am a mature young woman taking care of my destiny and sexual health. I have nothing to be ashamed of. I try to forget about Rosco. *Breathe in the silver, breathe out the black,* as a creepy yoga instructor once told me.

At four thirty, I slide into some jungle-print hipsters and a top that displays my sparkling navel. I put in my headphones, turn Billie Eilish up loud, and walk into town on a mixed cloud of trepidation and excitement.

CHAPTER TWENTY

Pulling out my earphones, I scan the beer garden. A band is playing Beatles covers and the beautiful people are out in force. I squeeze past a tall blonde girl in shorts that could double as a belt and order an orange juice.

'We've got to stop meeting like this,' says a voice beside me.

My stomach lurches. 'Remembered your wallet today, huh?' I snap, eyeing the beer in Cactus's hand.

'Can I buy you a drink?'

'I've already got one.' I lift my glass. 'As I'm sure you noticed before you offered.'

'Oh, fair go ... I—'

But I'm not listening. The breath rushes out of me as I see Adam come in.

You've got it bad, girl, murmurs Nansea.

He's wearing khaki pants and a faded blue shirt that sets off his platinum hair.

Cactus turns, following my gaze. His lip curls. 'You know him?'

There's something on his face I can't decipher. Anger and ... Is he worried? Well, he should be. I narrow my eyes at him. 'Yeah, I do.' It comes across with a hint of menace. Not waiting to see his reaction, I push through the crowd toward Adam.

His face lights up as I approach. 'Hey, where are you headed Nansea?'

'Nowhere special.'

'Me too, what a coincidence.' He pulls me toward him and gives me a lingering kiss. He raises his glass as we separate. 'Cheers.'

'Cheers.' I gulp my juice. Glancing over Adam's shoulder, I see eyes boring into me. *Cactus.* Beer in hand, he leans against the bar, his face a tight mask. The hairs on my arms prickle.

Adam takes my hand. 'What's wrong?'

'Nothing.' I dismiss Cactus from my mind as Adam's hand runs up my arm.

'So, tell me more about being a dolphin trainer. You must have lots of interesting stories.'

Dolphin trainer. Why had I told him that? I sip my drink and wait for inspiration to strike. 'Well, as I mentioned, I've just finished advanced dolphin training school. This is for dolphins that can already jump through hoops and balance balls. The next step is learning to carry people around the pool. It's all about positive reinforcement. Like training a puppy ...' I enjoy spinning the tale until it occurs to me I'm doing all the talking.

Get back on task, says Nansea.

'Did you help Abbey with many projects?' I ask.

'A few.' He looks over my shoulder. 'Check out that sunset. It's a doozy.'

I turn my chair around. I have to admit it's worth a look. The wind has died, and the Bay is orange glass. A yellow shaft of light beams through a low-lying cloud, illuminating the mountains. *Hallelujah.* This is Byron Bay at its most seductive.

'Let's go for a walk on the beach.' Adam pulls me to my feet.

As we run hand in hand across the road toward the sunset, the band strikes up 'She Loves You'. I'm not at all surprised. We could be in a romantic movie, it is all so perfect. Too perfect, as it turns out.

As we step onto the sand, Adam's phone rings. He rolls his eyes. 'Sorry. I'd better take it.' He turns away from me. 'Oh, yeah, okay.' He slips his phone away and I can tell from his face it's not good news. 'I'm sorry. Turns out I've got a gig tonight at a party.'

'Huh?' *But it's our second date. I've bought condoms.*

'Acrobatics. Unfortunately, I need the cash, I'm skint. Some other time? I'll call you.' He's in a hurry to leave. He gives me a quick kiss and turns away.

Well, that's it for the big date. Hope my party condoms don't go out of date before I get the chance to use them. I'm about to set off toward my backpackers when a figure steps out from the pub. It's Cactus.

My insides tighten. *What's he doing?* I duck behind a pandanus tree. He stares my way for a moment before walking away in the same direction as Adam.

I'm about to desert my pandanus, when another figure appears across the road. *Rosco?* What's going on? It's like rush hour in Surfers Paradise here. Rosco walks away in the same direction as Cactus. Is he following him?

Emerging from my pandanus, I scurry down the street after them. It's almost dark now and the half-moon glows in the sky behind the lighthouse like a giant slice of cheese.

I keep some distance from Rosco. A surge of rowdy teenagers crosses in front of me and I think I've lost him. But I see his broad shoulders disappear into a doorway at the end of the road. Following, I inspect the sign above the door. *Crazy Frog's*

Restaurant and Nightclub. Cheap Meals. Jungle Night Tonight.
I peer inside. It's crowded in there, though it's only seven o'clock. The lighting is low, so I should be able to mingle without being seen. A throbbing beat vibrates across the bar as I slip in.

'Nansea?' calls a voice beside me. 'Is that you?'

So much for inconspicuous. I spin around. It's Lars, the Swedish backpacker from the surf lesson. He's sitting on a semi-circular couch with six sunburnt girls.

'It *is* you.' He smiles. 'You look different to last time. Cool hair.'

I'm so pleased it's not Rosco, Adam or Cactus who's spotted me, I start to gush. 'Hey, Lars. You're still in Byron Bay. I thought you were moving on to Cairns.'

'I changed my mind. Byron Bay is the coolest. I will stay here until I have to go home for my doctorate research. Come and join us, there's plenty of room.' Lars pats the seat and the girls move along with disgruntled looks.

I take a seat. It's a good place to observe the passing parade.

Lars does the introductions. 'This is Juliette, she is from France. Nicki, from England. Rachel and Hannah from Israel, and Nyoko and Midori, from Japan. They are twins, as you can see.' The two Japanese girls have dyed blonde hair and halter-neck dresses. They smile politely.

'We are having the ten-dollar dinner,' says Lars. 'It is excellent value, will I order one for you? You can have chicken or beef. The drinks are cheap too. I am buying a round now. What would you like?'

I nod. 'Lemonade please. And chicken.'

Lars bounces away to the bar, leaving me with the girls. They immediately discuss him.

'He's into you, Hannah,' says Nicki, the English one, in a posh Emma Watson accent.

'Ee eez zo cute,' says Juliette. 'You should go for eet.'

I tune the girls out as I scan the room, looking for Rosco, Cactus or Adam. The bar is like a barn. It stretches into dark corners filled with clusters of shadowy people. I can't see them anywhere.

Lars dances toward the table with a tray of drinks. His face is painted in orange and white stripes. Black whiskers radiate from his nose.

'Roar.' He puts the drinks down and claws at the air with his hands. 'They are doing free face-painting over near the bar. It is for the jungle night. You should all go and get painted.'

The girls giggle. 'Maybe later,' say Nyoko and Midori together.

'Cool idea,' I say. If I get my face made up, I'll have less chance of being spotted. I get up and go over to the bar.

'What animal do you want, sweetie?' asks the face-painting girl, gesturing at her pots of paint.

'Zebra.'

'Too easy.' She strokes the paint on my face and holds up a mirror.

I smile as I see my black-and-white striped image. It's perfect. I wouldn't recognise me, myself. I should add face paints to my disguise grab-bag. The possibilities are endless. Then I remember I don't need a disguise grab-bag, I'm not a PI anymore. This is just for Abbey.

'Hey, cool, look at Nansea,' Lars calls as I come back. 'Come and dance with the tiger, Miss Zebra.' He jumps up, pulls me over to the dance floor, and pogoes up and down. He's like a tiger on a wasp's nest.

I jig around beside him, scanning the room.

Lars dances faster and faster until he is a blur of orange and black.

I'm dizzy just watching. It's like that fable where the tiger chases its tail until it melts into butter. I notice his pupils are so dilated, they almost cover his blue eyes. That explains why he's so manic.

'Have you taken something?' I yell over the music.

'Yah.' Lars bounces up and down. 'Some guy in the corner near the men's toilets has special biscuits. All natural, he says. Organic. No chemicals. Do you want me to get you some?'

I shake my head. I'd tell him to save some brain cells for his research, but I don't want to sound like his mother. As Lars pulls me round and round, I spot Cactus. He's sitting on a stool by himself, nursing a beer. His eyes slide straight over Lars and me. I guess we look like crazy jungle animals. I steer Lars further into the crowd. There's no sign of Rosco. Or Adam.

The bar gets busier and the music louder. We stop dancing to stuff down some overcooked corn and a couple of limp slices of chicken. I push it away half-finished. The drinks keep flowing and the girls giggle louder. An antelope, a jaguar, a chimpanzee, an elephant and two pretty cheetahs now sit at the table with me.

Through it all, I keep half an eye on Cactus. He doesn't move from his bar stool. When everyone has eaten, the staff push the tables together, making an elevated dance floor.

'Now it's time to party,' says the DJ.

I was under the impression I'd been partying already. I guess I've led a sheltered life.

'We're going to be giving out prizes all night. First prize of two private surf lessons with Rosie from Bay Surf goes to the best jungle dance couple on the next tune.'

'Let's go.' Lars pulls me up.

I resist. I'm exhausted, and I shouldn't be out on display, but Lars won't take no for an answer. Out on the dance floor, I force my aching body into an impromptu war dance. We get into the spirit of it, stomping and waving our hands and generally making fools of ourselves.

As the music fades away, the DJ makes his announcement. 'Winners of the surf lessons are ... the tiger and the zebra.'

Lars and I jump up and down, hugging each other, and push through to the front of the crowd to get our vouchers. As I turn with my prize in my hand, I see Cactus's shoulders disappearing through the door. *Damn, damn, damn.* 'Sorry, got to go,' I say to Lars.

He holds onto my arm, calling above the noise of the music. 'But Nansea, I thought you liked me. We've been having fun, haven't we?'

I pause.

But Lars' hand drops from my arm as two Japanese cheetahs pull him back onto the dance floor. Doing an excellent job of disguising his broken heart, he waves, turns, and begins to shimmy.

Breaking through the crowd into the open air, I glance up and down the street. Cactus has disappeared. *Top-notch surveillance, Olivia.* Now what? I wander up toward the beach, hoping I'll see him. The footpaths are busy, but there's no sign of him.

At the top of the street, I cross over to the beach. The moon is low in the sky and a sparkle of light runs across the sea toward it. I gaze out at the water feeling the energy of the dance still buzzing through me. My skin prickles. *The half-moon.* It's been three weeks since Abbey disappeared.

Something occurs to me. *Cactus has gone to get ready for his night surf. Like he did the night Abbey disappeared.* I chew my lip, imagining what might have happened …

Cactus is pumped up. He's had a few beers and takes off for a midnight surf. Abbey's in bed but she can't sleep. The full moon shines in her window so she picks up her board and heads for the beach. Cactus is out in the surf. He sees Abbey. She steals his waves in the daytime and now she's stealing them at night too. They argue. He snaps. He grabs her and holds her under and tows her body further out to sea, so it won't wash in.

For a moment, I'm so certain of it I want to confront him straight away. Make him tell me what he did. But what do I have? A wild hunch. I clench my fists. How do I get him to admit it?

A re-enactment, cries Nansea. *He'll freak out and spill the beans.*

This strikes me as an inspired idea. Yes, I will confront him in the surf, where he's not expecting it.

But beneath my surge of gung-ho fervour is a twinge of nausea. There's something impenetrable about Cactus. On one level, he's your typical macho sexist surfer. On another level, he is an enigma. He has to be hiding something.

CHAPTER TWENTY-ONE

By the time I've gone back to my room, picked up Abbey's surfboard and got to the beach, my gung-ho levels have declined. Leaping into the black water with a potential psycho killer doesn't seem as tempting anymore. Not to mention that being on a beach alone at night is a silly idea.

My hand tightens around Abbey's board as I remember what happened to me on the beach when I was fifteen ... I swallow, a sour metallic taste in my mouth. But I'm over that now. I've moved on. I can't live my life being scared of the dark.

I take a deep breath. I can do this. The shimmer of the moon on the water and the sweep of the lighthouse beam entice me on. I walk up the beach toward The Pass.

All is quiet in the water, so I put the surfboard under a tree and lean against it to wait. Music from the Beach Hotel drifts toward me, but the crash of the waves deadens it. The sound is relaxing, and I'm almost drifting off to sleep when a motor startles me. I peer out to sea. A large launch has anchored off Julian Rocks. Voices carry across the water.

There's movement near the shoreline. A surfer is getting into the water. *Is that Cactus?* It's too dark to see. The surfer paddles out through the whitewash, into the dark water beyond. I watch until he disappears into the night. *Is he paddling all the way to Julian Rocks?* A faint humming noise comes from the direction of the launch. It sounds like a small boat. I strain my eyes but both the surfer and the boat, if there is one, are shrouded in darkness.

I peer into the shadows. What to do?

Something fishy is going on out there babe, says Nansea. *You better check it out.*

I suppose she's right. As I get to my feet to investigate, another surfer runs down the beach, surfboard tucked under his arm. I shrink back into the darkness. The sweep of the lighthouse beam illuminates him. *Blond hair. Muscled arms.* It could be Cactus, but I can't tell from the back. *If this is Cactus, who's the other guy?* There are too many fair-haired surfers around here. This investigation is turning into a Raymond Chandler novel. Chandler's detective, Philip Marlowe, always has to wade through a sea of blondes to find his villain.

The surfer pushes his board onto the waves and paddles into the blackness. *What's going on out there?*

Go after him, squeals Nansea. *You'll never know otherwise.*

I eye the inky water.

As I'm building up to tackling the waves, yet another surfer emerges out of the shadows and runs to the water. Like the others, he vanishes into the darkness. I stare out at the water. Is there some kind of surfers' convention going on? Maybe I'd better not get involved.

What are you, an investigator or a mouse?

Reluctantly, I strip off my dress and glasses. I've reverted to my comfortable old Speedos, rather than the Bond Girl bikini. I do a heroic run to the water with Abbey's board under my arm, but stop dead, ankle deep in the warm water. *Too scary.*

Get in there, snarls Nansea.

Trying not to think of sharks, I launch myself into the water and paddle out. *Sharks. Sharks, sharks.* The hammerheads, tiger sharks and great whites of my imagination lunge toward me. If only I'd never seen *Jaws.*

It's different at night. I can't see the waves until they're almost on top of me. Luckily the surf is small, as I'm not at all keen on being washed off my board. It's scary enough on top of the water. The surge slaps me in the face, and then I'm out the back. Panting, I pause in the still water and peer around me. *Nope. Nothing to see, better get back to the beach.*

'Aaeeeyaa ...' A piercing scream bursts from my mouth as something touches my leg. I kick out and turn, preparing to jab it in its nasty, sharky eyes.

'Christ, you've deafened me,' says Cactus.

My pulse thuds as I sit up on my board, legs dangling into the darkness. Cactus isn't much of an improvement over a great white. 'Why'd you sneak up on me like that?' I yell.

Sitting up on his board, Cactus shows me the palms of his hands. 'Whoa. You're the one doing the sneaking around. It'd be funny if it wasn't so dangerous. You're following me and it's a bad idea. You're going to get yourself hurt.'

A lump fills my throat. 'Like Abbey, you mean.' I stare toward the shore. I'd been mad to come out here. I'll never out-paddle him if he attacks me.

'Yes, like Abbey.' Cactus's expression is unreadable in the darkness.

I shiver. That's practically an admission of guilt. I need to get far, far away from him. 'What are you doing here?' I force myself to say.

'Surfing, what else?' His voice is flat. 'Are you going to leave me to it?'

I hear the hidden threat ... *or?* That's enough for me, I'm out of here. Without a word, I paddle away, my arms slicing through the water. When I glance back, Cactus has vanished. I stop paddling and press my head against Abbey's board. Bile rises from my churning stomach. Just when I could have done with some encouragement, Nansea is silent.

Moonlight bounces off the saltwater droplets that cover the deck of the surfboard. The adrenaline seeps from my body, leaving me limp. I gaze at the shiny droplets and try to muster the strength to paddle to shore.

Suddenly my breath catches. The drops of light shimmer, forming themselves into curves and lines. It doesn't look random. Is there something scratched into the wax on the board? I sit up and stare at it. Gleaming silvery lines take the shape of jagged letters. I trace them with my finger. Is my imagination going overboard, or ...?

As my finger moves over the scratches, the letters emerge beneath my touch. They are untidy and ragged, but they are letters. N ... A ... I ... A ... D. At first it makes no sense, but it comes to me. *Naiad*, a female water spirit. I run my finger over the word again and again, the sharks and dark water forgotten.

Abbey scratched these letters in with her fingernails before she disappeared. They're a clue. If only she'd written something useful. Like *Cactus did it*. I paddle for shore, catching a wave into the beach, my mind whirling like a spin-dryer.

I'm cold now that the fright is wearing off and desperate for a hot shower. I walk back along the sand with Abbey's board under my arm. *Naiad*. What happened to Abbey?

The launch is still anchored off the rocks, but there's no sign of Cactus or the other two surfers. Maybe they're fighting it out, out there.

I hear something behind me as I trudge along. I half turn, but there's no-one there. My heart quickens. Is there a wallaby up in the sand dunes? Maybe it's not a fabulous idea to be walking on the beach by myself. I quicken my step, heading for the lights of Main Beach. I'm almost there.

Sand squeaks behind me. *That's not a wallaby.* I freeze, nerves prickling. I am swinging around when a body hits me from behind. It pushes me to the ground, knocking the surfboard from my hands. A hand presses on the back of my head, grinding my face deeper into the sand. Dampness comes off my attacker as they sit on my back. *They've been in the water.* I kick and struggle, but it's no use. They're stronger than me. Why did I come here by myself? I'm such an idiot. My head starts to spin.

'This is a warning.' A breathy voice whispers in my ear. 'Back off or ...'

'Ha ha. You are so crazy, Midori.' A faint voice carries toward me from down the beach, along with muffled giggles.

The weight lifts off me. I sit up, coughing, and see a shadowy figure run into the pandanus that lines the beach. I spit the sand from my mouth and breathe in shallow gasps, tears of shock springing to my eyes.

The giggling comes closer, and three dark shapes approach along the shoreline.

'Hey, is that you Nansea?' The voice is familiar.

The figures come into focus. It is Lars and the Japanese girls – a tiger and two cheetahs. They stop giggling.

'Are you okay?' asks Lars. 'You are all covered in sand.'

I nod. I'd rather not explain about the attack. 'Yes. Just, um …
rolling down the beach.'

Lars and the girls stare at me blankly.

'It's an Australian half-moon tradition.'

'Cool. Let's do it!' Lars flings himself onto the sand and starts
to roll.

I've never been so pleased to see anyone in my life.

CHAPTER TWENTY-TWO

Next morning, I gaze at the glimpse of ocean from my window. A small wave breaks onto the sand and two kids squeal as they run up the beach away from the surge. Everything seems innocent and happy out there, but it's not.

I turn to inspect myself in the mirror. My neck is stiff, and the side of my face looks like it's been sandpapered. *I'm okay.* I shouldn't have been out there on the beach by myself, but ... Now at least I know I'm getting somewhere. There's someone out there trying to stop me.

Naiad. I picture the word scratched on Abbey's board. It has to mean something.

The naiad is a huge diamond, says Nansea. *Or an ancient statue. Or a priceless painting.*

These all sound like something in a Nancy Drew or Sherlock Holmes book, but they don't ring true.

I replay the breathy whisper of my attacker over and over in my head. Who was it? Were they disguising their voice?

Cactus had threatened me in the surf. And I'd been attacked straight afterwards. It makes sense it was him. My attacker was strong, I know that much.

My brain feels all muddled; I didn't sleep well. So much was going through my mind. *The attack, Naiad, Fallen Angel.* My subconscious produced startling dreams, but no solutions. Yawning, I make myself an instant coffee, tipping a container of UHT milk into the cup. It tastes terrible, but it wakes me up.

Abbey's surfboard leans on the wall beside me, giving my room a cheerful holiday ambience. Kneeling beside the board, I run my fingers over the letters. *Naiad* ... It's a breakthrough of sorts, but it's hard to see where to go next.

It's a racehorse, says Nansea. *Or a huge luxury boat. Or a nugget of gold.*

I toy with the idea of ringing Rosco and bringing him up to date. Maybe he'll fill me in on what he was up to last night. The embarrassing supermarket condom incident hangs between us though. If our relationship was weird before, it will be ten times weirder now.

I know what he'd say anyway. He'd give me a hard time for being gung-ho and tell me to talk to the police.

You can find her, says Nansea. *No-one knows Abbey like you do.*

She's right. The trouble is, I have no idea where to begin. I make another coffee and go outside. Slumping on the bench in the sun, I massage my stiff neck. It's Easter Sunday. I have to go home tomorrow. Back to the *chain of causation* and *the agreement is void.*

I don't feel like the Olivia who left The Goldie two days ago. There's something surging through me. It's the thrill of the chase. Yes, I'm out of the box now. No-one is going to put me back in – and definitely not Rosco. I might only be a volunteer PI, but I've never been more determined to solve a case.

You've got this, babe.

I stand up. It's time for another visit to Abbey's house. There has to be something I've missed.

❀

The weather is changing as I pull up at Abbey's house. A fresh breeze makes the hammock dance. Out at sea, clouds are building on the horizon. A chorus of frogs croaks from the gully that runs down the fence line.

As I open the door, the mustiness of unused rooms makes me sneeze. I walk down the corridor to Abbey's bedroom. Nothing has changed. I scan the room for anything I've missed.

My eyes keep coming back to her computer. Sitting, I press the power button and wait for it to boot up. My gaze falls on her thesaurus, which is lying to one side of her keyboard. Abbey loves playing with words.

You can't beat a hardcopy thesaurus, I hear her say. *It's a writer's best friend.*

I pick it up and thumb through the index, the word *naiad* racing through my head. Maybe this will be my next breakthrough. My confidence suffers a setback when I find no entry for *naiad*. *So much for that.*

What about *fallen angel? Aha.* The thesaurus has two entries for this – *bad man* and *devil.* What about *plaything?* This leads to about a hundred different words, ranging from *billiards* to *skittles.* No light bulbs flash inside my head. It's a dead end.

I set the thesaurus aside as the computer screen flickers to life. It's an old computer and there's no password protection so I scroll through Abbey's files. There are hundreds of them. I can disregard the old ones, so I sort by date. I scan the recent folders: *eco tours, sustainable energy, whales* ... They sound like topics for her uni studies, or articles. My mouse moves over a folder

140

marked *Topple Cher.* I move on, but come back to it. The title is nonsensical, but something about it rings a bell.

My eyes flick to the thesaurus and my pulse beats faster. *Yes.* She *had* used the thesaurus. *Fallen = Toppled. Angel = Cherub. Toppled Cherub.* Clicking, I open the folder. It turns out to contain about twenty more folders. I click on one called *Fall Ang.* There is only one file in this folder, *Dev Marb.*

Of course. Fallen angel equals *devil, plaything* equals *marbles.* Abbey had been playing with words. How many times had I driven past the jutting peak of the Devil's Marbles without it clicking? And hadn't I seen that name somewhere else?

Scrabbling around in my bag, I pull out my tattered *What I Know* list and turn it over. On the other side is the application to join the Amalians. I read the short introduction to the sect.

About the Amalians – The Amalians own land at the Devil's Marbles outside Byron Bay. Here we will develop a retreat where group members can enjoy themselves in communion with our saviour, Amal.

It was under my nose the whole time.

My pulse thumps as I click on the file named *Dev Marb.* A document opens, but ... it's blank. It looks like Abbey created a file, but never wrote anything. Another dead end. Then I notice it's a read-only file. Why would Abbey have a read-only file with nothing on it? *Unless ...*

Invisible ink, says Nansea.

Correct. Only this kind of invisible ink doesn't react to lemon juice. I click on *show changes* and a box pops up asking for a password. Barely hesitating, I type in N-A-I-A-D, press enter, and the words appear.

Aliens before animals in battle for the rainforest.

My eyes fly over the rest of the piece. It looks like the start of an article.

A short drive from the seething coast lies the rainforest ... Passing through the hillside villages ... rocky peaks of the Devil's Marbles ... time stands still ... twisted vines ... rocky canyons ... Only those who wish to abseil down thundering waterfalls ... miraculous forest ... so impenetrable ... unexplored. A dubious development threatens this wilderness.

The article seems innocuous. But Abbey went to some trouble to make sure no-one read it. Was she concerned about repercussions? I tap my fingers on the table, then email the document to myself. I can figure it out later.

Outside, the first drops of rain patter on the tin roof. I yawn. Last night's exploits are catching up with me. It's unprofessional to nap on the job, but I'm not getting paid, so I do what I want. Turning the computer off, I lie on Abbey's bed. A whiff of lemon-scented soap wafts up from the pillow as I listen to the comforting beat of the rain.

When I wake, the room is darker. It's one thirty, but seems much later. The rain on the roof is now a deafening cascade. Walking out to the front verandah, I watch the water rush down the gutters and splash onto the grass. The frogs in the gully outdo each other in a crescendo of excitement. Beyond the hills floats a grey mass of rain-streaked cloud. I stretch and sniff the moist air. I love a tropical downpour.

My mind is clearer now, after the sleep. I need answers. It's time to talk to the Amalians again. Locking Abbey's door, I splash out through the puddles to my car.

CHAPTER TWENTY-THREE

The cult flag hangs like a wet rag outside the Amalian Centre. Climbing out of my car, I run to the shelter of the overhanging verandah and try the door. It's locked. Tacked to the door is a note – *Awakening in the Forest today. Call your spiritual guide for directions.*

I don't have a spiritual guide, but I have a fair idea where they'll be. The Devil's Marbles are about a forty-five-minute drive from here. I glance around at the outlying cottages, which must be where the cult members live. They appear deserted. This might be a good time for a poke around.

One of the cottages is larger than the others. Maybe that's Citra's. I dart through the rain and, sheltering under the overhanging eave, try the door. It's locked of course. I peer in the window but can't see anyone inside.

Squelching around the cottage, I try window after window. Water buckets from the gutters, drenching me. Finally, I find a high window that's been left ajar. If I stretch up, my fingertips reach over the edge of the sill. Can I get enough grip on the boards of the house to climb up?

Go for it, says Nansea. *You'll never get a better chance.*

Grabbing onto the windowsill, I scrabble up and push my

head through the opening. The toilet is below me. Feeding my hands through the window, I do a seal-like slide onto the bathroom floor.

'Ouch.' Bare-midriff tops aren't designed for rough detective work. My fake belly-button ring has fallen out, so I fasten it on again. I glance around. It's a standard bathroom, nothing suspicious.

What's that? I freeze as a noise from outside the bathroom echoes through the house. A squeaking. It's like ... nothing I've ever heard before. The squeaking stops for a moment and starts up again. It's like one of those secret sounds they play on radio.

I creep to the bathroom door and peer out. The loungeroom has white walls, white canvas chairs and white throw rugs. A surprise feature is the white surfboard propped up against the wall. I hadn't picked Citra as a surfer, but she is a Californian after all. The only splash of colour comes from a large picture of Amal. His hands are held out, Christ-like, in front of a hovering spaceship. He still looks like Benny from ABBA.

The squeaking sound is louder now. I scan the room and stop, my pulse thumping, as I catch a glimpse of movement on a table near the window. I frown as it comes into focus. It's a white mouse running around and around on a treadmill that needs oiling. How does Citra put up with the noise? *And what's with the mouse?* Is it a higher being – Amal in disguise?

'Hi mouse,' I murmur, stepping out of the bathroom.

It doesn't pause in its frantic race around the treadmill.

A kitchen and a bedroom run off the loungeroom. The kitchen is spotless. It doesn't look like it gets much use. The bedroom has a king-size bed covered in a white quilt. Glass bottles of essential oils are lined up on a bedside table.

I peer around and, spotting a wastepaper basket under the table, pull it out. There's a crumpled piece of paper in the bottom. Flattening it out on the bed, I read the violet scrawl of writing. *Dearest Citra, I'm so, so, so sorry I let you down. Please don't make me go. I will try harder in future. I love you so much, Angel.*

Interesting. But not relevant. I crumple it up and put it back in the basket. A quick snoop around reveals nothing else of interest. Well, that was a waste of time, but I suppose every investigation has its dud moments. Disappointed, I let myself out the front door.

On the verandah, I stop, my heart pounding. There's a dark shape against the wall that wasn't there before.

A snuffle comes from the shape. It's a guy, slumped on the ground, his tattooed arms wrapped around his legs. His brown hair is soaked from the rain. I venture closer. 'Are you all right?'

He looks up. 'Oh, hello.' His face would be handsome if it wasn't so glum.

'What's up?' I ask.

'My friend, Angel ...' He sighs, as if it hurts to say her name. 'She isn't allowed to see me.' He wipes his nose with the back of his hand.

Angel – she of the messy violet writing. 'Why can't she see you?'

He grimaces. 'She said it's forbidden. She has to break off all contact with non-believers.'

'She's your girlfriend?'

'Kind of. I met her here. I was doing the electrical work. We were getting on great. I thought she was going to come away with me, but now ...'

'Do you want me to pass on a message? If I see her?'

His eyes brighten. 'Yes, tell her Gary misses her. And I won't forget her.'

'Okay, I'll tell her.' I turn to go.

'Wait, there's more. Tell her she needs to get out. I'll be waiting here for her, in my car, every day.' He points toward the road outside the gate. 'There. Tell her I'll be right there. Every day.'

'Wow, this Angel must be special.'

A dreamy look comes over his face. 'I've never met anyone like her before.'

It's romantic, but there isn't anything I can do to help. 'Bye.' I rush out into the rain.

❋

Driving away, I turn my car toward the hinterland. As my wipers flick back and forth, I reflect on Abbey's article about the Devil's Marbles.

She seemed to be leading up to an exposé of some dodgy dealing behind the Amalians' new retreat. Did Citra try to stop her? I remember the cult leader's strong fingers on my arm as I tried to leave the Transformative Workshop. I wouldn't put anything past her. I think of the violet letter. *Please don't make me go.* She seems to enjoy a bit of psychological manipulation too.

I remember the body pushing me into the sand. I'd assumed it was a man, but could it have been Citra? She's tall, and strong. I drum my fingers on the steering wheel, thinking of the surfboard in her loungeroom. My attacker had been in the water.

Better watch your back, says Nansea.

The rain eases as I turn off the bitumen onto the potholed dirt road leading to the national park. I don't know exactly where the Amalians' land is, so my cunning plan is to drive around until

I find them. Rainforest crowds the road on either side, creating a dark green tunnel. Fat raindrops bounce onto my windscreen as my car brushes against the branches. A wallaby hops into the undergrowth as the car splashes through the puddles. I wind down my window and absorb the smell of wet earth.

Tucked among the trees ahead is the entry sign for Devil's Marbles National Park. I slow down. The Amalians' land won't be in the park itself. A drooping cardboard sign is tied to a tree on the corner of a narrow side road. Jumping out of the car, I lift it up, peering at the rain-smudged letters. The word *Awakening* and an arrow are barely visible.

Pulling my car over to the side of the road, I gaze up the muddy track. I shouldn't announce my arrival before I've had a chance to see what they're up to. I eye the deep puddles filling the wheel marks. My little car could get bogged in there too. No, I'll walk. I pull off my thongs, which are not going to be much use to me here. Grabbing Jacq's binoculars from the glove box, I squelch barefoot down the road, mud oozing between my toes.

It doesn't take long to regret leaving my car behind. The road shows no sign of ending and the mud makes it tough going. They could be twenty kilometres away for all I know. I shiver. I'm soaking wet from the constant drizzle.

I glance down to negotiate a puddle and spot a shiny black blob on my toe. *Ew.* It's an enormous leech. Gritting my teeth, I pinch it between my fingers and fling it off. It refuses to be flung. Each time I try to flick it off, it latches onto my finger.

Show it who's boss, babe, says Nansea.

I scrape the leech onto a tree and jog away before it can mount a comeback. It's three-thirty, but here in the rainforest, twilight is already falling. I'm considering retreating when I hear faint voices and music. Creeping forward, I duck behind a tree, putting my binoculars to my eyes.

Man, those guys are wild, whispers Nansea.

I have to agree. The scene looks like a mediaeval ritual, set to South American panpipes. In a clearing in the forest are about twenty blindfolded people. Their sodden gowns must once have been white. They are grouped in muddy pairs, hugging and kissing.

I recognise some of the people from the Transformative Workshop. There are the two overweight men, looking, in their gowns, like over-risen bread rolls. The uptight blonde is also here, not looking at all uptight anymore. The Amalian way of life must suit her.

A gong resonates through the forest and the muddy pairs separate. They mill around like dodgem cars until they bump into someone else and it all begins again. Some of the men gravitate suspiciously toward the better-looking women. Are they peeking out from under their blindfolds?

I'm so engrossed, I almost jump out of my skin when a hand appears on the tree trunk beside my face. I eye the long, red fingernails.

'You can join in, if you're so interested,' says a woman's voice.

CHAPTER TWENTY-FOUR

The cult leader is as scary as I remembered. No muddy robes for her – a sleeveless red sheath hugs her frame, outlining her well-toned biceps.

You should start weight training, babe, says Nansea.

I back away from Citra's hard stare, my pulse doing a rapid tap dance.

'I know you, don't I?' Her eyes flicker over me. 'You came to one of my workshops. You don't need to hide away here, we welcome new members. As long as they embrace the way of Amal.' There is a veiled warning in her tone. Grasping my arm, she leads me toward the kissing and cuddling Amalians.

Should I play along or confront her?

She whips out a blindfold, ties it over my eyes and pushes me toward the group. The gong sounds. I stop dead. *No alien worshipper is going to grope me.*

Too late. Hands grasp my arms and slide up and down. The distinctive smell of pig reaches my nostrils. I pull off my blindfold and back away. The annoying hippie from the transformative workshop stands blindfolded in front of me. His hands stretch toward me.

'It's cool babe.' He steps forward. 'I feel a deep sense of love and compassion for you.'

I step backwards again and notice Citra watching me, an amused smile on her lips. I stride toward her. I've had enough of this silly culty huggy stuff, I need answers. 'This isn't what I'm here for.' I raise my voice above the pan pipes, which are coming to a crescendo. 'What do you know about the disappearance of Abbey Watson?'

As I say this, the music stops, leaving me yelling into the silence. I gulp and glance behind me. Twenty pairs of eyes stare at me, their blindfolds on their foreheads or around their necks. What are my chances of making a quick getaway?

Pretty slim, babe.

The group moves forward as one. *What are they going to do? Grope me to death?* 'Are you all right, Citra?' My smelly friend steps forward, his eyebrows drawn together.

Luckily, he is one of the weediest men I've ever seen. Citra could toss him over her shoulder without drawing breath.

'It's all right, Ravi.' Citra has a note of impatience in her voice. 'All of you, return to the Awakening.'

Ravi shuffles off.

Citra snaps her fingers at one of her acolytes and the music starts again. She turns to me, her face impassive. 'Abbey Watson? The girl who was writing an article about our development?'

My heart thuds, but I try to sound tough. 'How many Abbey Watsons do you know?'

Citra smooths her silky hair. 'I don't know anything about her disappearance. Didn't she kill herself? That's what I heard. You think I had something to do with it? That's ridiculous.' Her voice is dismissive.

I'm beginning to doubt myself, but press on anyway. 'Abbey was about to expose your dirty dealing, so you got rid of her.' I stare Citra straight in the eye. 'Didn't you?'

'That's preposterous. We've got nothing to hide. Our development is legal. No threatened species showed up in the surveys. People like Abbey will never be happy.'

I mentally pull out my investigator's notebook. 'Where were you on the night of the last full moon?'

'Is that the night she disappeared? I have an alibi if that's what you're after. Any of these people can back me up.' She gestures at the group behind her. 'Every full moon, we dance all night in the forest. It's when the spirit of Amal is closest to us. Hundreds of people come, not only Amalians.'

'Well, naturally *they* would back you up. It doesn't mean it's true though.' Something else occurs to me. 'Did you see Cactus there?'

'Cactus?'

'He's a surfer, tall, blond ...'

Citra rolls her eyes. 'He may have been. There were at least a hundred there who'd answer to that description. Look, I'm sorry she's missing.' She speaks in a soothing voice. 'It's true we had some conflict. She kept coming back to our land, to try and stop the embassy development. She even brought a botanist here. We told her to get off, she had no right being here.'

'Who was the botanist?'

'The English guy who performs at the markets. I don't know his name.'

Adam. I frown. 'Does the word naiad mean anything to you?'

'Naiad? As in water spirit?'

I nod.

'Same as what it means to anyone else, I guess.' She glances behind her at the writhing devotees. 'I need to go. We're about to start our meditation session. Why don't you join us? You seem in need of guidance. Amal has room for all.' She puts her hand on my arm and lowers her voice. 'You can choose your own partner.'

I eye the white-robed men. The whole scene is a total turn-off. 'Thanks, but I'd better be going.'

'Have you still got your crystal from the Transformative Workshop?'

'Ah, no, I lost it in the surf.'

'It must have been the wrong one for you. Your ideal crystal guide will stay with you always.' Citra slips a hand down the front of her dress and pulls out a pouch. 'Here, this one should help.' She presses a quartz crystal into my hand and walks away.

I watch her go. Maybe I'd been wrong about her. I finger the crystal, half expecting it to pipe up with some words of advice, but it is as taciturn as my previous one. Maybe I'm not a crystal kind of girl. I stick it in my bra anyway – I need all the help I can get.

Trudging back up the road to my car, I reflect on what I've learnt. Adam was here with Abbey. I need to ask him if *naiad* means something to him. I could have it all wrong of course. Is it possible that Abbey just had an accident on her night surf? Surfing's a high-risk sport in the day, let alone at night. *But if that's what happened ... why did someone attack me on the beach yesterday? And is she still out there somewhere?*

I shiver in the evening breeze. I'd forgotten how tough investigating is. Right now, I'd rather be at home with a warm Milo.

The sun is slipping behind the trees, casting shadows across the road, as I get to my car. A sign to the Devil's Marbles National Park catches my eye. *Look-out, five kilometres.* I can get up there before dark. It might be a peaceful place for reflection, and I need some of that. I start my car and turn up the road.

I pull in at the look-out car park and wander over to the viewing platform. There's no-one else around. Standing on the edge, I lean over. A palm-filled valley stretches below me. It looks like a lost world. In the distance, the sea glistens in the fading light. If I walked off down that valley, I would disappear. Something about that appeals to me.

What now? Citra said Adam had been to the Devil's Marbles with Abbey. He didn't mention that. I should call him. See if he knows something he hasn't told me. I rub my arms as the wind sweeps up the hill. A falcon erupts from the cliff wall and spirals upwards.

As I walk back to my car, I glance at the information panel – *Welcome to Devil's Marbles National Park.* My hand is on my car door when a heading catches my eye. *Rare and threatened species of Devil's Marbles National Park.* I remember what Citra said. *There are no threatened species on our land.* But what if there are? It looks like there are some in the national park, and it's not far from here to the Amalians' land.

I step closer to the board and read about the threatened species found in the park. *The spotted quoll, Albert's lyrebird, the rufous bettong.* I'm about to turn away when another heading captures my attention. *New tree found, then lost again.* I read on.

In 1893 a logger found a tree in this area he'd never seen before. Curious, he sent leaf and fruit samples to the Botanic Gardens in

Sydney. The word came back – it was a new species. Botanists named it after a naiad, or water spirit, of Greek legend.

I stop there, my pulse thudding.

Naiad is a tree? says Nansea. *That's a let-down.*

A tree. Why didn't I find this out before? I read on.

In 1914 a disastrous fire swept through the Archives and the samples were lost. Despite many surveys, the tree was never found again.

So that's it. Naiad is a rare tree. A rare, possibly extinct, tree that Citra pretended she'd never heard of. Is a tree the cause of all this trouble? It's hard to imagine. Did Abbey discover it and try to stop the Amalians' development? Taking a park brochure from the box on the information board, I tuck it in my pocket.

Sitting on the bonnet of my car, I gaze out toward the rainforest. It seems huge and impenetrable now, but once it would have stretched all the way to the sea. In the valley, lights are winking on in the farmhouses. On the coast, the lighthouse beam flashes, then vanishes as it swings out to sea. The glow of the moon appears in the sky.

Okay, let's figure out what Adam knows. Pulling out my phone, I press his number.

'Adam here,' he answers straight away.

My stomach somersaults at the sound of his voice, but I'm not going to let myself get sucked in. I need answers. 'Hi, it's Nansea.'

'Hey Nansea, where are you? Sorry about last night. Do you want to meet up tonight?'

'I'm up at the Devil's Marbles National Park.' I wait to hear his reaction.

'It's beautiful up there, isn't it? Must be dark though, huh?' His voice is relaxed. 'What are you doing?'

'I've been having a look around, but I'm coming back to town now.'

'Why don't you come over to my place? I'll cook you dinner.'

I hesitate, but not for long. I can quiz him about his botanical survey when I get there. It will be easier face-to-face. 'I'll be there in about an hour. I need to have a shower. I'm covered in mud.'

'Have a shower here. I'd like to see you covered in mud.'

His words make my cheeks burn. 'Okay.' He gives me directions to his house, and I hang up. I sit on the car, trying to calm my breathing.

This is the third date ... But he's a suspect. My mind flicks to the unopened box of condoms in my bag. Am I meticulous, well-dressed Nancy Drew or a feisty, sexy Jane Bond?

CHAPTER TWENTY-FIVE

I turn off the coast road near a wooden community hall and wind my way up a rutted track through thick sugarcane. A tawny frogmouth flutters across my headlight beam, vanishing into the darkness.

A light in the distance gets closer, and my pulse races as I pull up outside Adam's ramshackle cottage. Is this a hot date, or a date with death?

Stay cool, be alert, says Nansea.

I check my reflection in the car mirror and wish I hadn't. My face is streaked with mud, there are leaves in my hair and my clothes are filthy. Licking my finger, I wipe some of the mud from my face.

'Why don't I do that for you?' Adam leans in the window and puts his lips to my neck.

My body turns to jelly. He might be a hot suspect, but he is a smoking hot kisser.

We make it from the car to his couch in an intense blur of kisses. My body is glowing, but my mind is in a whirl. I need to have it out with him. I summon my strength and pull away.

Adam pulls me back toward him. He strokes my cheek with one finger.

A shiver runs through me. 'I'm getting mud all over you.'

'A small price to pay.'

My heart thumps. I'm in too deep.

'What's up?' He strokes my arm.

'What does naiad mean to you?'

'Have you been reading the sign up at the Devil's Marbles?' He smooths my rumpled pink locks. 'Do you think I've found the lost tree?' He pulls his head back and meets my eyes. 'Or that Abbey found it?'

'Citra from the Amalians said she'd seen you and Abbey up there in the rainforest together.'

'Yeah, we were looking for threatened species. Abbey was hoping we'd find some so we could stop the development. No luck though.' He smiles, his eyes crinkling in the corners. 'There's more to you than meets the eye, isn't there, Nansea?' His voice is light, but I sense an undercurrent.

I force myself to keep going. 'What were you doing the night Abbey disappeared?'

Adam holds my gaze. 'I was up at the full-moon dance in the forest. It's an event organised by the Amalians.'

'Yeah. I've heard of it. Seems like everyone was up there that night.' *Everyone except Abbey.* 'I'd better have a shower.' I need some space.

Adam stands up. 'Shower's that way. I'll be in the kitchen making dinner. Grab some of my clothes if you want something clean.'

I sit on the couch for a while after he's gone, wondering what I've got myself into.

Standing under the shower, I try to wash away my doubts. Should I break it to him that I'm Olivia, a law student and amateur PI, not Nansea, the dolphin trainer?

Wrapping a towel around myself, I wander out into Adam's room, gathering up my scattered clothing as I go. Bra, knickers … crystal? I scan the floorboards for my crystal guide. This one has gone missing as well. What's wrong with me? I can't even look after a stupid crystal.

I get on my knees and peer under the bed, running my hand along to feel for my runaway friend. No crystal. Just some rubber cord. *Rubber cord?* I pull it out for a closer look. It's a surfboard leg rope with dolphins painted around its ankle strap. It reminds me of something. And my crystal is nestled in its crook.

'Hey Nansea, do you like your curry hot?' Adam opens the door and his eyes flick to the leg rope. 'What are you after?'

'Uh, looking for my crystal.' I hold it up. 'Found it.' I push the leg rope back under the bed.

He smiles. 'So, how do you like your curry?'

'Any way is fine.'

'Okay, leave you to it.' He shuts the door.

As soon as he's gone, I spring into action. *I'll do a quick search and carry on having fun.*

I pull open the drawers in his bedroom cabinet. Socks, boxers, T-shirts. I select a large shirt and pull it over my head. *What else?* His wallet is lying on the table beside the bed. I flick it open and see a piece of paper poking out of the pocket. With a quick glance at the door, I pull it out.

It's an article torn out of the local paper.

Miracle tree found again.

Many locals know the story of the naiad, the lost tree from Devil's Marbles National Park. This week the Sydney Botanic Gardens had some exciting news. The tree samples, thought to have been lost in the 1914 fire, have been found. A Botanic Gardens spokesperson said an intern found the samples in a disused storeroom. They can now confirm these samples are indeed the lost tree.

'When we analysed the samples, we made a thrilling find,' the spokesperson said. 'The fruit contains chemicals similar to those in Madagascar's Rosy Periwinkle, which is an anti-cancer agent. These chemicals may also have euphoric effects. It is truly a miracle tree.'

'Seventy per cent of plants with anti-cancer agents occur in the rainforest. Plants like the Rosy Periwinkle are big business, with sales bringing in about US$160 million a year. Closer to home, we only need to look at the Wollemi Pine, recently discovered in the Blue Mountains. Despite having no special properties, this ancient tree is a multi-million-dollar industry. Wollemi Pines are now sent all over the world.'

So, the naiad is a miracle plant, worth millions. *Is it worth killing for?* Maybe. But there's nothing to link Adam to the tree. As a botanist, he'd have an interest, that's probably all it is. I check for a date – the article's about two months old. And there's nothing to say that anyone's found a live tree. Slipping the article back in his wallet, I open the door.

Adam, wearing only a pair of faded board shorts, is in the kitchen, stirring a pot on the stove. I swallow at the sight of his bare chest.

He turns around. 'Well, hi there. Cool T-shirt.'

I twirl. 'I hear the big look is so hot this season.'

'Sexy.' Adam twitches his eyebrows at me.

Sexy. This makes me think of Jane Bond. My cheeks colour. But Jane Bond wouldn't be seen dead in a big T-shirt.

The spicy smell of the curry wafts toward me. My stomach growls most unbecomingly. My cheeks grow hotter as the sound echoes through the kitchen. I've had nothing to eat all day except toast for breakfast.

Adam smiles. 'It won't be long.' He points to the loungeroom. 'There's a glass of wine on the table out there for you.'

I wander out to the loungeroom, take a sip of wine, and sit on the edge of the couch. I've never known such a hectic couple of days. And there's still the sex question to consider. Am I Nancy Drew or Jane Bond?

Adam's house is shabby, but comfortable. Well-worn bean-bags are scattered across the floor and paintings decorate the walls. I peer at the name on the corner of one. *Adam McBean.* So Adam is an artist as well as an acrobat and a botanist?

The smell of food wafts in and my mouth waters. I'm so hungry and dinner is taking a while. There's a tin biscuit box on the coffee table. My stomach rumbles as I open it. *Mmm, Anzac biscuits.* I stuff two in my mouth, washing them down with another sip of wine.

Adam comes in with dinner at last. The food is tasty, and I unwind, though I'd enjoy it more if I didn't have to keep telling dolphin anecdotes. By the time I finish the curry, my whole body feels floaty and relaxed. 'What did you put in the curry? It had the most amazing flavours.'

Adam looks into my eyes. 'A bit of this and a bit of that.'

I drift from the table to a beanbag. Lying back, I examine a painting on the wall. It's a semi-abstract of a girl on a beach. 'Did you paint that?'

'Mmm. Like it?'

I nod. The longer I look, the more it grows on me. The colours are larger than life. I'm drifting into the picture. The sand is practically squeaking between my toes.

Whoa there, says Nansea. *There's something odd going on here.*

Shut up fusspot. I'm having fun.

Adam drops into a beanbag opposite me. He picks up my foot and strokes it.

I giggle. 'Tickles.'

Outside the window, the moon shines in. 'Look out there,' says Adam. 'It'd be beautiful out in the surf now.' His hand rubs my calf. 'Want to go for a paddle?'

'I didn't know you surfed.' For some reason, this makes me uncomfortable, but I can't focus on it for long. *Of course he surfs. He has a leg rope under the bed.*

'Mad not to, living here.' Getting to his feet, Adam pulls me up. 'Come on. I've got a board you can use.'

My inner worrywart kicks back in as I get out of my car at the beach. Adam parks beside me and climbs out.

Isn't it strange you feel so good? Nansea mutters.

I'm going surfing with a gorgeous guy. What's not to feel good about?

Adam and I walk down to the sand and put our boards beside the water.

No leg ropes? queries Nansea.

I'm not interested in such trivialities. The sea looks amazing. Bright flashes of silver blaze off the water along the moon's pathway. Sharks don't bother me. I can't wait to get in.

'Beautiful huh?' says Adam. 'I love it at night.' With a bounce, he flings his legs up into a handstand, and cartwheels along the shoreline.

I clap, whistle and raise my arms above my head, ready to do the same. Then I remember I can't handstand, let alone cartwheel. I'm pretty good in a headstand though, should I do one of those? No, it's not the same thing at all. And besides, the sand looks very soft and unsupportive. I lower my arms before Adam notices.

Good call, says Nansea. *That would have gone badly.*

'Come on.' Adam pushes his board out into the inky water.

The sea fizzes against my legs as I wade in.

The whitewash parts as I paddle, salt spray splashing up around me. We stop beyond the breakers and I crane my neck to look at the stars. The hulking tower of Julian Rocks glows further out at sea. It's wilderness out here, nothing but blackness all around.

'I like you Nansea.' Adam's face is in darkness, but his bare chest glistens in the moonlight.

A warm glow spreads through me. 'There's something I should tell you. My name is—'

A yell cuts through my confession. 'Hey, stop right there!'

Was that Nansea?

But no, Adam glances behind him. 'Sorry Nansea. Gotta go.' He paddles with rapid strokes away into the darkness.

'Come back!' A burst of adrenaline clears my mind, but I still can't figure out what's happening.

'Are you all right Olivia?' says a voice out of the night. A figure on a surfboard paddles toward me.

What's he doing here? says Nansea.

My mind implodes with confusion. It's Rosco.

CHAPTER TWENTY-SIX

I stare at the dolphins on the shower curtain as water pours down my face. They're very lifelike. It's almost like they're moving. Something about them bothers me. *There were dolphins on the leg rope under Adam's bed.*

I turn the shower off, put on a tracksuit and come out.

Rosco is leaning against the wall. He's thrown on a sweatshirt over his board shorts and his hair is still damp. He has that Ewok village argument look on his face again.

Is he thinking about the condom aisle? This shouldn't be a problem, but it is. *Everyone buys condoms, or if they don't, they should*, says Nansea.

I dismiss condoms from my mind. 'Take a seat.' I lower myself onto the bed.

He shakes his head. 'I'll get the chair wet.'

'So ... are you going to explain what happened out there in the surf?' I say.

'You had a lucky escape.'

'I was doing fine until you came along.'

Rosco clears his throat. 'Adam McBean has been dealing in a new narcotic that's flooding the market.'

I frown. 'What?' That was unexpected.

'Maybe he tried it out on you? Did he give you a drink? That's the usual MO.' Rosco pauses. 'Modus Operandi. Method of Operation.'

I snort. 'You told me what MO means the first week at Gold Star Investigations.' Did Adam dope me? I remember the way I'd felt – the euphoria. I'd almost done a cartwheel. I've never attempted a cartwheel before. My last trace of euphoria evaporates.

'I've been following him for some time now. He's been supplying boats offshore as well.'

Was that Adam, paddling out to the boat that night? 'But why didn't you tell me you were following Adam?'

'You two seemed ... close.' Rosco meets my eyes.

He's thinking about the condom aisle. I slump back on the bed. I'd been an idiot to trust Adam. 'What about Abbey? Did he do something to Abbey?'

'Maybe.'

I shiver inside my tracksuit, remembering the hand pushing my face into the sand. Was that Adam?

'It shouldn't take long for the police to pick him up. Keep your doors locked, won't you? And call the police if he tries to contact you.'

A new narcotic ... My gut clenches. 'I might know where he's getting the drugs from.'

Rosco raises his eyebrows.

'It's the miracle tree, the naiad. I think he found it.' I tell him about the clue on Abbey's surfboard, my attack on the beach and my trip to the rainforest.

Rosco shakes his head. 'You're crazy. Why didn't you call the police? Or me at least. You don't have to do it all by yourself.'

I flush. 'Abbey is my friend.'

Rosco gives a small nod. 'But I'm the one getting paid for this.'

Does he think I'm undercutting him? 'Maybe Adam ... did something to Abbey because he wanted to keep the tree secret so he could exploit it himself.' *Abbey.* 'Maybe the suicide note was a letter she wrote about something else.' I feel ice in my chest.

Rosco sighs. 'Maybe. But leave the rest to the police, all right? They'll track down McBean. When are you heading back to the Gold Coast?'

'Tomorrow.'

'You'll be safer there.' He opens the door and vanishes into the night.

The room is much colder without him. I don't feel like Nancy Drew or Jane Bond anymore. I've stuffed things up, but that's not the worst thing. I blink as tears trickle down my cheeks. For the first time, it feels like I might never find Abbey.

CHAPTER TWENTY-SEVEN

American Indian chanting has replaced dolphin calls in the lobby of The Waveroom.

While I'd rather go home and try to forget the mess that I've made of all this, there's one more thing to do in the Bay. Yesterday, I'd made an appointment with Luna to have my chakras balanced. I need to talk to her about Ashok.

Sitting on the puffy couch, I inhale the incense. Who knows, maybe I'll feel better after some chakra realignment. It can't do any harm. It will be good to see Luna too.

Luna emerges from a side room, wearing a white singlet and floppy pants. I'm still sceptical, but her aura of radiance and calm is impressive.

Her eyes light up. 'Hey Olivia.' She gives me a hug. 'Great to see you, what are you doing here?'

'I'm your next appointment.'

She flicks through her appointment book. 'No you're not, I've got someone called Nansea. She booked online. Funny name.' Her eyes meet mine. 'Oh, right. You're undercover?'

I nod.

She narrows her eyes. 'What are you working on? You're not investigating me, are you?'

I laugh. 'No. Just the usual. Cheating husband. Thought I'd

get my chakras balanced while I'm down here.' I feel bad lying to Luna, but I don't want her to get her guard up.

'In that case, come through here.' She shows me into the side room. As I step through the door, some of my frazzled edges drop away. The pastel colours and lavender scent are soothing me already.

'Feng shui,' says Luna, reading my mind. 'The Waveroom is designed to ensure calmness and clear thought.' She gestures to a stool in the centre of the room. 'Sit here while I get organised.'

I'd been looking forward to a lie-down, but it doesn't look like it's going to happen. I perch on the stool instead. 'Are you still working on the boat with Sea Shepherd?'

Luna draws the blinds. 'I'm taking a break, but I'll go back. It was intense. I mean, I'm ready to give my life for whales, and it's totally the right thing to do, but, man, those Antarctic seas are rough.'

'So, have you given up yoga instructing?' When I first met Luna, she was involved in a bizarre Byron Bay yoga feud.

'I'm still doing some on the side, but I've realised chakra balancing is my life's work. Anyone can teach yoga.' Luna lights a row of coloured candles. 'How long is it since you last had your chakras aligned?'

'This is my first time.'

Luna freezes, taper in hand, her eyes wide. 'What? That's crazy. You need to get it done every three to four months. How often do you get your car serviced?'

I shrug and wriggle on the stool. So far, this isn't as relaxing as I'd hoped. 'When it needs it.'

'Well, you're taking more care of your car than your body. You can replace your car. This is, like, the only body you've got.'

I mentally roll my eyes. I didn't come here for a lecture.

'Okay.' Luna's tone implies she is rolling up her sleeves, ready for a grease and oil change. 'In that case, I'm going to have to give you a deep cleansing before I can balance your chakras.'

This sounds like the prelude to some extra costs. Like when the hairdresser insists I need a conditioning treatment before she can cut my hair.

'There's no extra charge.' Luna reads my mind again. 'Close your eyes and try to relax.'

I squeeze my eyes shut and Luna begins a high-pitched chant, which morphs into a rapid gibberish. *Too weird.* I open my eyes a fraction.

Luna's hands sweep down the sides of my body as she chatters away. 'I've discovered I'm originally from Sirius, the blue star. We use a special language for healing there.'

If she's from Sirius, I'm a dolphin trainer called Nansea.

'It works better if you try not to resist.'

I snap my eyes shut. This is all very well, but how am I going to raise the topic of Ashok?

'Okay, that's cleared you up.'

My body feels exactly the same.

'I'm going to start the balancing now. Lie on the bed while I prepare the oils.'

That's more like it. I lie on the white-sheeted bed that stands against the wall.

Luna takes seven oil lamps from the table at the front and arranges them in a semi-circle around the bed. She kneels to light them. 'There's one for each of the major chakras.' She picks up some crystals from a glass shelf. 'The crystals will channel my healing energy.'

I feel a cool touch as she places a purple crystal on my forehead. 'Amethyst for the crown and brow chakras. Lapis lazuli for the throat chakra. Rose quartz for the heart chakra. Tiger eye for the solar plexus and hematite for the root and sexual chakras.'

This last is a shiny black and gold crystal, which she places on my lower abdomen. The crystals rise and fall with my breath.

'The crystals will release your innate intelligence and clear blockages. Close your eyes and try to keep your mind clear. I may touch you if you need stronger healing.'

She chants again. It's relaxing with the scent of the oils and her soft voice singing. The chanting pauses. 'Oh dear.'

'What?' I murmur from my half-asleep state.

'Your chakras are congested. Only the first two and the sixth are functioning at all.' Luna has the tone of a doctor delivering difficult news.

I'm tempted to ask *how long have I got?* 'What does that mean?' I say instead.

'Well, have you been, like, having negative thoughts? Perhaps you've been experiencing low self-esteem, or had trouble expressing yourself?'

My eyes spring open. 'How did you know?'

'It couldn't be any other way with your chakras like this.' Luna shakes her head. 'I'll do what I can, but you need to have a regular tune-up. Yoga and meditation will help, if it's all you can manage.'

I nod, as if I plan to ramp up my usual intensive yoga and meditation routine. Luna continues chanting and I drift off into a half-asleep trance.

'I've finished now. Allow your body to return to awareness.'

I struggle up through layers of consciousness.

'What's the significance of the tree?' she asks.

My eyes fly open. 'What tree?'

'I saw a tree suspended above your forehead as I worked on you.'

'Can you read my mind?'

'No, but your spirit guide tells me some things.'

My spirit guide? Maybe my crystal is talking to her. I'll never get a better opening ... 'Wow, that is so incredible you can see a tree. I've been thinking of joining Forest Friends.'

Luna breaks into a broad smile. 'Have you? I'm the secretary.'

'That is such an amazing coincidence.'

'It's not a coincidence.'

Is she onto me?

'Everything happens for a reason. The universe is showing you its plan.' She pauses. 'Did I see you at the meditation session for Ashok? You look a bit different – the pink hair and all. You ducked off before I could say hi.'

'Yes. I don't know Ashok well, but I wanted to be, like, with him, you know?'

Luna nods.

'Sorry I was late. I guess you know Ashok pretty well?'

'Ever since he's been in Byron Bay. He's the one who started Forest Friends.' Luna's eyes light up. 'He's so inspirational.'

'It's sad about his accident. Strange the way it happened.'

Luna gazes into my eyes. 'That's what I feel too.' She touches my forehead. 'I was right about your sixth chakra. Your intuition is working.' Her eyes flick around the room as if checking we're alone. 'I think one of the developers did it.'

I draw in my breath. 'But who would do that?'

'Forest Friends is a threat to people trying to make a fast buck out of Byron Bay. Ashok doesn't pander to big business. Hits them where it hurts. It's the only thing capitalists understand. That's what he taught me.'

'I agree. What do you find works best?'

A look of caution comes over Luna's face. 'Our methods are confidential, until you join. But you can look at the forest campaigns down south to see the sort of thing that works. That's where Ashok came from. He learnt about direct action in Victoria and Tasmania.'

'Wow. I'd love to join Forest Friends. It sounds like you're really making a difference.'

Luna narrows her eyes. 'This is for, like, investigation reasons, isn't it?'

I feel my cheeks flush.

Luna gives a small smile and shrugs. 'I figured. Well anyway, things are up in the air until Ashok's back on deck.' She moves away from me to blow out her candles.

'Have you heard anything about how he is?'

Luna turns back with a radiant smile. 'Yes. Haven't you heard? Right after our meditation session he woke up and checked himself out of hospital. Shows you the power of positive vibrations. That's why it's so important to keep your chakras balanced.'

A wave of dizziness sweeps over me as I climb off the bed. Maybe my chakras are draining blood from my brain.

Luna puts her hand on my arm as we walk out into the reception area. 'Over the next few days you should notice the difference. You'll feel less sluggish, more positive and focused.

Do you want to make an appointment for your next balancing?'

'I'll give you a call.'

Luna puts her hands together beneath her chin. 'I send you love.'

What's the correct response? 'Peace out.'

CHAPTER TWENTY-EIGHT

I have almost no memory of the time between leaving The Waveroom and turning up at Nan's. That chakra balancing did something to my brain. Luckily my body pilots me to her door.

Jacq's boisterous welcome is just what I need. She brandishes a small ukulele at me as I come in the door. 'Look what Donald gave me. Listen to this.' She plays 'Happy Birthday'. 'It's the only tune I know.'

'That's awesome. Can't wait until it's my birthday.'

Nan appears, wearing a plastic frangipani behind her ear and a flower-patterned kaftan. Her eyes flicker over me: she hasn't seen my Nansea Version Two makeover before. 'You look ... exotic, Olivia.' She rushes out to her ukulele lesson. I wish I had her energy.

After dinner, Jacq goes to bed early, while I slump on the couch trying to summon the strength to do some prep for uni. Or at least to break out the vitamin C and get rid of the pink hair. No, I can't be bothered. I'll do it in the morning. I'm half-asleep watching Netflix when Nan comes back from her ukulele lesson.

She eyes me from the kitchen. 'Do you think I could pull off pink hair?'

'Totally.'

She fingers her short, blonde hair. 'I might give it a try ...'

'Pink hair won't go with your Aloha vibe. You'd need to switch to new wave or pop rock.'

Nan tilts her head to one side. 'It's not out of the question ... I'll discuss it with Donald.'

I hope Nan and Donald don't become pink-haired pop rock ukulele players. It wouldn't surprise me if they do though. At eight o'clock, I lie on my bed and pass out, having done no preparation for the week ahead.

*

Hot sun on my face wakes me. I claw my way up through layers of sleep to find myself staring at a clock that says eight-thirty. *It can't be.* I scrabble around for my phone. Yes, I have half an hour to remove my fake tan and pink hair, find some clothes, drop Jacq off at school and get to uni.

My phone beeps and a reminder flashes up on the screen. *Nine am. Ten-minute talk on an aspect of criminal law.* This doesn't compute. I read it again. My stomach lurches. *How did I forget this?* I'm supposed to be giving a presentation in my criminal law lecture this morning. It is now eight thirty-five. *Aargh.*

I waste five minutes trying to locate a vitamin C tablet to crush and mix into my shampoo before giving it away as a bad joke. I then waste another five minutes scrubbing at my face without shifting my fake tan. *Forget tan and pink hair, clothes are more important.* I dig through our cupboard, but all my normal clothes are in a dirty tangled heap in the corner. Washing must have been on my to-do list.

I scan my room. Surely there's something here apart from tie-died skirts and bare-midriff tops? *No.* I throw on my bell-bottom pants and a bare-midriff top and run into the kitchen.

'Hi Livvie. I didn't want to wake you, you looked tired.' Jacq, bless her heart, is finishing a bowl of Rice Bubbles in front of the TV.

At quarter to nine, we rush out the door. I drop Jacq at school, zoom around the corner to uni, park my car and run toward the lecture hall. The lecturer's voice drifts toward me. I'm late.

My designated seat is down the front, but I creep into the back of the hall and take a vacant spot. The eyes of the girl next to me widen. She nudges the girl beside her and inclines her head in my direction. Another set of eyes peers at me and I hear an intake of breath. I gaze straight ahead as nudges and whispers spread through the hall like a Mexican Wave.

It's just pink hair, folks. And fake tan. And a fake butterfly tattoo. And a bare midriff top. Move along, nothing to see.

'And now for today's presentation ...' Professor Anderson glances at her notes. 'Miss Grace will enlighten us on an aspect of criminal law.' She inspects the front row. 'Are you there, Miss Grace?' She looks out into the hall.

There is nothing else for it. I get to my feet and, straightening my back, stride down the aisle toward the stage. The professor eyes me as I approach, taking in the tattoo, the pink hair, the tan, the bare midriff, the bell-bottom pants. For a moment I'm tempted to turn and run.

Be cool, babe, whispers Nansea. *You've got this.*

I smile as I climb onto the stage. 'Thank you Professor Anderson.' I have no idea what I am going to say. 'The key principles of criminal law are ...' I pause under the gaze of hundreds of eyes.

Go girl, says Nansea.

I take a deep breath and ... Rosco's face appears in my mind.

Rosco had an ad hoc method of on-the-job training. He dispensed random facts whenever they came to mind. On my first day at Gold Star Investigations, he'd leaned back in his chair. *Olivia, PIs might not be police, but it's still important to know the key principles of criminal law.* He'd ticked them off on his fingers.

I hold up four fingers. *Finger one.* 'Presumption of innocence.' I put one finger down. *Finger two.* 'Burden of proof.' *Finger three.* 'Right to remain silent.' *Finger four.* 'Double jeopardy.'

I gaze out at the lecture hall. *Well, that leaves about eight minutes to go.*

'The aspect of criminal law I will be expanding upon today is ...' My mind turns to Adam. 'The presumption of innocence. In effect, this means you must consider someone innocent until proven guilty.'

The lecturer lowers her eyebrows.

She's not impressed, but I race on before she can interrupt me. 'Let's imagine you think someone might have dosed you with a drug that induces euphoria. To presume innocence, it would be best to assume you ate something you shouldn't have. To do otherwise would be unconscionable. Or, if you were attacked on the beach, you can't assume the person who may or may not have given you drugs did it. Even if they engaged in misleading or deceptive conduct. Or, if your friend disappeared in the surf, it doesn't follow that this person did something to her ...' *Or that she's dead.* I trail off. *Four minutes to go.*

I move on to Cactus. 'You also can't assume that because someone hates female surfers, they attacked your friend in the surf.' *Citra.* 'Neither can you assume that because someone has a nasty way with mind control, they attacked your friend.' *Ashok.* 'Or that because someone is annoying and pompous, they are guilty of anything at all. That would be far-fetched and fanciful. It would, in fact, be pure puffery.' I eye the clock. My time is up. 'In conclusion, this is what is meant by the presumption of innocence.'

There is some scattered applause. I presume it's sarcastic, but Professor Anderson nods. 'Thank you, Miss Grace. A novel approach, but not without its merits. I appreciate that you have developed some interesting, though unlikely, scenarios.'

I blink. 'Thank you. On a personal note, I expect my normal appearance to resume tomorrow.' As I walk over to my usual seat, murmurs spread around the hall.

Sophie sweeps her eyes over me as I sit. 'I didn't know you were a closet hippie, Olivia.'

I flounce my pink hair at her. 'Like my look?'

'I want pink hair, it looks sick.' Her eyes fall on my stick-on butterfly tattoo. 'Maybe I should get a tatt as well.'

After the lecture, Sophie and I head for the cafeteria. Sophie tilts her head and inspects me as I sit down with my sandwich. 'There's something different about you. Not the hair and the tatts. Something … internal. Your eyes look brighter.'

'That would be the chakra balancing. You should try it. Release all those block—'

There's a knock on the window beside our table. A suntanned face peers through the glass. *Rosco. What's he doing here?*

Sophie smooths back her blonde hair and wiggles her fingers at him.

Rosco beckons at me.

Sophie raises her eyebrows. 'Where have you been hiding *him*, Olivia?'

Rosco beckons again, more urgently.

I sigh. 'I'd better talk to him.' I get to my feet and walk outside. 'What are you doing here?' I hiss. It's weird seeing Rosco at uni. He seems larger than life against this ordered environment. It's like finding Han Solo behind the counter at the bank.

Rosco clears his throat. 'I thought I should warn you, the police haven't picked Adam up yet.'

Wings flutter in my chest at his name. 'You could've called.'

'I wanted to see you. To make sure you're okay. After what happened in the surf and the doping and all.'

'I'm fine. It's nice of you to take an interest.'

Rosco pauses. 'You look ... well.'

'I had my chakras balanced.'

'Right, that explains it. Not.'

'Why would Adam want to see me anyway?'

'Is there any reason he'd think you're a threat to him?'

'Not really.'

Rosco's blue eyes search mine. 'If there's anything else you remember ...'

At that moment my chest lurches. *The leg rope under his bed.* He'd sprung me looking at it.

'What is it?' says Rosco.

The students rush out of the cafeteria toward their classes. 'Torts time,' calls Sophie.

'I should go. It's just ... he had a leg rope under the bed. It had dolphins painted on it. It's probably nothing.'

'You think it's Abbey's? She wasn't wearing a leg rope the night she disappeared, was she?'

'That's the thing. She always used to. Why would she have left it off? Especially for night surfing.'

'So, if it is Abbey's, it links him to her disappearance.'

My heart thumps. If Adam is connected to Abbey's disappearance ... *Did Adam do something to Abbey?* I stop right there. I can't think about that. Not right now. Not while I'm at uni.

'I'll check it out,' says Rosco.

Giggling girls jostle past on their way to class. I take a deep breath. 'I need to go.'

'Yeah, okay. Take care.' Rosco raises his hand and walks away.

A queue has formed outside the lecture hall. 'Is that your boyfriend, Olivia?' asks Sophie, as I join her.

'No, he's not. We used to ... work together.'

'He's super cute. Want to introduce me?'

I grit my teeth. I have no desire to match-make Sophie and Rosco. 'Um, yeah. Or you can find him on Bumble? He's into trainspotting though, so unless you want to spend a lot of time looking at trains ...'

Sophie's nose crinkles. 'That's weird. He doesn't look like he'd be into trainspotting.'

'He collects china cats too.' I pause. 'Oh, and I've never seen him with a girlfriend.'

'Huh. Is he ... gay?'

'Yes, I think so. Almost definitely.'

'That's a shame.'

I don't take in much of the Torts lecture. My head is spinning. *What if Adam tries to finish what he started in the surf?* And if he's guilty ... If that's Abbey's leg rope under his bed, does that mean she really is dead?

CHAPTER TWENTY-NINE

The moon reaches the top of its arc, glittering on the glassy waters of the Bay. In the distance, pinpoints of light gleam from dark hills. Twisted vines snake into shadows. A sugar-glider lands on a tree with a soft thump, its tongue laps at the bloody sap. A lone surfer rides a wave into shore. The lighthouse beam sweeps around again, lighting up his face, his platinum hair ...

I sit up, my pulse racing. Did something wake me? Nan is at Donald's, so it wasn't her. I listen, but all is quiet. It was a dream, that's all.

I lie back down, staring at the ceiling. I sit up again. Was it Jacq? She's been waking up with nightmares while Mum and Dad are away. And she fell asleep in Nan's bed tonight, watching a movie on her big-screen TV. I should check on her. Turning on a light, I pad down the corridor in my purple bed-shirt and peer into Nan's room. Jacq's pink cheeks on the pillow and the snuffle of her breathing calm me.

What's that? A floorboard creaks behind me. I swing around, my heart pounding.

A hand presses over my mouth. 'Don't scream,' says a man's voice. A voice with an English accent.

Adam. I struggle, kicking out, trying to bite him.

'It's only me: Adam. Calm down, Olivia.'

If only the baseball bat wasn't outside, leaning up against the balcony where Jacq left it.

'You're not going to scream, are you?

I hesitate.

'Olivia, it's me. I'm not going to hurt you.'

I stop struggling and shake my head. I need to know why he's here. He takes his hand away and I turn around, my pulse racing.

Adam's face is stretched with tiredness. His platinum hair pokes up at odd angles and his clothes are rumpled. 'Sorry to scare you. I didn't want to wake your sister up.'

'How did you find me?'

Don't let him know you know, says Nansea.

What? What do I know?

'I googled you. It's not that hard,' he says.

'But ... you don't know my real name.' *Should I kick him?*

I told you to start weight training, says Nansea.

Adam steps toward me.

I step backwards. 'How did you know my name?' I whisper.

Adam lifts his shoulders. 'The photo on Abbey's wall. You were so cute, you two. I asked her who you were. She told me all about you and the things you got up to together. I didn't recognise you at first, but it clicked eventually.'

My cheeks flush, remembering my dolphin trainer story. 'When did you realise who I was?' Had I fooled *anyone?*

'That night you turned up at my place, all covered in mud. You looked like the girl in the photo. You haven't changed much.'

'I'm not a dolphin trainer.'

'You'll always be a dolphin trainer to me.'

'But … this isn't my house. The address isn't online.'

'I found out you were at uni.'

'You followed me?'

He nods.

I swallow. 'You've got a nerve. Showing up here. After you drugged me. I should ring the cops.'

Adam's brown eyes widen. 'I didn't drug you.'

'What, you dropped something in my wine by accident?' I remember Jacq is still sleeping and lower my voice. 'I was doped.'

Adam shakes his head. 'I didn't …' His brow wrinkles. 'You did seem less uptight.'

I snort. 'I am not uptight.'

Adam's face clears. 'You ate one of my biscuits, didn't you?'

I blink. 'Two.'

'They're special biscuits.' He pauses. 'I sell them.'

I narrow my eyes.

Remember the presumption of innocence, says Nansea.

I suppose he could be telling the truth. 'You shouldn't leave them lying around if you don't want people to eat them.' I step away from him. 'Come away from Nan's room. We'll wake my sister up.' I head for the loungeroom.

He speaks from behind me. 'How was I to know you'd help yourself?'

I swing around and hiss at him. 'What was in them? Naiad berries?'

'I figured you'd work that out. Yeah, Abbey and I found the tree while we were doing surveys on the Amalians' land. The berries are amazing, but they're bitter. I was experimenting with different ways to take them. Biscuits were my latest idea.'

I remember what Lars said in the nightclub. *Some guy in the corner has special biscuits.* 'You've been selling the berries?'

'It's hard to make a living from acrobatics and botany. Gotta hustle where you can.'

I examine his face in the dim light from the streetlight outside. 'So, what are you doing here?'

'I couldn't disappear without telling you ...' His voice is soft. 'I didn't do anything to Abbey.'

I wait – it sounds like there's more to come.

'It was my fault though. I left her there. In the surf. We'd had an argument. We had a lot of arguments, but that night was the worst ... about the tree. She wanted to tell everyone, to get it protected, to stop the development. I wanted to keep it quiet, so I could sell the berries, at least for a while. I needed the money. She went off for a surf to calm down, but I followed her out there.' He lowers himself onto the couch.

I stay standing. 'So, what happened?'

'We argued again, and I left her. When I found out she hadn't come back, I couldn't tell anyone I'd been the last person to see her. It would have all come out about the tree. I didn't see how it would help for me to get involved. I know it makes me look bad, but it's the truth.'

I let out my breath. I believe him. He's done some dodgy things, but he's not a killer.

'We'd taken the berries together, and gone to the pub. She was ... pretty out of it.'

'Abbey never used to take drugs.'

'People change. They weren't really drugs, anyway. They were ...'

'Organic?' I sit in the chair opposite Adam and my hands find my knitting. I toy with the needles. Here's my weapon if I need it. 'Do you think she vanished on purpose?'

Adam lifts his shoulders. 'Abbey is a dreamer. It got her down, the way the town was changing. The big money moving in. The fights over development. She thought of leaving, but she didn't know where to go.'

My knitting unravels as I pull at it. So, hers wasn't the perfect life I'd imagined.

'I guess I wasn't always a good friend to her,' he says. 'Part of me was pleased to see her wising up. You know, getting real.' Adam gets off his chair and drops to his knees in front of me.

A wave of heat goes through me as he takes my hand. Despite everything.

'I know I'm an idiot Olivia, but I wanted to see you again before I get out of here.'

His hand is warm, and I don't want to let it go, even though I know I should. 'Where will you go?'

He shrugs. 'They tell me it's a big country.' His eyes meet mine and the air between us sparks.

Go for it, babe, says Nansea.

But I am not Nansea, not here in this room. I'm Olivia, and I have responsibilities. Jacq is asleep down the corridor. And besides, he might not be a killer, but he knew things about Abbey. Things that might have helped us find her. He lied. I need to get rid of him before I do something stupid. I drop his hand just as my phone rings.

Adam watches me as I walk across to the kitchen counter and pick it up.

'Are you all right Olivia?' It's Rosco.

'Yeah, I'm fine. You woke me up.' Adam's eyes meet mine, but I keep my face blank.

'I've been tipped off that Adam McBean was seen on the Gold Coast. I wanted to check up on you. Keep your doors locked.'

'Thanks, I'm okay.' I give a fake yawn.

'Also, Ashok's given a statement. They weren't able to get much sense out of him for the first couple of days after he regained consciousness. Memory loss. But he's positively identified Adam as his attacker now.'

An icy chill washes over me. I look over at Adam. He doesn't look like a killer.

'There's something else. The police found the leg rope under Adam's bed.'

I eye Adam, trying to look unconcerned. *Go on.*

'Mrs Watson has identified it as Abbey's leg rope. She says she always wore it. It's not exactly proof, but it does link him to her disappearance.'

I speak before I can stop myself. 'He's here. Tell them to come quickly.' I bang the phone down, avoiding Adam's eyes, my heart beating like a machine gun. *Am I a loose end he's about to tie up?*

Adam walks toward me. His hand touches my chin.

I grit my teeth as I meet his eyes, a sick feeling in my gut. 'Is that why you went out with me? So I'd fall for you and not suspect you?'

Adam's hand drops and his face pales.

A bitter taste rises in my mouth.

'At first, maybe, yes. But I fell for you Olivia, I did. I wouldn't have come here tonight otherwise.'

My throat is tight. 'You'd better go.'

'All right, I will.' Adam walks toward the front door.

'It was you who attacked me on the beach, wasn't it?'

Adam stops dead, his hand on the door. 'No. I don't know anything about that.'

I'm not sure if I believe him or not. I turn away until I hear the door bang. Then I get dressed and wait for the police.

CHAPTER THIRTY

Dawn is glowing in the sky outside when I go into the bathroom and find a jar of vitamin C tablets to crush into my shampoo. I've hardly slept. It's a bit of a job removing the dye and the fake tan, but one hour later, when I look in the mirror, there's no trace of Nansea left.

I march out of the bathroom. Last night, I told the police all I knew. Adam is out of my life forever and I'm fine with that. I stop mid-stride as a wave crashes over me. *Abbey.* If Adam's a killer, then Abbey is dead. I'll never get to tell her what she means to me. Wiping my eyes with the backs of my hands, I take a deep breath. I can't break down now.

Going into our bedroom, I gaze at Jacq's pink cheeks on her pillow. I need to stop all this sleuthing around and get back to reality. I have responsibilities. *Jacq, uni, Mum.* I have to pull myself together.

Rifling through the wardrobe, I gather up a pile of diaphanous hippie clothes. Dumping them into a plastic bag, I put them in the corner of my room ready to take to Vinnies.

Grabbing my uni wear, I go out to the loungeroom and set to work ironing. I don't usually iron my cargos and T-shirts, but today I do. By seven-thirty I've finished ironing and done the background reading for today's lectures. By eight o'clock I've planned a study schedule for the next two weeks. I've also printed out colour-coded spreadsheets for Nan, Jacq and me, to track our movements. I sit on the couch with a piece of toast. What else can I achieve this morning?

Warm hands creep over my eyes. I scream, my fragile peace shattering.

'Livvie?' Jacq pokes her head around my shoulder. 'I didn't mean to scare you.'

I squeeze her in a hug until she pulls free. My pulse takes a long time to settle.

While Jacq eats her cereal, I go into our room and sort my socks and knickers into colour-coordinated piles. Nan's landline rings in the kitchen and Jacq answers.

She chats away, giggling every now and again. After about ten minutes she puts the phone down.

'Who was that?' I call out.

'Rosco,' comes the small voice.

'Rosco?' I come out into the loungeroom. 'What did he want? Why didn't he talk to me?'

Jacq shrugs. 'He wanted to know if you were okay. I said you were. He's *my* friend now. He says he'll give me surf lessons if you bring me to the beach. Will you Livvie? Please? Please?' Jacq has always hero-worshipped Rosco. She thinks he looks like Prince Phillip from *Sleeping Beauty*.

What's he up to? I sense a conspiracy behind this. 'We'll see.'

My uni day passes in a fury of efficiency. I listen hard, take immaculate notes, and try to catch up on my reading in between lectures.

Sophie touches me on the arm as we leave the Torts lecture. 'Coming to the cafe?'

'No, I have to go to the library.'

'Are you all right, Olivia? You seem ... different.'

'Yes, I'm just very busy. I have to do my assignments for Crime and the Criminal Process, Torts, and Principles of Public Law.' I toss my neatly brushed hair and straighten my ironed T-shirt. 'I got behind, now I'm getting serious.'

I'm still holding it all together when Jacq goes off to play at a friend's house after school. I'm fine when I find one of Adam's platinum-coloured hairs on the couch. I put it in the bin and keep right on studying. It's only when the radio plays 'Dog Days Are Over' that my efficiency crumbles. I remember him leaping onto the trampoline – *it was fun jumping over you*. I throw myself onto my bed and sob until a wet patch the size of a dinner plate spreads out beneath my head.

I know Adam isn't worth crying over, in fact I'm not sure if that's why I'm crying. Maybe it's just that all of a sudden ... life is so, so deathly boring? I sob and sob in shuddering gasps, trying not to think about the real reason I'm crying. I haven't found Abbey. I've failed her. She's gone.

❀

'You look glum, Olivia,' says Nan when she comes home from her ukulele jam.

I'm at the kitchen table, reading a law textbook. 'Got a lot of work to do,' I grunt.

Nan cocks her head. 'You know what they say about all work and no play. When did you last go out on a date? You haven't told me anything about your date in Byron Bay.'

Date in Byron Bay? Oh yes, I'd forgotten my excuse for the first weekend in Byron. 'It didn't work out. I don't have time for dating. Did you know we all get marked on a bell curve? It's not enough to know the work. I have to be better than the other students and they spend every spare moment studying. If I fall behind this year, I won't be in line for internships, and ...'

Nan sniffs and plays a short riff from 'Somewhere Over the Rainbow' on her ukulele. 'That's all very well, but if you get too stressed, you'll end up getting sick and where will you be then?' She plucks her ukulele. 'Why don't you try keeping a journal? My therapist suggested it and I find it helps to reduce stress.' She perches on the couch and segues into 'Happy'.

It seems to be working for her. Perhaps I'll give it a go.

CHAPTER THIRTY-ONE

Olivia's Private Journal.
Keep Out or You Will Be Cursed by the Spirit of the
Mummy (This means you, Jacq)

*Wednesday: Cleaned the flat. Discovered the teapot was
supposed to be silver and the bathroom tiles were green, not
grey. Realised cleaning is a fruitless activity. Cleaning one part
makes other parts look dirtier.*

*Rosco rang, but only to talk to Jacq about surfing again.
He's up to something, but I'm too busy to worry about Rosco
and his little games.*

*Modified Mum's spreadsheet to track movements every
fifteen minutes, instead of hourly. I'm sure this will result in
some efficiency gains.*

*Thursday: Decided knitting is the path to peace. Finished
winter jacket for Nan's terrier, Kevin. Gave it to her to muted
appreciation.*

*'Haven't you got anything better to do with your time
Olivia? Wouldn't you rather I babysit Jacq so you can go out on
the town?' she said.*

Some people will never be happy.

*Added another column to the spreadsheet to take Kevin's
movements into account.*

Friday: *Concentrated efforts on knitting a winter scarf for Jacq. If winter fails to arrive, can always give it to Vinnies. There must be someone out there who would appreciate a scarf. Skyped with Mum and Dad. Weird conversation as usual. I didn't tell them about Abbey.*

'The root of suffering is attachment', said Mum.

'Crime is common, logic is rare,' said Dad, quoting from Sherlock Holmes again.

I'm not sure if these comments were on point or pointless. Mum and Dad used to be so sensible. They never used to quote Buddha and Sherlock Holmes at me. What's going on over there in Kathmandu? Why aren't they coming home?

Have decided to dodge their calls for the foreseeable future. I can't talk about Abbey to a background of chanting monks. And there's nothing else I want to talk about.

Saturday: *Rosco rang and talked to Jacq again. Tried to ignore pleas by Jacq to take her to beach for long-awaited surf lesson. She has stuck up pictures of surfers all around our room. She's also propped Abbey's board in the corner of our room, so she can look at it at night. Which means I have to look at it at night. Which is making it hard to sleep.*

Jacq refuses to wear the scarf I have knitted for her. Suggests I find someone else to give it to. This is the thanks I get for all those hours of selfless work.

On the positive side, the spreadsheet is working well to coordinate the household. I can make further efficiency gains if I divide it into five-minute intervals. Nan, Jacq and Kevin are already having trouble accounting for their movements though, so I'll need to build up to it.

Sunday: *Concentrated on the ironing. Asked Nan for advice on the best way to deal with wrinkles in cotton but was cruelly dealt with.*

*'I'm going out to hula dancing lessons with Donald, Olivia.
I don't have time for ironing. You should buy wash and wear.'*

*Jacq appreciated her ironed underpants though. She wants
me to iron them fresh every morning now, so she can put them
on warm. I hope I'm not creating a rod for my own back.*

*Rosco rang again to speak to Jacq. I'm not going to be able
to hold off on the surf safari for much longer.*

Monday: *Have decided to stop writing this journal. My life is
too ...*

The journal ends. I couldn't decide if my life was too boring,
too hectic, or just too frigging sad.

On Monday night I discover Jacq in the loungeroom, cutting
up the magazines with Abbey's articles that I'd stashed under
my bed.

'What are you doing?' I scream. 'Those are mine.'

Jacq blinks. 'I'm making a collage.' Pictures of surfers she's cut
from the magazines are strewn across the couch. She is clearly
keen to expand on her current surf poster repertoire.

'I'm sorry, I didn't mean to yell at you. It's just, those are
important to me. I'll cut out the articles I need to keep, and you
can use the rest.'

'Can I stick some pictures up on the wall in here?' she asks.
'There's not much room left on our bedroom wall.'

'Sure, why not?' Nan can always take them down if she
doesn't like them. I find some blu-tack and sit beside Jacq to cut
out Abbey's articles. It's therapeutic, the cutting, like I'm back in
pre-school.

My eyes focus on Abbey's name at the top of an article. I blink
rapidly as the letters swim. What a shambles I've made of my

investigations. It's lucky I'm not a PI anymore – I may not be very good at it.

On the coffee table, Nan's *Gold Coast Times* is still open at an article I'd read this morning. *Multi-million-dollar alien embassy gets green light*, reads the headline. The Amalian development is scheduled to begin soon.

It's not over yet, says Nansea. *You need to find the tree.*

I'm not having any of it. *Go away. I have no need for you now.*

Look what happened the last time I listened to her. What's the point anyway? I don't care about the tree. I only want to know what happened to Abbey. And I don't know what to do next.

Come on, says Nansea. *You can't stop now. What would Abbey do?*

That's a low blow. Abbey would find the tree and stop the cult developing the land. But that's Abbey. It's tiring trying to save the world. I yawn.

Nan stalks in and looks around at the pictures on the wall. 'What's going on here?'

I give her a summarised version. 'Jacq's making a surfing collage and I'm ...' I glance at Abbey's articles. 'I don't know what I'm doing. I guess ... I guess maybe I haven't finished yet.'

'With ukelele,' says Nan, 'you never finish, you just progress.'

I consider this. 'That's actually quite relevant. Have you ever considered setting yourself up as a guru?'

'Who knows what's in store for me. Life is a crazy adventure.' Nan's phone tings. 'Time for—'

'Ukulele lesson?'

'Correct.' She wanders out.

I stare at my magazine clippings. Have I missed something? Is

Abbey's article about vegetable gardens a coded message? Unlikely. What about 'Cunning ways with plastic-free wraps'? No.

'Are you going to stick those up on the wall?' asks Jacq. 'That's what investigators usually do.'

It's not a bad idea. 'Why not?' I grab some blu-tack and stick Abbey's articles up, stepping back to admire my handiwork. Tipping my head to one side, I cross my eyes. *Okay, chakras, do your thing.* No, nothing. Maybe my chakras need extra boosting. What did Luna say? *Yoga and meditation will help, if it's all you can manage.*

'They're not straight, Livvie.'

I uncross my eyes and blink at Jacq. 'Can you straighten them up for me? I'm going to meditate.'

'Okay.' Jacq jumps to her feet.

I sit, close my eyes, and try to quiet my mind. Five seconds later, my eyes fly open. It's my turn to cook and I haven't got the chicken out of the freezer yet.

'Have you finished meditating?' asks Jacq.

I nod. 'I'll get the dinner on.'

Later, after Jacq is in bed, I make myself a Milo. I go out into the loungeroom and stare at Abbey's articles on the wall. For some reason my mind turns to Dad's Sherlock Holmes quote – *Crime is common, logic is rare ...*

Logic. That's what I need. Surely I can figure this out. I scan Abbey's words. She is such a skilled writer, there's not a word out of place. Her piece on the Devil's Marbles development didn't read as well, but I suppose it was just a draft. Picking up my phone, I open the document I'd emailed to myself from Abbey's computer.

Aliens before animals in battle for the rainforest.

The rainforest is only a short drive from the seething coast, but it is a different world. Heading west from Byron Bay, you pass through the hillside villages, then climb to the peaks of the Devil's Marbles. Here, time stands still. Tangled vines snake from the canopy to the shadows below. Steep-sided rocky canyons twist and turn. Only adventurers who wish to abseil through thundering waterfalls can access these. This miraculous forest is so impenetrable, much remains unexplored. A dubious development threatens the borders of this wilderness.

I look from my phone to the articles on the wall. All the finished pieces are spare, to the point. The one on my phone, though, is flowery, overflowing with adjectives. My fingertips tingle. Is my intuition chakra warming up?

Tapping my phone, I highlight all the adjectives in Abbey's article. *Seething, hillside, twisted, steep-sided, rocky, thundering, miraculous, dubious.* I scan the highlighted words, but nothing comes to me. I guess I'm clutching at straws. What if I expand my highlight to include the words after the adjectives? I tap again. *Seething coast, hillside villages, twisted vines, steep-sided rocky canyons, thundering waterfalls, miraculous forest, dubious development ...*

Miraculous forest ... Could that be the miracle tree? As I read the highlighted words again, they make a kind of sense. They sound like directions. Are they a description of how to get to the tree? It's an odd way to leave a message, but it's the sort of thing Abbey would do.

Running into my room, I rummage through the brochures I

picked up in Byron Bay. *Aha.* Here's the one on Devil's Marbles National Park. The map in the brochure is small, but ... My pulse leaps – a shaded area near the park boundary is labelled Rocky Canyon. I check Abbey's article on my phone. *Rocky canyon. Tick.*

If my theory is correct, somewhere in that canyon will be *thundering waterfall.* I check the map again. Some wiggly lines show the river dropping over waterfalls. *Tick.*

All going to plan, somewhere near the waterfall will be ... *the miracle tree.* My heart does a shimmy of excitement. And if my theory is a bunch of twaddle? Well, I'm not Sherlock Holmes.

The miracle tree. While the tree itself is not important to me, maybe it will lead me to Abbey. Or, at least, if I find it, I can stop the Amalian development, which is what Abbey wanted.

So, I need to get in there, but how? I'll need help. Someone who knows the area. Not Rosco – he'd want to stop me. Besides, I'm not ready to deal with that kind of complication. I don't know what he's up to with Jacq and this surf lesson thing, but being with Rosco is fraught.

I study the map. There are a lot of cliffs. That means ropes. I only know one person who's into rock-climbing. I don't like him much, but at least I can trust his green credentials. He will be keen to save the tree from development. I find Ashok's number and dial. Not expecting him to answer, I press the speaker button and start washing up.

'Hello, this is Ashok.'

Hands still in the sink, I speak into the phone. 'Oh, hi, this is Nansea, Abbey's friend ...'

'Yeah, I remember you.' The voice coming out of the phone is as irritating as ever. His accident hasn't improved his personality.

'I was glad to hear you've recovered from your accident.'

He laughs in a sarcastic way. 'It wasn't an accident. I was mugged. I hear McBean's done a runner.'

'Yeah, I heard that too.' My stomach clenches. I hang up the saucepans while it settles. 'Well, the reason I rang you was about the tree.'

'The tree?' He sounds enthusiastic now. 'Have you found out something about it?'

'Maybe. What do you know already?'

'A little. When you told me how Abbey had written *Fallen Angel's Plaything* in her notebook ... It clicked for me later – she meant the Devil's Marbles. I knew McBean did a flora survey up at the Devil's Marbles with Abbey. The Miracle Tree is a Byron Bay legend, so I know the story. It all fell into place. He got rid of her so he could have it to himself.'

'So you went looking for him?'

'Yeah. I went to the Beach Hotel, but he wasn't there. I figured he'd be out surfing. I found him at Tallows, right on sunset. Tried to get him to admit what he'd done to Abbey. He attacked me. Held me under. I'd be dead now if that dog walker hadn't pulled me out of the water.'

I swallow. *Would Adam have done that?* What do I know? I scrub at the benches. *He had Abbey's leg rope under his bed.* 'Do you know the Devil's Marbles area well?' One of my over-zealous wipes pushes a glass to the floor. It shatters with a crash. *Damn.*

'Better than most. I live near the park and I'm always in there exploring. What are you doing?'

'Nothing.' I drop the Chux and pick up the phone, dancing around the remains of the glass in my bare feet. 'Have you ever heard of a place called Thundering Waterfall?'

'In Rocky Canyon? Yeah, I've heard of it, never been there.

That's where you think the tree is? How'd you work that out?'

'Abbey left a message behind. It took me a while to figure it out. Do you want to go there with me?'

'We'll need ropes. It will be tough – you up to it?' Ashok sounds dubious.

Hell, yeah, says Nansea.

'Uh, yes.' *Am I?* I'll have to be. 'What about this weekend?' It's Nan's weekend for looking after Jacq.

'All right. Come around to my place on Saturday morning. It's on the way.' He describes how to get there. 'I'll organise the gear.'

'Okay, see you there.' A splinter of glass digs into my foot as I put the phone down.

CHAPTER THIRTY-TWO

Ashok's house is about half an hour's drive from Byron, out toward the hills. On Saturday morning, I wind my way along the potholed dirt road, past the fluttering prayer flags and rainbow-painted fences. At a sign reading *Hudson's Creek Co-operative*, I get out of the car and open the heavy steel gate. A narrow track leads off into an old banana plantation that's being reclaimed by the rainforest. The air smells of lantana and dust.

Ashok told me his house was the third one I'd come to. I drive past a tepee and a yurt and pull up outside a wooden house that's still under construction. Ashok is outside working in the vegetable garden. His red hair streams out from beneath a broad-brimmed felt hat. A kookaburra perches on a tree above, waiting for worms.

He looks up as I drive in. His face is paler than before, which makes him look even more prophet-like. He stares at me as I get out of the car. It's obvious he has no idea who I am. Last time he saw me, I was Nansea. Today, I'm dressed for practicality. My loose T-shirt and khaki shorts accessorise with an orange AFL cap I found on the beach.

He frowns as I walk over, his green eyes squinting in the sunlight. The penny drops. 'Nansea? What happened to you? You've gone all white.'

He can talk. 'Yeah ...' I stick to the cover story. 'We've had a sick dolphin. I've been in the inside pool with it for a while.' I hope he won't recognise this pale version of me from Abbey's beach ceremony. Not that it matters at this stage, but it would be awkward.

Luckily, he seems to have a poor memory. 'Come inside. I'll get my stuff.' He winces.

'Are you all right?'

'I get a headache when I'm in the sun. The quacks tell me it should improve. It was a fair whack that pommy gave me.' He props his spade against the stairs and kicks the mud off his boots. Opening the screen door, he stands aside to let me in.

Ashok's house is an eccentric mixture of old and new. Parts look like they've been there for centuries, while others are still unfinished. Spiders swing from the timber beams and a winding vine pokes through the roof like a hanging basket. Weight-lifting equipment clutters one corner. That explains his muscular arms.

I gaze around. Posters from environmental campaigns plaster the walls. *Save Daintree, Save the Tasmanian Forests, Save Ningaloo.*

Ashok disappears into the next room. Returning with a rope over his shoulder, he walks straight out the front door. I trot after him. 'We'll take my car.' He gestures toward his battered four-wheel drive. 'There are some rough tracks out there.'

I climb in and plant myself on the ripped seat, pushing aside a pile of Forest Friends brochures. The car coughs and takes off down the driveway.

Ashok drives in silence, his hat pulled low to block the sun, which streams through the windscreen.

I struggle to think of small talk. Giving up, I gaze out the window. After a while, I see the national park sign ahead. Ashok turns down the road where the Amalians did their Awakening. Swinging the wheel, he veers onto a steep side-track.

I'm pinned to the back of my seat as we drive up a near-vertical slope. The engine makes a desperate high-pitched squeal, but Ashok's face is calm. I guess he's done this kind of thing before.

As we reach the top of a ridge, he points to a valley on our right. 'Rocky Canyon's in there. We'll have to walk soon.'

The road deteriorates. Ashok eases the four-wheel drive through holes that would have swallowed my car. Pulling over to the side of the track, he gestures toward the rainforest. 'It's that way.'

'Are you sure?' The trees are so thick around us, we could be anywhere.

'Yep.' He glances at a map he'd placed on the dashboard. 'Let's go.'

The forest looks impenetrable, and we are so far from civilisation ... I glance at Ashok and my heart thumps a little faster.

You sure you want to do this, babe? asks Nansea.

I swallow. I've come this far, I need to see it through.

Ashok pulls a backpack out of the boot, along with a rope, which he slings over his shoulders. He vanishes into the forest.

I push my way after him. It's arduous. Waist-high ferns and spiky vines ensnare me at every step. I'm scratched from head to toe and my legs are trembling with exhaustion by the time I catch up to him.

He is standing at the top of a roaring waterfall, which

cascades into a shadowy canyon below. He glances over at me. 'You've abseiled before, right?'

You bet, says Nansea.

I hesitate. 'Yes.' I try not to look at the spot where the water is pounding into the pool. It makes me queasy. My sole abseiling experience was five years ago at school camp and it hadn't gone well. I'd frozen halfway down the small cliff and burst into tears. A teacher had to climb up on a ladder to help. Still, I am older now …

And hardened to terror, right? says Nansea.

Wrong. My eyes are drawn to the bottom of the waterfall. It's a long way down. I'm tempted to tell Ashok to go on without me, but I'd never find my way back to the car.

Ashok raises his voice above the rushing of the water. 'You go first, I'll follow.' He hands me a harness.

'Isn't there an easier way?' I try not to whimper. 'Surely Abbey and Adam didn't come this way?'

'They must have. It's the only way into the canyon. What's the problem?' Ashok checks my harness, pulling at the buckle. 'You're good to go.'

I'm sure he knows what the problem is. I swallow with difficulty and take a step backwards toward the cliff as Ashok feeds out the rope. An important question occurs to me. I come to a standstill. I can't take another step until I know the answer.

Yeah right, says Nansea.

'How will we know the tree when we find it?'

'I've got it covered.' Ashok pulls a plastic bag out of a pocket in his heavy cotton shirt. Inside is a piece of paper with an artist's drawing of a slim-trunked tree. Next to the tree are detailed drawings – heart-shaped leaves and a cluster of berries. 'I photocopied this from a botany textbook.' His voice is quiet. I can hardly hear him over the crash of the water. 'It's based on the only specimen ever found.'

He puts the drawing away. There's something reverential about the way he treats it, even though it's a photocopy.

'It means a lot to you, this plant, doesn't it?' I'm trying to prolong the conversation. Delay the moment when I step backwards over the cliff.

'Yes, but I don't want to exploit it, like everyone else.' His voice is bitter. 'I want it to exist for its own sake. Imagine being one of the only people who have seen the naiad.' His eyes drift over my shoulder toward the canyon.

My gaze follows his. 'But … if we can find it, they might grow it in the Botanic Gardens. Like the Wollemi Pine. That would be good, wouldn't it?'

Ashok glances at me, his face impassive. 'Yeah, well, we'll see what happens. We've got to find it first anyway. After you.' He gestures down the waterfall.

'But …' No, I don't have anything else to say. I grit my teeth, turn my back to the drop again and put my feet into the rushing water. I take a tentative step backwards. It's scary. The water buffets me and the rocks are slippery beneath my feet. I can't do this. I can't. But I have to. For Abbey.

Come on, says Nansea, *you've got this.*

I exhale in a rush, cling to the rope behind my back, and let it through my fingers, inch by inch. I am over the edge now. *I'm over the edge.*

Looking up, I see Ashok staring at me. He makes a *hurry up* gesture. I let a little more rope through, focusing on keeping my breath steady and not looking down. I keep on edging down, my pulse thumping. *I can do this.* Finally, my feet find horizontal ground. *I did it.*

Unclipping the rope from the harness, I give Ashok a thumbs-up. I'm too traumatised to celebrate. I'm just glad to be in one piece and not halfway up a cliff. After a while, my heart calms enough for me to take in my surroundings. *Wow.* This place is incredible. It's like a green cathedral.

Luxuriant ferns cover the steep canyon walls. They hang over the top, filtering the sun, like green stained-glass. The river splashes over smooth, round boulders, its sound echoing around me. I've never been anywhere so beautiful and wild before.

It doesn't take long for Ashok to land beside me. He pulls down the rope and winds it up, slinging it over his shoulders as before. Only when he's done that does he stop to take in the canyon. Then he does an odd thing. Touching his hands together in prayer position, he bows his head for a moment. As he looks up, his eyes slide sideways to me and he lifts his shoulders. 'It's a powerful place.'

For the first time, I see what Abbey saw in him. He has hidden depths. 'How much further is it?' I ask in a low voice.

'Not far, about three k.' He sets off downriver with long strides.

I trot to keep up, working hard to stay upright on the rounded rocks that line the canyon floor.

After about an hour, the sound of a waterfall becomes louder and louder. The air ahead fills with fog-like spray. It must be a big one. I hope there's an easy way around it. Abseiling is now at the very top of my least-favourite things list. Soon we reach the place where the canyon drops away. I peer over, watching the stream burst into rainbows as it hits the rocks below. It has to be twenty metres down. *What now?*

I glance at Ashok, but his eyes aren't on me. He's staring at a crack in the rock at the side of the waterfall. Out of the fissure grows a tree. Its pale silvery trunk stretches, smooth-barked, toward the sun.

The tree isn't thick, but it's tall. How can it grow there, within the rock? Straining my neck, I follow its trunk upwards. Clusters of purple berries dangle between glossy leaves at the top. Some of the berries have fallen to the base of the tree. Moving forward, I touch my fingers to its cool trunk. A shiver of excitement runs through me. 'Well, hello there. You've been hard to find.' *This is it.* The miracle tree. I turn to Ashok, but my smile freezes as I see him.

His eyes shine with a fervour I recognise from images of men waving guns.

My pulse skips a beat, but I pretend I haven't noticed anything. I raise my voice above the noise of the waterfall. 'It's amazing to see it, isn't it?'

He moves to stand beside me, his eyes on the tree, his shoulder brushing mine. 'I've got something I need to tell you.'

I've got a feeling I'd rather not hear what's coming.

'It wasn't Adam who killed Abbey,' he almost whispers.

Killed? I look into his pale eyes and my mouth goes dry.

'I was following them. I found her out there in the surf … alone.' His voice is flat.

'What, why?' I glance over his shoulder, up the canyon. Can I outrun him? *Doubtful.* And if I do, how will I get back up the waterfall?

'She was … involved with Adam.' He pauses. 'I loved her.'

'But they weren't ...' I falter. *What do I know? Only what Adam told me.*

'... and she wanted to tell everyone about the tree,' Ashok continues. His eyes are far away, back there in the surf with Abbey. 'I took her by surprise, held her under. I didn't want to ... I loved her so much. But it was her own fault. She wouldn't listen. She broke the rules.'

The rules? Acid rises in my throat. I struggle to control myself. I can't break down now. 'And the note?' I whisper. 'The note she left?'

'She wrote it to me, to break off our relationship. After that ... I had no choice.' Ashok gazes up at the tree with an awed expression. 'Can't you see? This is one of a kind. What will happen if everyone knows it's here? They'll never be able to protect it. People will be in here all the time, trampling through the river, collecting berries, taking samples. Taking the whole tree.' His voice is high with hysteria.

'But ... we can tell the authorities. They can keep its location secret and protect it from development.'

Ashok's hand shoots out and grasps my wrist. He picks up a berry from the ground, 'Do you know how much this is worth, investigator?'

I shake my head, my brain numb. *Investigator?*

'Oh yes, I know who you are. I thought you were a cop or a private investigator when I saw you at the ceremony. I was right, wasn't I?'

'No, I'm no-one, just Abbey's friend.'

Ashok's eyes are contemptuous. 'You've got nothing to gain by lying now. Do you know how much this is worth?' he repeats, thrusting the purple berry under my nose.

I pull away, but his grip is too strong.

'Millions. There's only one way to protect it. The way it's been protected for hundreds of years.' Ashok's eyes burn with a fanatical light. He grasps me by the shoulders and pulls me the short distance to the edge of the waterfall.

'It was you who attacked me on the beach, wasn't it?' I'm trying to buy time.

'I tried to warn you, but you wouldn't listen.' His voice drops and he gazes over my shoulder. 'Why wouldn't you listen?'

I have a feeling he's not talking to me. 'But what about Adam? He knows where it is.'

He twitches and his eyes come back to me. 'I doubt we'll see him around here again. So, it's only you and me. And soon, just me.'

I kick out at him, but his hands dig into my shoulders, making me wince with pain. He meets my eyes for a moment as I teeter on the brink of the drop, but it's not me he sees.

'I'm so sorry Abbey,' he says.

He pushes me, but I don't fall. I grasp at his arms, finding strength in desperation. *If I'm going, you're coming too.*

His eyes widen with fear as he staggers, half-leaning over the cliff edge with me clinging to him. He shakes his arms to get me off, but the movement unbalances him. He topples toward me.

Time stops as we float, locked together like lovers. I open my mouth to scream, but no sound comes out.

CHAPTER THIRTY-THREE

I float above the forest. The moon is a bright yellow half-ball. It glitters on the distant sea. Pinpoints of light reveal a small town. In the streets, bare feet shuffle and dance to the twang of a banjo.

My eyes open. Moonlight streams into the canyon through gaps in the canopy. Shafts of light bathe my face. *Moonlight?* Last I knew, it was daytime. Pain squeezes my chest. I close my eyes against the light, waiting for the pain to go away. *Abbey.* What did Ashok say ...?

I float up again. My body is lying among the rocks, a pale shape beneath me. Along the ridge, a dance party throbs in the rainforest. Rusty kombis and station wagons jam the dirt track. The steady doof, doof, doof carries down the valley.

My eyes open again. The moon has moved on and my face is in shadow. *That's better.* My hand is beside my face. Curling my fingers, I touch my cheek. It's wet with a sticky substance. I wiggle my toes. They work. Beneath my back is something soft. I swivel my eyes from side to side. An arm is flung out beside me. *My arm?* I wiggle my fingers. *Not my arm.*

I close my eyes, remembering our sickening plummet off the cliff edge. Prying my eyes open again, I attempt to roll onto my knees. A blinding flash of pain sweeps through me. *My leg, something wrong with it.* I wriggle sideways, sliding off the soft thing underneath me.

Raising my head, I see the soft thing. It's Ashok. His head is covered with blood. My stomach churns and tears flood my eyes. 'What were you thinking?' I yell. His image goes out of focus.

When I open my eyes, the moon has moved again. Ashok moans.

It all comes back to me, what he said at the cliff. He killed Abbey. He held her under. 'You're pathetic,' I hiss at him. 'You didn't own her.' Tears prick at my eyes. I grit my teeth, pushing thoughts of Abbey down. I need to get out of here. I will think about Abbey later.

I sit up and scan my surroundings. The waterfall rises high above me, its roar filling my head. As I watch the water drift down in slow motion, I re-live my fall. We had tumbled from ledge to ledge, locked together. In the end, Ashok had cushioned my landing. *Karma.*

Everything is out of focus. It takes a while to realise this isn't because of my injuries. My glasses are gone. I feel around, but can't find them. I push myself to my knees, nursing my sore leg. How will I get out of here? My phone is still in my pocket. I pull it out, but its screen is cracked, and nothing happens when I press the power button. There's probably no reception anyway.

Crawling to the river, I drink from it like a dog, sucking down mouthful after mouthful. Splashing water over my face, I wash away the blood. My head seems all in one piece.

My eyes fall on a bunch of berries lying on the riverbank.

They glow purple in the light of the moon. *The miracle tree.* They've fallen from the waterfall. I pick them up. They are the size of a grape and shiny on the outside. Slicing one with my thumbnail, I break it open. Inside, succulent-looking crimson flesh surrounds a black seed.

My brain ticks over. I felt good after I ate Adam's biscuits. Will the berries dull the pain enough for me to walk out of here? I pop two in my mouth and bite. A sharp, sweet-and-sour taste spurts onto my tongue. I spit out the pip. My stomach rumbles. It's been a long time since I've eaten. *Maybe a couple more?*

I can't stop. I demolish the whole bunch. I wait, but apart from a slight clenching of my guts, nothing happens. I gather up a few berries and stuff them in my pocket. I might need a top-up later.

My sore leg buckles, but holds as I climb to my feet. *How do I get out of here?* I'm going to have to go downstream. Ashok had a map. I limp toward him. He is lying still with his eyes closed, but he moans as I feel in the pocket of his shirt and pull out the map. 'You needn't think I'm going to carry you out of here,' I say.

He moans again.

I restrain myself from kicking him, though I would very much like to.

Maybe a small kick? says Nansea.

Strangely, she sounds a lot like Abbey. I eye Ashok. He deserves way more than a kick, but he's in terrible shape already. He'll get his punishment once I get out of here. I grit my teeth and unfold the map. It's hard to make sense of it in the dim light, especially without my glasses. At last I find the tiny words, *Thundering Waterfall.* I trace the path of the stream downstream with my finger. It looks like there are about eight kilometres until it intersects with a road.

Eight kilometres. On a graded track with two working legs, it would take about two hours. On a rough creek bed in semi-darkness, with a bodgy leg, maybe eight. I'm tempted to sit down again. But who's going to find me? No-one knows where I am. And besides ... I glance over at Ashok. He's harmless at the moment, but that could change. I hobble toward the trees that line the river and select a walking stick. A faint humming in my ears tells me the berries are taking effect. *Good.*

I set off downstream, but it's slow-going. At every step, pain sears through my leg. I keep myself going by reminding myself I'm moving away from Ashok and toward civilisation. Soon, the canyon widens and the forest thickens. I stagger along, sighing with relief as the berries deaden my pain. Tangled vines grab me. They don't want to let me pass.

I fantasise I'm Nancy Drew in a Costa Rican rainforest. *Where are the missing monkeys?*

A soft thump brings me back to my senses. A glider the size of a cat lands on the tree beside me. It scratches at the bark with a dainty paw and pokes out its pink tongue to lap at the sap. I stretch my legs and a twig snaps. The glider scuttles up the tree, into the darkness. I scan the forest. In the silvery moonlight every leaf is in sharp focus, even without my glasses.

I swing my head from side to side. As I rotate, the sounds change, like a siren rushing toward me and away again. Every sound is magnified. On the other side of the hill, a dingo howls. I howl back.

What an outlandish accent you have, it replies in Abbey's voice, and scampers away. That was strange.

I rotate my head again, my ears picking up vibrations. Downstream is a faint *doof, doof, doof.* As I register this, I realise

I've been hearing it for some time. I stagger on toward the music. I make it to the next tree, and the one after. Rustles of forest creatures tell me I'm not alone. Thorny vines rip my arms and legs, but it doesn't matter. I'm on my way home. A bulging tree trunk takes the form of a dwarf.

Hey ho, hey ho, it's off to work you go, says Nansea/Abbey.

The music becomes louder. The moon vanishes behind the clouds and a light rain falls. I tilt my face to catch the drops on my cheeks, licking them as they roll toward my mouth. *Delicious.* I gaze up at the sky. It's beginning to lighten; dawn can't be far away. The music is loud now. My internal organs vibrate as I hobble faster.

In the pre-dawn greyness, I stumble into a clearing full of hundreds of bodies. Wet and muddy, hands held high, faces lost in the music, they are dancing in the rain.

As the music enters my body, I push my way among them. The first rays of sunlight seep over the horizon. The ground steams as the warmth hits it and mist envelops the crowd. I'm pushed this way and that as the music intensifies. We are one organism, one mind. I lose my stick, but it doesn't matter anymore. I put my hands in the air and dance.

I hear someone give a high-pitched 'Yee-hah!' and suspect it is me. The crowd whirls around me.

Faster, faster, says Nansea/Abbey.

I'm on a roundabout. At any moment, it will fling me off.

A cool hand encircles my upper arm. I blink as a familiar face comes into focus.

'Is that you Nansea? What have you been doing? You look terrible.'

Citra's beautiful face swims as my legs collapse beneath me.

CHAPTER THIRTY-FOUR

My head is throbbing when I wake, but I'm lying in a comfortable bed with the rain pattering on the roof. This is a huge improvement on my previous situation.

You made it out, says Nansea.

But Abbey didn't. My chest clenches. Ashok killed her. I thought I'd already accepted that she'd gone, but I guess a secret part of me was still holding onto hope. Tears trickle down my face as I remember my last words to her. *Butt out of my life.* Now I'll never get the chance to tell her she was right. I *have* been putting my life on hold.

I try to open my eyes, but they're glued shut. On the second attempt, I prise them open and evaluate my situation. My ankle is large and cumbersome under the sheets. It's been bandaged. The room is blurry. I feel around for my glasses, but remember I lost them at the waterfall.

Although the room is dim, a warm, yellow glow wafts from some candles in the corner. It must be evening. I've been asleep all day. As I raise my head, it vibrates like a chainsaw. I take in my surroundings. I know this place. I'm in Citra's bedroom. *What am I doing here?*

It comes to me. Citra found me at the half-moon party. She

rescued me. I hear low voices outside. Citra and someone else, a man. I can't make out what they're saying. I need to get closer.

As I slide my feet to the ground, the room shimmies and sways. Clutching the bed head, I push myself to my feet. I'm wearing a white gown, which trails on the floor. I look around, but there's no sign of my clothes. With a painful shuffle, I limp to the door. It is locked.

My head spins. Am I a prisoner? *Why?* I press my ear against the keyhole.

'What are we going to do with her?' I recognise that voice. A piggy aroma drifts through the keyhole with it, confirming my guess.

'We need to make her one of us,' says Citra. 'I found the berries in her pocket. She knows where the tree is. She'll stop our development if we let her go. Imagine the benefits if we can use the tree ourselves. It *is* on our property.'

My body turns to ice. No sooner do I escape one homicidal maniac than I'm captured by another. Ashok is still lying in the canyon. I need to tell the police what he did to Abbey.

'But how?' It's Pig Man again.

'We'll bring her to the gathering. It's in her own interests. She is a lost soul.'

'But what about ...?' The Pig Man's voice is muffled, and I don't catch the end of his sentence.

'Trust me. Once she's at the gathering, that won't be a problem. You know how it works.'

The voices become louder, and a cautious instinct makes me retreat to the bed.

'She hasn't done the training though,' says Pig Man. 'We've been preparing for weeks.'

'She is tired, hungry and emotionally drained. She'll be open to it.'

'You are so wise Citra.'

Teacher's pet, says Nansea.

Jumping into bed, I pull the covers up to my nose and squeeze my eyes shut. The door opens, bringing with it a waft of incense and pig smell. Two sets of footsteps enter. I keep my eyes shut.

'She's still asleep,' says Citra. 'Is it all organised?'

'Yes, they're all waiting for you.'

Citra puts her hand on my shoulder. 'Nansea. It is time to wake now. We are having a gathering to celebrate your recovery.'

I decide to play along. I'm in no state to bust out of here. I open my eyes. 'Where am I?'

Citra looks serene. Her black hair is piled up into a bun and a frangipani blossom is tucked behind her ear. The scent of sandalwood and rose emanates from her skin as she bends over me. 'You are in my house. I brought you here to recover. You're looking much better.' Her dark eyes gaze into mine. 'It was so strange when you wandered out of the forest. You had sticks in your hair and scratches all over you. You were like a creature of the forest ... a dryad.'

'Thanks for bringing me here. I appreciate it. I'd better go now though. I need to get back to the Gold Coast.'

'Of course,' says Citra. 'But first, join us for our prayer meeting.' Her hand rests lightly on my arm, but I sense the strength in it. It's not a request.

Pig Man hovers behind her wearing a green hair band, which holds his straggly brown hair back from his face. I could take him down, but not the two of them together.

'Okay,' I say. 'But after that I'll get going.'

Citra smiles. 'It won't take long.' She puts out her hand to help me to my feet. I wince as my foot hits the ground. Making a break for it isn't looking like a good option at this stage.

Outside, it is dark and still raining. Pig Man produces an umbrella and holds it over us as Citra leads me across the grass to the main building. Drumming drifts through the rain toward me and I hold up my long gown to keep it off the wet grass.

Inside, the meeting room is dimly lit with flickering oil lamps and the air is thick with incense. About fifty people sit around the walls, swaying to the beat of a drum played by a bare-chested, sinewy man. Without my glasses, their faces are a blur.

Citra motions for me to sit and I wedge myself into a gap on the floor. Beside me is one of the overweight men from the first workshop. His fleshy arm presses against mine as he sways to the drums. He still looks like he'd be better suited to a Gold Coast tour bus.

I scan the room, looking for the route to a quick getaway. The door is closed though, and Pig Man stands in front of it with his arms folded. The drums are mesmerising, which I suppose is the desired effect. The vibrations ripple through me and my body moves to the beat.

Citra stands at the front of the room and gestures to the drummer, who softens his repetitive beat. When all eyes are glued to her, she speaks. 'Welcome Amalians. Still your minds and open yourselves to Amal. We are here to invite his presence among us.' She speaks slowly, emphasising every word.

It is strangely compelling.

'We are so close now to our goal, Amalians. When our embassy is built, Amal himself will join us here on earth.'

I glance around the room. Everyone has their hands in the air as they sway to and fro.

'Give thanks to Amal ... give thanks to Amal ... give thanks to Amal,' Citra chants.

The group chimes in. 'Those who are not with us are doomed. Amal is our saviour.'

'Approach now to feel his gift of light,' Citra says.

Tension fills the room. Everyone is waiting for something to happen. *But what?* The fat man next to me gasps. Reeling forwards, he falls to his stomach. Pulling himself up, he crawls toward Citra.

She places her hands on his head. 'Be healed!' she cries, raising her voice so it vibrates around the room.

The man cries out and raises his hands in the air, tears running down his face. 'Thank you Amal,' he yells. 'I am healed.'

After that, mayhem pretty much ensues. The drumming gets louder and louder and the smoke from the incense fills my nostrils. One by one, people crawl toward Citra, screaming and crying as she touches them on the head.

There is a collective madness here. The Amalians are dancing to the beat of the drum now, their faces gleaming with sweat. It's like a pagan ceremony; the hysteria is infecting me too. My heart thumps. I am so tired and overwrought, and the chanting and drumming is getting under my skin.

I find myself on my feet, waving my hands above my head. The pain in my ankle has almost vanished. My body becomes one with the rhythm of the drum. I am dancing for Amal. It seems like a reasonable thing to do. I notice Citra's gaze on me, and she gives me an approving smile. This makes me feel warm all over. I step up my dancing efforts. I have no idea why I was so suspicious of Citra. She is amazing. So kind and generous.

As I dance, I see something – a face that was hidden by the crowd. It reminds me of something. Something important, but I can't remember what. I dance a little closer. The face is blurry, but familiar. For some reason it makes my heart ache. I dance closer, focused on the blurry face. Halfway there though, I forget what I'm doing. It doesn't matter. I'm here with Citra. I am dancing for Amal. It is all beautiful. I twirl and wave my hands.

As I twirl, my foot catches on a small vase containing incense. The incense falls onto me, burning my foot. *Ow.* I am suddenly not quite so euphoric. The blurry face is still in front of me. My heart thumps. For a moment, I forget about Amal. *Can it be ...?* I dance closer, my mind clearing. Her hair is cut shorter and I've never seen her wear a white robe before. But as her face comes into focus, there is no doubt about it. My heart explodes out of my chest. 'Abbey?' I whisper. Joy rushes through my body, from my fingers to my toes.

Abbey is sitting in a beanbag, nodding her head to the rhythm of the drums, her face blank. She looks spaced out.

I've never seen her look like this, and for a moment I doubt myself. I shuffle closer, waving my hands, acting like I'm still mesmerised. When I get near her, I touch her shoulder. 'Abbey,' I hiss.

Abbey shrugs my hand off without looking at me. 'I'm Angel.'

Angel? That was the name of the girl Gary the electrician was waiting for. *Tell her I'll be here, every day ...*

I pinch the top of her arm.

'Ow. Leave me alone,' she mumbles, still swaying to the drumbeat, her eyes unfocused. 'I'm already healed.'

'Angel,' I say. 'Gary said to tell you he loves you. He's waiting outside.'

'Gary? I told him to go away.'

'Abbey. I know what Ashok did to you.'

She frowns at the mention of Ashok's name. 'I hate him.'

'Me too. I squashed him. In the canyon. He won't be going anywhere now.'

At this, her mouth twitches and her head comes up. Her eyes focus on me and widen. 'Olivia?' she whispers.

'Uh huh.'

A light comes on inside her.

She looks like Abbey again.

'What are you doing here?' she asks.

'It's a long story. How about we get out of here first? Let's go find Gary.'

She nods. 'But you squashed Ashok?'

'Yep. I flattened him.'

'Good.' Abbey's mouth curls into a smile. 'No-one messes with Olivia.'

I smile back. 'I'm so pleased to see you.'

'Me too you.'

'Okay, do like I do.' I put my hands in the air.

Abbey stands up and puts her hands in the air. She meets my gaze and rolls her eyes. 'Can you believe this scene?' she whispers.

My mouth twitches in reply. *She's back.* I dance across the room, twirling and whirling like a dervish. My bandaged foot and over-long robe hinder me only a little.

Abbey dances in my wake, doing her best impersonation of a blissed-out Amalian convert.

Our dancing excites the group further. One after another they follow suit, whirling and screaming in delirium. My ears ring with the noise. Even Pig Man deserts his position near the door to join in with the dance.

'I am healed,' I cry out as I zigzag toward the door, trying not to be too obvious. Reaching the door, I dance in front of it, feeling behind me for the doorknob. It turns. I meet Abbey's eyes, and with a twirl, slip through the door without looking back.

Abbey follows me out into the night.

'Run.' Grasping Abbey's hand, I pull her toward the road.

A red Corolla with fat tyres stands beside the gate. True to his word, Gary is behind the wheel, dozing. That's one devoted admirer.

'Gary!' squeals Abbey, as she jumps in the front seat.

He jolts upright as I dive in the back.

'Nansea, Angel,' calls Citra from behind us. 'Don't go, you belong here with us. You'll regret this.'

'No we won't. Go, Gary!' screams Abbey.

With a screech of wheels, we take off into the night.

CHAPTER THIRTY-FIVE

'Olivia, you would not believe what's happened to me since I last saw you.' Abbey swings around in her seat as we roar away from the Amalians. Her hair flaps in the wind.

'I've been having a super-weird time too.'

'It can't be as weird as what's happened to me.'

'It could. Yesterday Ashok pushed me off a cliff, but I squashed him. After that I took some naiad berries and thought I was Nancy Drew until Citra captured me. Can you beat that?'

Abbey smiles. 'Woah, that's what happened to me too. Except substitute surf for cliff and skip the Nancy Drew part. Also, I would kill to squash Ashok.'

'You shouldn't have skipped the Nancy Drew part, that was the best bit. Apart from squashing Ashok, which was also awesome.' I squeeze her hand. 'So, tell me everything.'

Abbey squeezes my hand back. 'Of course *you'd* rescue me, Ol! Thank you.'

'What about me?' says Gary.

Abbey leans over and pats his cheek. 'You too.'

'So, Ashok said he pushed you under in the surf...'

'Yeah, Ashok was crazy jealous about Adam.'

'Were you and Adam together?' This shouldn't bother me, but it does.

'No. Not that I wasn't tempted. I mean, have you met him?'

I nod.

'Then you know what I mean.' Abbey's eyes widen. 'Hey, did you two ...?'

'Yeah, he jumped over me at the market and things progressed from there.'

'Classic pick-up,' says Abbey. 'Who can resist being jumped over?'

'He said you and he were just friends.'

'Yeah, that's right. Just friends. Adam is not exactly ... reliable though. He did try it on, but I was with Ashok.'

My gut clenches.

Gary's neck goes a little red.

'So, how did you get away from Ashok?' I ask.

Abbey gives me a long look. 'Come on, I've been training for this my whole life.'

I remember her underwater lap of the pool at the swimming carnival. 'You held your breath?'

Abbey smiles. 'Yeah. He pushed me under, and I just went limp. When he went away, I swam into shore and ... I didn't know what to do. I was kind of freaked out. I didn't want to go home, in case Ashok was there. There were some backpackers in the car park, and they said they were going up to the full-moon dance. So, I jumped in their van and we headed up there.'

'And Citra captured you?'

'Yeah, she kind of homed in on me as soon as I got there. We'd met before, when I did the survey up there. She said she'd keep me safe and it seemed like a good idea at the time.

I wanted to chill, somewhere Ashok wouldn't find me. And, it's embarrassing, but … I guess I was brainwashed.' Abbey frowns. 'I didn't think I was that kind of person. Turns out I am.'

'It nearly happened to me.' I remember the beat of the drums, Citra's hypnotic voice. 'I only snapped out of it when I got burnt by the incense.'

'It's kind of a bummer I had to leave,' Abbey says. 'I was looking forward to making some half-alien kids with Amal.'

Gary flashes her a sideways look.

'Joke. You're going to have to get to know me all over again, Gary. I'm not Angel anymore.'

Gary smiles. 'I like this version better.'

Abbey rests her head on his shoulder. 'Thanks for the getaway.'

'Abbey?' I say.

'Yeah.'

'I'm sorry I told you to butt out of my life. You were right. I have been putting my dreams on hold.'

Abbey looks back at me. 'I shouldn't have said that. It's your life. I was going through a weird phase. I blame Ashok, he messed with my head.'

As we drive over the Queensland border, I remember that my car is still back at Ashok's place in Byron Bay. It seems like a lifetime ago that I left it there. How will I get it back?

'You do know Rosco is crazy about you though, don't you?' says Abbey.

'He's not. He ghosted me after I left the agency.'

Abbey frowns. 'Well, that's strange, but I'll eat my half-alien baby if I'm wrong.'

'Hope it's tasty,' I say.

'Olivia.' Abbey's voice is stern. 'I am never wrong about these things.'

I don't believe her, but as we head north into the night, I remember how Rosco looks when his hair falls over his eyes. Like Han Solo after he battles the giant otter.

CHAPTER THIRTY-SIX

Three days later, my cuts and bruises are healing well, but the inside of my head is taking longer. I wake every night from dreams of falling. In a bizarre role-reversal, I run across the room and climb into bed with Jacq. It's the only way I can get back to sleep.

Each morning she wakes up and smiles when she sees me there. 'Did you have a bad dream again Livvie? You know it's not real, don't you?'

Unfortunately, it was. They'd retrieved Ashok from the canyon. He'd broken his leg, so he wouldn't have made it out alone. He confessed what he did to Abbey. He also admitted Adam hadn't attacked him in the surf. He'd just fallen off his board and hit his head.

It turns out Ashok has a history of violent behaviour. He'd left Victoria in a hurry and changed his name after an incident at a blockade. A logger had been injured by a spike Ashok had put in a tree. They hadn't been able to pin it to him, but he'd found it prudent to lie low.

I've been in a strange place since I got back from Byron. I've rescued Abbey. But, like the song says, I still haven't found what I'm looking for.

Abbey and I are meeting up at a McDonald's in Surfers this afternoon. McDonald's was Abbey's choice. I was shocked, but she told me she's not a vegan anymore.

'Olivia,' says Nan as I'm going out the door. 'You need cheering up. I've organised a blind date for you this evening.'

I come to a standstill. 'What? No way. I am not going out with one of your friends' weirdo grandsons.'

'This one isn't like that, Olivia. It's time to go out and have some fun.'

I point at the door. 'I'm going out. And I'm going to have fun.'

Nan snorts. 'You're eighteen. You're in the prime of your life. You'll thank me for this.'

'No, I wo—'

Nan holds up her hand. 'I am not taking no for an answer, Olivia. You're meeting him at the Metro Bar at five. Just for drinks, unless you decide to go on for dinner. I'll pick Jacq up from school, so you have the afternoon to get ready. Do try to make an effort.'

I sigh. Nan is an unstoppable force. I don't have the energy to resist. 'Fine, I'll do it, but it won't cheer me up. How will I know him?'

'He said he'll be wearing a shark tooth around his neck.'

My stomach sinks. *A shark tooth around his neck?* 'Why? Is he a shark hunter?'

'There's nothing wrong with wearing a shark tooth.'

'A reasonable person would say there is nothing right about wearing a shark tooth. It is, in fact, a not-insignificant character flaw. It could even be ruled unconscionable.' My life might be a shambles, but at least my law-speak is progressing.

'Oh, stop talking like a lawyer. Get out there and live a little.'

Something about the way she says this reminds me of Nansea. I haven't heard from her since I left Byron and I miss her feisty voice. 'Okay, I'll go. But it will be awful. I'll be scarred for life and it will be your fault.'

Nan smiles smugly. 'We'll see.'

✿

I catch a bus to McDonald's because my car is still stuck in Byron. The police say they'll drop it back to me this week, which is good of them.

It's a stunning autumn day as I get off the bus and walk along the beachside path toward Cavill Avenue. The sea is shimmering, and sunbathers crowd the beach. For once, the Queensland tourism slogan – *Beautiful One Day, Perfect the Next* – isn't far off the mark. As I walk in the door of McDonald's, I see Abbey straight away.

She is sitting on a corner couch, and it looks like she's eating some kind of hamburger with the lot. She smiles at me and waves, her hair bouncing around her glowing face.

'You look well,' I say as I sit.

Her smile broadens. 'So frigging thrilled to get away from the alien-worshippers.' She gestures at me with her hamburger. 'All I got there were lentils and carrots, so now I can't get enough junk food.'

I get myself a thickshake and we reminisce about our escape from the Amalians.

'Did Amal look like Benny from ABBA to you?' I slurp on my drink.

'Oh my god, totally.' Abbey laughs. 'The tight white suit and the bowl haircut. And I was planning on having his baby.'

She laughs and pauses to stuff some French fries in her mouth. 'Can't believe Citra got off scot-free.'

Abbey and I had told the police how Citra had brainwashed us, but they hadn't been able to make any charges stick.

'Did you see they're putting together a new development proposal?' I say.

Abbey rolls her eyes. 'They say it will protect the tree. We'll see.'

The miracle tree is in the hands of the government now. It made the front page of the papers, but interest died away quickly. A few radio stations chased Abbey and me for interviews, but we weren't interested. They found a botanist from the Botanic Gardens to give a rave instead. *The most exciting botanical find for 200 years*, he'd said.

A bidding war between drug companies was in progress. There were rumours of high-level government wheeling and dealing to ensure maximum profitability. Security guards had been posted out on the canyon after some berries made it onto the black market.

'Guess Ashok wasn't too far wrong about the way things panned out,' I say. 'Didn't justify throwing me over a cliff though. Let alone what he did to you.'

'No, if anyone ever deserved a good squashing, it was him. Hey, big news. I'm switching from environmental science to psychology.'

'Why?'

'Two reasons. It was a pretty out-there experience getting brainwashed by the Amalians. I've been reading up on it. Did you know about a third of the population are joiners and followers?'

I shake my head.

Abbey eats more fries and continues. 'They want to give away their power. That's why they succumb to people like Citra. She's an accomplished hypnotist too. Once you respond to a hypnotic suggestion, it only needs to be topped up once a week or so to keep you in its power. It made me realise how important it is to understand how the brain works.'

I nod. 'And the second reason?'

'Ashok. He did the same thing to me.'

'Brainwashed you?'

'Sort of. He was super controlling. That's why I stopped coming up to the Goldie and seeing you and Mum. He told me the Gold Coast was bad for my spiritual development.'

'That's true.' I slurp on my thickshake. 'Couple of days back on the Goldie and you're already eating at Maccas.'

'He wanted to cut me off from everyone. He went mental when I hung out with Adam. I don't know why I let him do that to me. I need to learn to stop giving away my power.'

I think of how I'd given up my PI dream. 'Maybe I need to learn that too.' There's one thing still puzzling me – the leg rope under Adam's bed. 'Why weren't you wearing a leg rope, that night in the surf? You usually do.'

She frowns. 'I was.' Her face clears. 'Oh yes. That leg rope was a present from Adam: he painted the dolphins on it. We argued that night. I said I was going to report the tree and he said he'd dig it up and take it out of there. I don't think he meant it, but I believed him. I went ballistic, so I took the leg rope off and threw it at him. Sounds funny now, but it made sense at the time.'

'So, you and Gary?' I ask. 'You're a thing?'

Abbey shakes her head. 'He's a cool guy and obviously he's ready to go the extra mile, full marks for the rescue. But ... after Ashok, I need to take a break from guys and figure out what's right for me. I'll check back in with him down the track.'

'Sounds like a good plan.'

Abbey and I finish off our food and get to our feet. She puts out her arms and we hug.

'Love you, Ol,' she says.

'Love you too.'

'I'm not going to tell you what to do with your life, but ... you are an excellent investigator.'

'And you will be an excellent psychologist.'

Abbey puts out her little finger. 'Friends forever.'

I link my finger with hers. 'Friends forever.'

CHAPTER THIRTY-SEVEN

As I get back to Nan's, I groan. It's time to get ready for my blind date, and there's nothing I feel like doing less.

In our room, I put on my special occasion normcore outfit – full-length cargos and a newish T-shirt. *Pretty average look, babe*, I imagine Nansea saying, and she would be right.

I won't be revisiting Tan Magic or dying my hair pink any time soon, but perhaps I can resurrect some of Nansea's clothes? Cargos and T-shirts are still my staple, but there's nothing wrong with mixing it up, right? Going to the corner, I pick up the garbage bag full of clothes and empty it on the floor. A diaphanous rainbow spreads across the carpet.

Five minutes later, my silky skirt swishes around my ankles as I hobble toward the front door.

'Wait.' Nan runs toward me, a frangipani in her hand. 'Your date will be looking for someone with a frangipani in her hair.'

I eye the flower. 'You'd better not have set me up with a member of your ukulele orchestra.' There's no-one in the group younger than sixty.

'Don't be silly. I just want to make sure you find each other.'

I've never worn a frangipani in my hair before. But as its scent wafts toward me, I decide today is a day for new things. 'Okay.'

Nan fixes the flower behind my ear with a bobby pin. 'There. You look beautiful.' She smiles with satisfaction. 'Enjoy your date.'

'Don't worry, I won't.'

The Uber drops me off in Surfers and I make my way through hordes of excited tourists to the Metro Bar. Inside, I scan the crowd. A middle-aged man with slicked-back hair and a half-unbuttoned shirt gives me the once-over. I eye the gold chain hanging across his hairy chest. *No shark tooth. Phew.*

I head for the bar. With any luck, I've been stood up. I'll get a drink and duck off.

I'm about to order when my eyes catch on a guy with blond hair and broad shoulders. I freeze. *Rosco. What's he doing here?*

He's sitting at a side table with his head down, working on a newspaper crossword. I hadn't picked him as the crossword type. The waitress smiles at him flirtatiously as she puts his beer down. A pang of something which must be indigestion knots my gut.

I don't want to deal with Rosco. I'm moving out of his line of sight, when his head comes up. We eye each other warily. I see a chain around his neck. There's something dangling at the end of the chain. Could it be ...? Surely not. Nan wouldn't do that. Would she?

Rosco's eyes come to rest on the frangipani behind my ear. He raises his eyebrows and makes a thumbs-up sign.

I stare at his chain. That does look an awful lot like a shark tooth. I know Nan is an evil mastermind, but this is ridiculous. Grinding my teeth, I walk over to him.

'You must be my blind date,' he says.

I roll my eyes and lower myself onto a chair. 'Hi, I'm Olivia. Fun fact – my grandmother is a psychopath.'

He smiles. 'Now do you believe in synchronicity?'

'This isn't synchronicity, this is Nan's warped version of an excellent idea. Out of all the bars in all the world ...'

'You have to hobble into this one.' Rosco's mouth quivers with amusement. 'Can I buy you a drink?' He slides a credit card from the pocket of his blue shirt.

'I'll have a mocktail.' I wave my hand, trying to catch the waitress's attention.

Rosco glances up and instantly catches her eye. 'A mocktail over here please.' His teeth flash.

'Dowdy,' he says, turning back to me.

I glance at my outfit. 'That's a bit offensive. I did try.'

He gestures at the crossword. 'Eight letters.'

'Oh. Frumpish?'

He nods with satisfaction, scribbles it in, and puts down his pen. 'Finished.'

'So ...' we say, at the same time.

'You go,' I say.

'You're more-or-less back to the normal Olivia now, I see.'

He holds my gaze, and my stomach flutters. 'What's with the shark tooth?'

'Why?' Rosco keeps a straight face. 'Doesn't it make me look macho?'

'No, it makes you look like you chose the wrong souvenir of your Gold Coast holiday.'

'All the hipsters are wearing shark-tooth necklaces these days. You need to keep up with the trends. It's ironic.' Rosco smooths his hair with a mock-gigolo gesture. 'What's with the frangipani?'

'It's Aloha style. I've out-hipstered you. Hawaii is the new

Melbourne.' I push my straw around, making the ice tinkle in my glass. 'I can't believe Nan set me up on a blind date with you. How did she get you here?'

'She must have set up a fake profile on Bumble. I arranged a date with a frangipani-wearing girl who wasn't your Nan.'

'What did she look like?'

'Kind of like ...' Rosco ponders. 'Emma Watson.'

I raise my eyebrows. 'Nice. You must be disappointed.'

'No.' Rosco sips his beer. 'How about you?'

Disappointed doesn't cover it. I'd need Abbey's thesaurus to find a word for the feeling of being on a blind date with an ex-boyfriend who ghosted me. An ex-boyfriend who, to be honest, still makes my pulse beat faster. I pick the lemon out of my drink and gnaw it back to the rind.

Rosco's mouth twitches. 'You have a grand gift for silence, Watson,' he murmurs.

It's a quote from Sherlock Holmes. *The Man with the Twisted Lip.*

The waitress appears and picks up our glasses. 'Shall I get you another two?'

'No, we're not staying,' I say.

'I was joking,' says Rosco. 'About Emma Watson, I mean. I ran into your Nan in Surfers. She set you up.'

I frown. 'You knew you were meeting me? So, why did I have to wear the frangipani?'

Rosco shrugs. 'It suits you.' He drums his fingers on the table, and leans toward me, fixing me with his blue eyes. 'The thing is Olivia, I agreed because ... I have something to talk to you about.'

I shift back on my seat. This sounds like a prelude to a dressing-down.

'You found Abbey,' he says.

I nod. Did I invade his territory? He was the one who was supposed to be finding her, after all.

'Well done.'

I blink. I wasn't expecting that. 'Thanks.'

He clears his throat. 'It's made me realise ... I need a female partner.'

I stare at him.

'For the business,' he adds. 'Your job's still there.'

Is he saying he wants me back?

'An equal partnership, if that's what you want.'

He is. I want this so much, my chest aches. But nothing has changed. Jacq still needs dropping off at school. Nan is still unreliable. Mum and Dad are still in Nepal. Rosco still ghosted me. And yet, when I try to say no, my voice seizes up.

'I can't wait forever though. Business is booming.'

I should say no, but the word won't come out. I cough. 'Can I have a few days?'

'What's a few days between friends?'

He smiles at me and for a moment it feels almost like it used to when we played Star Wars. *May the horse be with you.*

He gets to his feet. 'Shall we say until Sunday?'

CHAPTER THIRTY-EIGHT

Jacq is on fire with excitement. I've given in to her pressure for a weekend in Byron Bay. She pogoes up and down beside me as I press Rosco's number on Friday night. I still feel weird ringing him, but I can't expect Jacq to do this by herself.

'Ask him, ask him!' Jacq nudges me with her shoulder.

'You're not going to Byron Bay this weekend, are you?' I ask, when he picks up.

'Nah.' Rosco's voice is dry. 'They're predicting a six-foot swell and southerly winds.'

'Oh.' I shake my head at Jacq and the corners of her mouth droop.

Rosco laughs. 'Where else would I be in those conditions except Byron Bay? Geez Olivia, get real.'

I give Jacq the thumbs-up and she squeals with excitement. I make the arrangements for Jacq to have a surf lesson with him and end the call.

He didn't mention the job offer again. Neither did I. I should have told him I can't do it, but the thought made me nauseous.

It's not like I'm enjoying uni. Thanks to my spreadsheets, I'm keeping on top of the work now, but it still doesn't thrill me. I don't know if I'm cut out for law. Being a PI is what I want more than anything, what I've always wanted. But there are so many obstacles. Not least of which is I'd have to work with Rosco again.

After dinner, I knit like a demon to dampen my rising panic. Rosco will expect an answer this weekend. What will I say? Am I waiting for the universe to reveal its plan?

'Is that scarf for an elephant, Livvie?' asks Jacq.

I hold it up. The scarf is long enough to go twice around an elephant's neck. 'No, I'm going to find a cold whale to give it to this weekend.'

'You're silly,' says Jacq. 'It's too early for whales.'

❁

'Can we go up in the lighthouse, Livvie?' asks Jacq, as we pull out of the driveway on Saturday morning.

On the forty-minute drive to Byron Bay I answer about a hundred questions. The impending surf lesson with Rosco is the major topic.

'Does Rosco ride really big waves?' she asks as we turn off to Byron Bay.

'Yeah, I reckon.'

'I'm going to get a barrel. Have you ever got a barrel?'

'No way.' I imagine being inside a moving tunnel of green water. 'I don't think I'd like it.'

'I would.' Jacq pulls her cap over her eyes.

I can see it won't be long until Jacq overtakes me in the surf stakes.

I tune into Lighthouse FM as we approach the town. It's the spiritual hour with Luna and I come in on the tail end of a discussion of astrology.

'That's awesome news we're out of the Mercury in retrograde cycle, Luna,' says the interviewer.

'You can say that again, Gopal. It's been, like, total chaos. We're now in the shadow phase, where the influence of Mercury is lessening.'

'That's fantastic, so it's full speed ahead?'

'Yep. I've spoken to a lot of people who've found it a difficult time. Everything that can go wrong, does go wrong.'

I smile as I pull into the beach car park. Luna might have her head in the clouds, but she can be spookily accurate.

We are meeting Rosco at the Clarke's Beach Cafe. He is sitting at a table under an umbrella doing a crossword again. Faded zinc cream plasters his face and his hair hangs in wet strands across his forehead. He gives me a small smile, then gives Jacq a broad one. She's right, he's her friend now.

'How're you going, tiger?' He punches Jacq lightly on the shoulder. 'Ready to hit the waves?'

Jacq nods, her eyes alight with hero worship.

'Okay, let's rip. Don't worry about her, Olivia, she'll be fine. I won't push her off on anything over six foot.' Seeing my face, he corrects himself. 'I mean six inches.'

Jacq skips along beside Rosco onto the sand, carrying a foam board. Rosco turns and gives me a thumbs-up. I wave and tuck my board under my arm.

I'm on my own mission. I haven't lost the voucher I got for my jungle dance with Lars. It's time for my individual surf lesson with Rosie. I've been languishing in intermediate surfer level for too long. It's time to take things to the next level so I can surf the big waves with Abbey.

On my way up the beach, I see someone I'd rather not run into. Cactus. He has his board under his arm and is dripping wet. There is no way to avoid him as he's coming straight toward me.

He raises one hand when he sees me. 'Hey, Nansea. Haven't seen you round. We should catch up for a drink. I owe you a beer.'

We haven't crossed paths since he threatened me in the surf, and now he thinks we're on beer-drinking terms? 'Nah. I'm right thanks. Consider your beer debt void.'

He shrugs. 'Your loss.' His eyes drop to my board. 'Keep out of the way of the real surfers, ay?'

I narrow my eyes. 'There are all sorts of things wrong with that statement. Not insignificantly, I am a real surfer. A reasonable person would say, you'd better keep out of my way.' As I toss my head and continue up the beach to my lesson, I can feel his eyes boring into my back.

Cactus might not have hurt Abbey, but it would not be far-fetched or fanciful to say that he's a nasty piece of work. If I were a PI, I'd be keeping him on my go-to list of undesirable characters.

❄

Jacq and I are lying on our beds in the backpackers watching television when there's a knock on our door.

Rosco pokes his head inside. 'Sunset-viewing time.'

'Do we have to? I'm pooped.' It's been a big day of surfing. After my lesson with Rosie, I kept going for another two hours, practising all the moves she taught me. I can hardly be bothered operating the TV remote, let alone viewing the sunset.

'You see Jacq, what did I say? Olivia can't hack it. Joking,' Rosco adds, as I grab a pillow off the bed to throw at him.

'Weakie,' says Jacq.

Rosco and Jacq have developed a chummy relationship that mainly involves taunting me.

I drag myself off the bed. 'Okay, let's do it.'

As soon as we're at the beach, Jacq runs to the shoreline to build a sandcastle. This leaves Rosco and me alone. The water is gold, and a colourful group of bongo players provides a background beat. It's beautiful, but it's weird to be sitting here with Rosco.

We sit about a metre apart and stare at the sunset, as if it takes up all our attention. *Yep, that's a sunset that demands total focus all right.*

He will expect an answer from me tomorrow about coming back to the agency. But how can I? There aren't enough hours in the day. And besides, things are still awkward. Look at us now. It's like there's a Plexiglass shield between us. I dig up a handful of sand and trickle it over my feet. Why did he ghost me?

Rosco breaks the silence. 'You look like you're a million miles away.'

My heart thumps. If I don't ask him now, I never will. It will hang between us forever like a rotting albatross. I need to know. 'Why ...' I clear my throat. 'Why did you ghost me after I left the agency?'

Rosco blinks. 'What?'

'You didn't reply to my messages.'

'I did.' Rosco looks baffled. 'You didn't reply to me.'

'That's rubbish and you know it.'

'It's not rubbish. I messaged you heaps of times and you never replied.'

I look out at the sunset. Why is he lying?

'I did it,' says a small voice. 'It's my fault.'

I hadn't seen Jacq come back.

She drops onto the sand at my feet and looks from me to Rosco and back again. Her face crumples. 'I did that,' she whispers. 'I deleted his messages. All of them.'

Rosco and I stare at her.

Jacq speaks quickly. 'I blocked his number. I unblocked it when he stopped calling, so you wouldn't know.'

The bongo players reach a wild crescendo as the sun sinks below the horizon.

'You what?' I say.

Jacq dissolves into tears. 'I didn't want you to marry Rosco and leave me all alone with Nan,' she wails. 'Mum and Dad left me. If you marry Rosco, you'll leave me too.' Tears run down her face. 'I'm sorry, Livvie.'

I wrap her in my arms and stroke her hair. 'It's okay. I understand why you did that.' It's kind of impressive. Sneaky, but impressive. She could have a bright future as a PI if she doesn't launch her own Silicon Valley start-up. 'I'm not marrying Rosco. And I'd never leave you all alone with Nan.' Inside me, something stirs – a mixture of anger and ... I glance up at Rosco.

He raises his eyebrows at me and opens his mouth in a wide circle. *Crazy*, he mouths.

I smile at him over the top of Jacq's head and he smiles back. Our smiles go on until the light fades from the sky. I feel like my whole body is smiling.

After a little while, we get up. Jacq and I hold hands as Rosco walks us back to the backpackers. She is quiet and runs inside as soon as we get there. Rosco and I stand under the streetlight. I'm drained, but at the same time, more peaceful than I've been for a long time.

'Well ...' says Rosco. 'That was bizarre, right?'

I shake my head. 'Sorry about my crazy sister. Guess she takes after me.'

Rosco laughs. 'Guess so. I always replied to your messages, Olivia. And I always will.'

It's still complicated between us, but a creeping warmth fills my chest. 'Me too. I'll always reply to yours.'

'One of us should have picked up the phone and cleared things up,' he says. 'I hate personal phone conversations though. It's okay for work, but ...'

'I know. I hate ringing people too.'

'I figured you wanted a clean break.'

'I figured *you* did.'

We stare at each other and my heart goes thump-a-thump.

'What's up with your parents? When are they coming home from Nepal?'

'I don't know. Mum's having ... a midlife crisis.'

Rosco nods. 'My Mum had one of those. She reinvented herself as a wedding planner.'

'I wish Mum would reinvent herself as a wedding planner, instead of teaching monks in Nepal.'

'My Mum said she wanted to rediscover her own greatness.'

Rediscover her own greatness ... 'I like that.'

Rosco and I smile at each other as we stand under the streetlight. *What now?* It's not like we can just pick up where we left off. Too much has happened since then.

'Want to have a barbecue later?' he asks. 'I'll bring sausages.'

Sausages. I suppose that's one place to start. 'That would be cool.'

We give each other one more long smile, then he waves and walks off.

Jacq is curled up in a ball on the couch when I come in. I don't have the heart to be angry with her. She's seven years old. She doesn't know any better. *Rediscover her own greatness* ... I know who is to blame for all this.

While Jacq is in the shower, I Skype Dad.

His face appears and he waves. His beard is longer than it was and a colourful beret perches on top of his shaggy hair. 'How are things going there, Olivia?' The connection is crackly.

'It's complicated.' I start with my misgivings about uni, how Jacq is missing them both. There's a crackly pause when I finish talking.

'I'm sorry, it's hard to hear you. The connection, and the monks are chanting ...' Cymbals clash over and over behind him. 'The monks are practising the Lama Dance again. It's time for evening prayers.'

He's about to go.

'Goodnight darling. Remember, when you have eliminated the impossible, whatever remains, however improbable, must be the truth.'

It's another quote from Sherlock Holmes, and it is more-or-less relevant to my current situation. But I need to have a real conversation. 'No. You can't go.'

Dad's face flickers. He's about to do the Cheshire Cat thing.

'This is important.'

His face flickers again, but he's still there.

'You need to come home. Jacq isn't coping. I'm not coping. I don't want to study law anymore. I want to be a PI. It's what I love. I'm good at it.'

'But your mum ...' The cymbals clash again.

'Dad, listen. You know how I told you about a girl who went missing?'

'Yes.'

'It was Abbey. I found her. I found Abbey.'

Dad is quiet for a moment, his face frozen. 'You should have told us, Olivia. Why didn't you tell us that Abbey was missing?'

I clench my hands. 'How could I? You're over there. And you keep vanishing. How could I talk to you about Abbey like *this*?' I wave my hand at the screen.

'I'm sorry Olivia. That must have been hard for you.' Dad takes a deep breath. 'I'm so glad she's okay. How—'

I interrupt him. 'I can't keep doing this, looking after Jacq. It's not fair.' I can tell him the whole story about Abbey later; right now I need something else. I talk faster. I need to get this all out before the connection dies. 'It's not fair on Jacq and it's not fair on me.'

'Hasn't Nan been looking after Jacq?'

'Nan has her own life. She has Donald and ukulele. She doesn't have much time for us.'

'Oh.' Dad frowns. The cymbals clash again.

'I've figured out what went wrong, why Mum cracked up. Her life is ridiculous. I know, because I've been living it. That spreadsheet she has, to get through the week, it's crazy. She doesn't have a minute to herself.'

'But ... she's so good at it.'

'Yes, she is. And because she's so good at it, we've all let her do it. You need to help. I'll help too, but I'm not doing it all. Why don't you ever make Jacq's lunches? Why didn't you ever used to make mine?'

Dad blinks. 'I'd be happy to make the lunches. I didn't realise ...'

'And you need to help with the school drop-off and pick-up.'

Dad nods. 'Of course I will.'

'And take Jacq to soccer.'

'That's fine. I didn't know there was so much to do. I'm sorry, I feel like I've been off in my own little world. I should have helped more. And this is what's wrong? Why she … had a midlife crisis.'

'I'm sure of it. Mum's been doing all this stuff since I was a baby. That's eighteen years. She's over it. It's your turn now. She needs time to figure out who she can be. She needs to rediscover her own greatness.'

Dad looks shell-shocked. 'She's so efficient. It never occurred to me she wasn't coping. I'll talk to her. I'm so sorry Olivia, I feel like I've really let you— ' The connection fades and dies.

CHAPTER THIRTY-NINE

Rosco knocks on our door around seven.

I open the door and for some reason I blush at the sight of him.

He blushes too.

We stand there staring at each other like two awkward beetroots. Things should have got less weird since we cleared up the ghosting thing. Instead, we have ascended to next-level weirdness.

Luckily Jacq is too excited about the barbecue to leave us in this excruciating limbo for long. She jumps off the couch and rushes up to Rosco. 'Have you got sausages?'

'I've got a surprise,' Rosco says.

'Sausages?' asks Jacq.

'Yes, but something else too.'

I've had enough surprises, but I pull on a sweatshirt and slide my feet into thongs. 'Okay, let's do it.'

The moon is high in the sky and the lighthouse beam razes the water as we pull up at The Pass car park. A family group is barbecuing, but otherwise the place is deserted.

'What's the surprise?' cries Jacq. 'Tell us now. Is it ice-cream?'

'You'll have to wait.' Rosco grabs something from the boot and runs to the beach with Jacq in pursuit.

Jacq's cries of 'What is it? What is it?' get fainter and fainter as they leave me behind.

'Thanks guys.' I trot after them.

On the sand, Jacq is jumping and snatching like a frisky puppy at the bag Rosco holds above his head.

'Do you want to see what it is?' says Rosco.

'What?' squeals Jacq.

Rosco pulls something from the bag. 'It's ... sparklers.' He flicks a cigarette lighter, lights the stick and steps back as a blaze of light flickers out.

Jacq claps and screams with excitement.

'Here's one for you.' Rosco hands Jacq a sparkler and lights it for her. She takes off down the beach, waving it around her head like a demented firefly.

My eyes follow her glow. Jacq is like a rubber ball: you can't keep her down for long.

'Here.' Rosco lights another sparkler and hands it to me.

I wave it in fiery circles, loops and swirls. For once, my mind is quiet. A surge of warmth spreads through my body. It starts in my stomach and flows up to my head and down to my toes. I know what Luna would say. *Your chakras are unblocking.*

I take what seems to be my first full breath in months – and bizarrely, a tear trickles down my cheek. I have no idea what that's about.

Rosco wipes my cheek with his thumb. 'Can't win a trick, can I? I never thought the sparkler would make you cry.'

I blink and the tears stop. My sparkler fizzes out. My cheek feels warm where he touched it. 'I love the sparkler. It's ...

everything's been so full-on.' I gaze out to sea. Across the bay, the mountains loom against the sky. Citra and her gang will be dancing up there. Maybe I'll join them one day. Once I've trained myself to resist brainwashing.

My phone buzzes with a message. It's Mum.

Hello darling. We've booked the tickets home. Your father said I need to rediscover my own greatness. I'm going to start a hiking business. I always wanted to do that. Buddha says your work is to discover your work and with all your heart give yourself to it. If you want to be a PI, you should be a PI. You will be great at anything you do. Your dad told me about Abbey. I'm so sorry I left you to deal with all this on your own. I'll make it up to you. Love, Mum. And thank you. xox

I smile. *Your work is to discover your work.* Her stay in Nepal has produced a positive transformation after all.

Jacq runs back and Rosco hands her another sparkler. She races off down the beach again.

'So, it's been a few days ...' says Rosco. 'Are you coming back to the agency?'

'Give me another sparkler.'

He lights one and places it in my hand.

Using my whole arm, I carve fiery letters in the sky. They flicker, fade into smoke, and blow away on the breeze. I can still see them though. A glowing *Y, E,* and *S.*

I'm back in the game.

The beam of the lighthouse catches Rosco's face. His hair is falling over his eyes and he looks like he's just defeated the giant otter.

I'm not sure whose idea it is, but somehow we seem to be kissing. I feel like I'm on a rollercoaster and I never want to get off. It's all the good feelings at once, like spring days and ice-cream and—

'Ew, gross.' We pull apart as Jacq rushes up the beach toward us.

Rosco squeezes my hand. 'We're going to be the A-Team, Olivia.'

We might be, or we might not. I foresee a whole bunch of trouble ahead. Right now, though, I'm looking forward to rediscovering my own greatness.

ACKNOWLEDGEMENTS

I would like to give my heartfelt thanks to everyone who has helped to bring *Trouble is my Business* to publication. I wrote most of this novel throughout the strange year that was 2020. At times like this, I'm more grateful than ever for the connections and friendship of the writing world.

The whole Wakefield Press team has been a joy to work with. Special thanks to Jo Case, for her enthusiasm and skilful editing, Poppy Nwosu for her fabulous publicity and Liz Nicholson for her beautiful cover design. The artwork of Olivia was created by the talented Jessie Brooke.

Many readers have offered wise advice and encouragement on various iterations and aspects of this story. Thank you to Helen Burns, Jane Camens, Jessie Cole, Siboney Duff, Michelle Taylor, Jane Meredith, Bronwyn Birdsall and Kayte Nunn.

Thank you to my wonderful agent, Jane Novak, for finding this series a happy home at Wakefield Press and for being such an insightful and helpful reader.

My family: John, Simon, Tim, Sue and all my extended family too. Thank you for your love, support, and understanding. It wouldn't mean anything without you.

And finally, thank you to you! I hope you've enjoyed reading Olivia's second adventure as much as I enjoyed writing it.